THE *Secret* OF HAVERSHAM HOUSE

THE *Secret* OF HAVERSHAM HOUSE

JULIE MATERN

SWEETWATER
BOOKS
An imprint of Cedar Fort, Inc.
Springville, Utah

ISBN 13: 978-1-4621-2207-3

Published by Sweetwater Books, an imprint of Cedar Fort, Inc.
2373 W. 700 S., Springville, UT 84663
Distributed by Cedar Fort, Inc., www.cedarfort.com

LIBRARY OF CONGRESS CATALOGING-IN-PUBLICATION DATA

Names: Matern, Julie A., 1964- author.
Title: The secret of Haversham House / Julie A. Matern.
Description: Springville, Utah : Sweetwater Books, an imprint of Cedar Fort,
Inc., [2018]
Identifiers: LCCN 2018004485 (print) | LCCN 2018006785 (ebook) | ISBN
9781462129027 (epub, pdf, mobi) | ISBN 9781462122073 (perfect bound : alk.
paper)
Subjects: LCSH: Adoptees--Fiction. | Man-woman relationships--Fiction. |
England, setting. | GSAFD: Regency fiction. | LCGFT: Historical fiction. |
Romance fiction. | Novels.
Classification: LCC PS3613.A8254 (ebook) | LCC PS3613.A8254 S43 2018 (print)
| DDC 813/.6--dc23
LC record available at https://lccn.loc.gov/2018004485

Cover design by Shawnda T. Craig
Cover design © 2018 Cedar Fort, Inc.
Edited by Breanna Call Herbert and Jessica Romrell
Typeset by Kaitlin Barwick

Printed in the United States of America

10 9 8 7 6 5 4 3 2 1

Printed on acid-free paper

For Todd and the kids.

Part One

One

ふふふ ふふふ

Emily Louise Davenport was a most fortunate woman for her era—she had been able to marry for love.

Her father, Lord Davenport, was an earl whose wealth was large enough that she was not required to fall on the family sword and marry for more practical reasons. So she married John Charles Haversham because she loved him and not for his five thousand a year or the title he would inherit.

John loved Emily in return and was a warm, kind, and generous husband, which was surprising in view of the fact that his mother and father were quite the opposite. Together, John and Emily lived at Haversham House, John's newly built, tasteful estate in southern Wiltshire, some good distance from his ancestral home. It seemed to all the world that they had been blessed with more than their fair share of life's blessings.

Though just nineteen when she married, Emily was mature in intellect and accomplished in the arts and languages. If she had a fault, it was that she cared too deeply.

John Haversham was twenty-four when they married, a towering young man of dashing good looks. They complemented each other in every way and were much feted wherever they went.

All seemed idyllic until, at length, it became apparent that the young couple could not produce an heir. As their friends began to fill their nurseries, Emily's heart became increasingly heavy when her own prettily decorated nursery remained barren and empty.

After seven long and painful years, Emily's hitherto excellent spirits were so downcast that on the advice of their doctor they removed to the Continent to experience a change of air and scenery.

Rather than frequent the more popular watering places, John decided on a place he had visited once in his youth—an out-of-the-way village in the south of France that boasted a grand villa on its outskirts and that his mother had condemned as being too far from good society.

He rented the house, complete with its French servants, and they departed, leaving everything and everyone behind and beginning a new life away from English society and its expectations.

The beauty of the surrounding mountain landscapes and colorful ocean views did much to elevate Emily's state of mind, and she began to take a renewed pleasure in painting and riding out with her husband, simple pleasures she had ceased at home. As her health improved, they ventured out to visit the village and enjoyed watching the bustle of the weekly markets, with their displays of fragrant cheeses, glossy fruits, and resplendent pastries. John took courage as he witnessed the joie de vivre creep back into Emily's soul.

They had been settled in this charming residence for nigh on five months when they made the acquaintance of a young, Italian gentlewoman who John feared might cause Emily's progress to unravel. She introduced herself as Signora Grimaldi and explained that she had come into the country for her confinement. This disclosure stabbed at the tender heart of poor Emily Haversham, but she bravely introduced herself and her husband to the young expectant mother as good manners dictated.

From that time on, John would change their daily routine in order to avoid the young woman, but in spite of his efforts, they would often meet Signora Grimaldi as they walked in the village square as though she had been waiting for them. It was obvious that these meetings pained Emily as she witnessed the steady change in the young woman's figure, but John was proud that his wife did not shun the lady who was outwardly bright and polished but who seemed to reflect a veiled sadness.

At length, the lady in question disappeared from their society and John assumed that her time had come and that she had delivered her child. He and Emily continued on with their easy lifestyle and quite forgot the lady until one day in September, some two months later, as they were sitting on a stone bench in the square, she approached them holding a babe in her arms.

John heard Emily gasp as Signora Grimaldi drew near and, perceiving his wife's distress, rose to lead her away from the difficult encounter. However, the proud new mother called out to them, and rather than seem ill-mannered, they both perched back upon the stone bench. Emily courageously fixed her face into a false smile and by silent agreement left John to address the lady directly.

"My dear Signora Grimaldi, we offer our congratulations. We quite thought you had returned to your home in Italy," he declared.

"Oh, no," she explained in her heavily accented, lilting voice. "I have been in my confinement and have found it so advantageous a climate for the baby that I have remained here. My husband joined me shortly after the happy occasion but has now returned to our home. I will follow him soon."

John was annoyed that she seemed completely ignorant of Emily's strained appearance and discomfort and was alarmed when she addressed Emily to ask, "Would you not like to hold my baby?"

He noticed a look of utter horror flit across Emily's delicate features and her sapphire blue eyes shine bright with frightened tears. He came rapidly to the rescue, exclaiming, "Mrs. Haversham is not feeling in good health today, so it might not be wise—"

Ignoring his protestations, Signora Gimaldi placed the infant in Emily's stiff arms.

John pivoted to deliver Emily from the child, but as she received the full weight of the baby, he was perplexed to see her expression transfigured from sorrow to unadulterated pleasure. It was as though Emily's broken heart commenced to heal the moment she looked down upon the infant, who returned her gaze with liquid brown eyes. He peered into the blanket to behold curly, black hair that framed a tiny face with delicate cheeks and rosebud lips. The baby was smiling gently back at the fragile woman who held her. It was obviously love at first sight, and John was uneasy that this event would undo Emily's progress when the baby had to be returned.

"I think you had better take her back, Signora Gimaldi—" he began, but Emily interrupted him.

"Just a moment more, John," she quietly pleaded.

"As a matter of fact," the child's mother ventured, "I need to run an errand at the post office. Would you mind tending her while I attend to the matter? I gave my nurse the afternoon off."

John looked at his wife with a quizzical brow, begging her to refuse—to make an excuse—but she returned his stare, imploring him to agree. So, in spite of his fears for his wife's well-being, he reluctantly consented.

They sat in the sun, a counterfeit family tableau, Emily cooing over the pretty child as they awaited the return of her mother. It was evident that Emily was utterly smitten and that the warm presence in her arms was beginning to heal her. He fretted as she rocked and sang gently to the baby even as he anxiously searched the crowd for the return of the mother.

The bell in the clock tower rang, and John realized that Signora Grimaldi had now been gone for the better part of an hour. *What could be keeping her?*

He stood to better search for the baby's mother in the crowd, glancing at his wife, who was careless of anything around her. He groaned inwardly.

John dropped down beside her, ill at ease, at which time the child began to whimper. Emily gathered the baby up to comfort it against her breast, and as she did so, the fine linen blanket surrounding the child came loose, and a piece of paper, hitherto unnoticed, fell lightly to the ground. John stooped to retrieve it and, opening it, read aloud:

Dear Mr. and Mrs. Haversham,

I have not been entirely forthcoming about myself and my circumstances, for which I apologize deeply.

I am an Italian national from a prominent family who found myself in some trouble. The gentleman responsible is unable to come forward and accept responsibility, therefore I did not tell him of my condition. To remain at home would have brought shame to my family, so I concealed it from them. I arranged to travel to France with my maid to meet some friends. After a few weeks, I told them that I had urgent family business to attend to back in Italy but would return to them at length. I did not. Instead, I came here to bear the child and prayed fervently that I might be forgiven of my sins and find a family worthy to take her. I could not let her be given to strangers.

It is inconceivable that my family should know anything of this situation. Consequently, I have assumed an identity to protect their honor and have come to this small place where there is little chance of anyone recognizing me.

The first day I met you, I felt that you were the people who should raise my child as your own, and as I came to learn that you had no children, I felt that God was confirming that decision.

I have spent the last weeks with her, loving her, delighting in her, and I will hold those memories close to my heart forever. Now the time has come to return to my friends and family, and I thus give her to you as a gift from God.

I have refrained from naming her so that you might choose her name. I have no doubt that you will love and protect her.

Sincerely,

Isabella

By the end of the recitation, he could hear Emily weeping openly, and he raised his eyes to see her clutching the child to her bosom. As she clung to the baby, he noticed a small birthmark peeking through the child's curly hair.

He leaned back, emotionally spent. Their prayers had been answered, though not in the way he had expected, and although there would be many details to discuss about such an unorthodox adoption, for now he would bask in the delightful moment.

"We received her in France, and she is of Italian descent," sniffed Emily, "let us name her Francesca—it means 'French' in Italian—as a constant reminder that she is a divine gift."

"It suits her very well," he agreed.

Lifting Emily from the bench, they began their walk back to the villa.

For a moment they walked in silence, but the silence could not work itself into contentment for a new weight pressed upon John's shoulders. There was something of a delicate nature they needed to speak of.

John cleared his throat and placed a protective arm around his wife. "Of course," he said at last, his voice lowered, "she can never learn of her true origins if she is to survive in English society."

"Your mother . . ." whispered Emily.

"My mother, yes, the queen bee of society. But society at large is without mercy in such cases."

Emily locked eyes with him, kissing the baby's head and putting her finger to his lips. "That, my love, is a conversation for another day," she said. "Another day."

Two

ENGLAND

Eighteen years later

If I didn't love you so much I would be terribly jealous!" proclaimed the rather plain young woman who had just burst through Francesca Haversham's bedchamber door without so much as a knock. "You shall be the belle of the ball tonight," gushed the young lady, whose name was Annabelle, cousin to Francesca. "You look magnificent!" she continued without the least hint of guile.

Francesca turned on her stool, a deep blush of pleasure creeping over her features. "You look very lovely too, Annabelle," she said kindly as she appraised her cousin's appearance.

"Oh, I look all right, but you will have every young man swooning. I will be more than satisfied to entertain those who are awaiting their turn to dance with *you*!"

"Now, Miss Haversham, I haven't quite finished your hair," complained Mary, her lady's maid, who had been patiently waiting for the conversation to end.

"Oh, I am so sorry," said Francesca, obediently turning to face the dressing table mirror while throwing a mischievous look of exaggerated contrition at Annabelle.

Annabelle Haversham smiled impishly back and watched the maid dress her cousin's hair. Reflected in the mirror was a lovely heart-shaped face with rosy cheeks.

The maid had dressed Francesca's thick, wavy tresses into the most delightful crown, adorned with fresh flowers. Annabelle saw Francesca reach her fingers behind her head, pulling down a tiny wisp of hair to hide a blemish on her neck, a habit she had developed in her youth.

Annabelle could not help but notice the contrast between her own looks and that of her cousin. She sighed. No one would notice *her* tonight. She looked at her own reflection in the glass and saw a round, pale face with fine hair pulled back into a bun ringed with thin braids. She had bitten her lips and pinched her cheeks just like her cousin, but the effect was not as charming. She smiled with resignation and as she did so, her countenance lit up with the beauty of good nature. She would do.

Coming out balls, a rite of passage for the female gentry, were highly anticipated events, and they had been planning this one for months. This was Francesca's debutante ball, and no expense had been spared.

Annabelle looked down at her gown with ineffable satisfaction and smiled again. It was of the purest silk, soft as a whisper, and the design was so exquisite as to make her heart take flight. She had never before worn such a gown, not even at her own coming out ball. Francesca, who had an elegant style and impeccable taste, had helped her choose the dress and it made her feel like royalty.

She glanced over at her cousin's gown. It, too, was of the finest silk and had much detail in the bodice of fine embroidery and small silk flowers. It fitted her small frame to perfection.

"Is it to your liking, Miss Haversham?" asked Mary as she placed the last fresh flower into her hair.

"Oh, Mary you are an artist!" she said, turning this way and that to admire her hair. "It is just as I had imagined, only better! Thank you!"

Mary blushed with pride as the beautiful girl bestowed her approval and exited the room.

A knock on the door signaled the arrival of Francesca's mother, Emily Haversham, who appeared holding a jewelry case. The two girls gasped in anticipation.

"Are those Grandmama Davenport's jewels?" asked Francesca in a reverent tone.

"Yes, my darling. As you know, it is the tradition to pass on these particular jewels at the time of coming out."

Annabelle watched as Emily opened the old-fashioned catch of the antique case to reveal velvet beds of shining stones, glimmering like stars in the heavens on a clear night. She peered at them in awe.

Emily delicately lifted the heavy diamond choker out of the case and placed it around her daughter's neck. The pear-shaped jewel hanging from the center settled into the indentation of her collar bone as if it had been commissioned for her.

Emily bobbed down to regard the effect of the jewels in the mirror, cheek to cheek with her daughter.

Annabelle was struck, not for the first time, by their differences; the mother's skin so ivory white, the daughter's a light olive; the mother's eyes a striking sapphire blue and the daughter's a rich, chocolate brown ringed with thick, black lashes. *The variance must hale from generations long past,* she thought. In other ways, such as their hair and build, the two women were very similar, she acknowledged.

She noticed Emily's eyes glistening with tears as she gazed at her daughter's image in the glass. Annabelle's heart ached for such sentiment in her own mother.

"Annabelle, you look very handsome this evening. That dress is most becoming, and your hair suits you very well." Her aunt smiled.

Annabelle glowed at the praise from her beloved aunt Emily. Would that her own mother were so free with compliments! "Thank you, Aunt," she responded gratefully.

Emily wiped her cheek and clapped her hands together, saying, "Now girls, it is almost time to come down. Francesca must be ready to greet her guests, who will begin arriving in less than half an hour, and I fear you should both take some refreshment before the festivities begin lest you faint from so much dancing and so little nourishment." She gave them both a motherly smile, her eyes flashing with merriment.

"Oh, Mama!" exclaimed Francesca. "I could not eat one morsel even if you encouraged me very much. I am far too excited and nervous to eat."

"Well, at least take a little water then. I do not want us to be the talk of the county because the debutante fainted at her own ball!"

"Although . . . it might be useful if there were a particular gentleman whose attention we wanted to attract," suggested Francesca with a playful glint in her dark eyes. Her mother shook her head and departed the room, laughing gently.

"Do you expect Phillip to dance with you this evening?" asked Annabelle. She referred to Phillip Waverley, second son of Sir William Waverley, a very great man in the county whose estate abutted the Havershams'. Consequently, Francesca and Phillip had grown up together and were great friends in their youth. Annabelle had long held a candle for Phillip and had been dismayed to notice that he had been little able to hide his attraction to Francesca on his return from Oxford the summer before. In his absence, Francesca had blossomed from child to woman in a most distracting way. Though Francesca appeared to be completely ignorant of the change in Phillip's feelings, Annabelle had graciously extinguished her candle.

"He did ask permission to have the first dance with me when he came to tea last Thursday," she replied with excitement.

"Do you favor him, then?" asked Annabelle, suddenly intrigued.

"To be sure, I think very highly of him, but I consider him more as a brother than a suitor! And he, I, as a sister! He was merely being kind, as is his way. Dear Phillip. But tonight is about *new* possibilities, is it not, cousin? My circle of acquaintance is so very limited here, and I know that Mama and Father have invited many old friends from various parts of the country."

"And their sons!" laughed Annabelle.

"Yes! And their sons. I aim to dance with *all* of them to broaden my associations. It will be an adventure! I do not believe that the purpose of a coming out ball is to secure a husband but to experience what the world has to offer in the way of suitors. Do you not think so, Annabelle?"

"Oh yes," she sighed, longingly. The possibilities were so very exciting.

"We must marry, of course," added Francesca, "but we are so fortunate that we will not have to endure an arranged marriage."

"That is true," said Annabelle, "but Father has made it clear that although I will have some choice in the matter he does expect my husband to possess a great deal of land. He is of the opinion that land is very important to the upper classes and will protect us from future financial upheaval. If I fall in love with a vicar's son, he will not approve of the match."

"Then you had better marry Phillip!" Francesca laughed, unconscious of the irony.

"Come now, we should seek some water as Mama suggested," said Francesca as she gathered up her dress and checked her appearance in the long glass, "or else we will be swooning for the ugly men as well as the handsome!" Annabelle took her arm and they both exited the room, giggling like school girls as they swept down the hall and the grand staircase.

At the bottom of the stairs they found Katherine, Francesca's cousin on her mother's side. Katherine looked most becoming in a silver-gray silk gown, but as usual her countenance was less becoming with its haughty lip. She was quite a beauty, but she suffered from a jealous disposition that resulted in a perpetually pinched expression. She had the misfortune to feel that any praise of another was a slight to her; indeed, she seemed to find offense in every quarter. This tendency to ill humor had prevented the closeness that might otherwise have existed between the cousins.

"At last!" sighed Katherine. "I have been waiting upon you these last twenty minutes!" she exclaimed. "You look very well cousin," she said grudgingly, addressing Francesca.

"Why thank you, Katherine," replied Francesca. This was praise indeed coming from her sour cousin. "You look particularly lovely this evening too."

Katherine nodded her regal head in agreement and turned her attention to Annabelle. "Annabelle, your maid has managed a miracle with your flat, dull hair."

Used to Katherine's underhanded slights, Annabelle took her comment in stride and chose to accept it as a compliment. "You are most kind, Katherine."

"Come, let us find some refreshment before the guests arrive," suggested Francesca, and she threaded her arm through Annabelle's on her way to the drawing room.

◦◦◦◦

It seemed to Francesca that the receiving line was interminably long, and she was extremely anxious to begin dancing. Eventually, however, her mother gave her leave to commence the dancing portion of the evening.

As previously planned, she began the evening's festivities with her old friend, Phillip Waverley. He was most young ladies' dream of the ideal suitor, she had to admit. He was taller than the average man, with very broad shoulders, wavy fair hair that he wore a little longer than was fashionable in the country, a rugged jaw, and green eyes. This evening he looked particularly dashing in his white breeches and royal blue coat. Francesca enjoyed the first two dances with him in a friendly camaraderie. It was a fine way to begin her ball and helped to calm her nerves.

Her next partner was a son of her father's friends from Scotland. He was a gangling youth who had not yet grown into his eyebrows and Francesca had to control an urge to laugh as he kept stepping on her toes.

Released from his embrace, she turned to her next partner, another stranger. He was rather short and portly and had a very unfortunate lisp, which caused him to eject a little spittle as he spoke. This was very distressing as Francesca was at pains to remain polite but needed to keep turning her head to save herself from the spray. How she would laugh with Annabelle when it was time for refreshment.

As she danced with partner after partner, she became more at ease with being the center of attention. Several of her partners were exceptionally handsome, she noted, but not so agreeable. Several more were exceptionally agreeable but not so handsome.

All too soon it was time for supper. She led the way into the dining hall on her father's arm.

"It appears that you are having a pleasant evening," whispered her father with a twinkle in his eye.

"Oh, Father, you know very well that I am in heaven! I think we should have a ball every month!"

"Alas, then there would be no inheritance to pass down to you, my sweet girl," he replied.

"Touché!" she returned.

He led her to the table and at his signal the company began to eat and drink and make merry. Katherine sat at the piano and provided music as they ate, for she was an excellent pianist.

Unfortunately, Annabelle was too far down the table to converse with, so Francesca had to hold in all her humorous tales until dessert, when all were more free to move about the room.

"Bella, my dear, are you having as much fun as I?" she inquired when they were able to speak together.

"Oh, my goodness, yes! I have never seen so many handsome men in all my life! One wonders where they have all been hiding!"

"Is there one gentleman whom you prefer above all others?" encouraged her cousin.

"No! I think I have fallen in love with at least a dozen men in the last half an hour alone!" she exclaimed before bursting into her beautiful, musical laughter. "But what about you? The debutante? Has anyone captured *your* heart?" Annabelle asked in a conspiratorial tone, upon which opening Francesca shared with her the more amusing tales of the evening.

After several minutes of private conversation, Francesca happened to look over her cousin's shoulder, where her attention was immediately captured by a newcomer who was standing just outside the doorway to the supper room.

"Annabelle, do you know who that is?" she asked urgently. Annabelle turned her elegantly styled head to cast a glance behind her. Her eyes opened wide in surprise and she nodded.

"Oh yes!" she said with barely concealed excitement, "I met him at Mrs. Sunderland's house in Bath last summer. He is the son of a Baronet from Gloucestershire. Mr. Langley Ashbourne. Do you not remember me mentioning him to you last year?"

"Oh, I do, I do," she replied thoughtfully. "He is your mysterious 'Mr. Fine,' is he not?"

"Mr. Fine," as Annabelle had nicknamed Mr. Ashbourne, was average of height and slight of build, but his face was the face of Adonis. A beautifully defined, angular jaw, intelligent eyes, and black hair styled in the latest fashion that shone in the candlelight. His beauty was almost painful to behold. Every feature was even and pleasant. Francesca did not know that she had ever seen his equal. She was quite at a loss for words. She felt Annabelle examining her with amused curiosity.

"He is fine, is he not?"

"I think you understated his qualities, Annabelle."

He was standing in the doorway, observing the masses as they dined and visited with one another. His air was unhurried, and he perused the room with a quiet confidence. Francesca could barely drag her attention away.

"We could importune grandmother for an introduction, as I believe he is an acquaintance of hers," suggested Annabelle.

However, before they could approach, Lady Augusta Haversham, Francesca's grandmother, was seen gliding across the room to the gentleman in question.

"Aha, you will get your introduction, I think," declared Annabelle.

Francesca returned her gaze to her grandmother and the elegant young gentleman. Lady Haversham was evidently welcoming him to the ball, and he appeared to be apologizing for his late arrival. Her grandmother turned and indicated her granddaughter with her gloved hand. The gentleman flitted his attention in the direction indicated but did not linger on her person, rather surveying the whole area. When his gaze landed, it was on Annabelle, at whom he smiled in recognition. As his lips parted, his face creased in the most attractive of expressions, and for Francesca, time seemed to stand still.

"He has a most pleasing smile; wouldn't you agree, cousin?" Annabelle sighed.

Francesca shook her head. Apparently, she had been so lost in reverie that she had missed the intervening conversation with Annabelle and did not know to what she referred. She recklessly wished that Mr. Ashbourne would bestow such an expression of pleasure upon her. Her heart quickened in anticipation of an introduction, but rather than accompany her grandmother across the room, he bowed and turned to leave. Her disappointment was acute.

❧❧❧❧

Lady Augusta Haversham floated across the room and grasped Francesca's hand. "Did you see the young man to whom I was talking, my dear?"

With a trembling voice, Francesca responded as nonchalantly as possible, "I did Grandmama. Is the gentleman not hungry?"

"No indeed. He is late because his horse threw a shoe and he had to stop in the village at an inn, the Kings Arms. He is lodging there this evening. Are you acquainted with him?"

"*I* have had the pleasure Grandmama," interjected Annabelle. "I met Mr. Ashbourne in Bath when I was there with Mrs. Sunderland."

"Is that so? How fortunate." Lady Augusta's tone was irritated, and turning to Francesca, she continued, "I knew his grandmother well, she was a girlhood friend and I met him several times over the years when I visited her. It must be five years since I last saw him. He has greatly improved in the intervening years." She turned back to include Annabelle in the conversation. "It appears that he was at Oxford with your cousin William, Annabelle. Isn't that extraordinary? Has William never mentioned it?"

"No," exclaimed Annabelle. "He has not!"

Francesca, still in a trance-like state, was not participating in the conversation at hand but was instead gazing at the doorway that had lately held the young man.

"It was I who invited him to come to your ball this evening. I very much hope that you will make his acquaintance, my dear. Now, I must go and speak to Lady Candelow." With that endorsement hanging in the air, she slipped back to the table she had recently departed.

"Well, I wonder that William never mentioned the connection," exclaimed Annabelle. "I am sure I brought up the association, Francesca. Francesca!"

"What? Oh, excuse me. I cannot imagine what is the matter with me," she murmured. "I feel quite light-headed."

"I believe Mr. Langley Ashbourne has cast a spell on you," she teased.

"I believe he has."

❧ ❧

As the official refreshment portion of the evening drew to a close, Francesca's father gave an emotional speech, which left both Francesca and her mother dabbing at their eyes. He then invited the guests to resume their dancing.

Francesca anxiously scanned the ballroom for the newcomer, Mr. Ashbourne, but could not find him in the dense crowd. She glanced at her dance card, dismayed to see that she had no room left and that she was promised to the rather portly Mr. Bonnington-Smythe for not one but *two* waltzes.

Mr. Bonnington-Smythe found her, though she made a rather sorry companion since she was continually searching the room for Mr.

Ashbourne. She was only half listening to his talk about the weather, but he seemed more than content with the sound of his own voice and did not appear to expect much of a reply, so it was of little consequence. As they completed a set, she suddenly glimpsed the gentleman in question standing by a glass door that was open to let in a much-needed breath of air from the gardens. Mr. Ashbourne was talking with Katherine rather intimately, his head bowed to hers. An unfamiliar and fierce rush of jealousy sprang to her breast. She shook her head to try to dispel it and return her attention to her dance partner, but alas, she could not. Against her will, her eyes hunted for them as her partner twirled her around and around. Mr. Ashbourne, she observed, was touching Katherine's arm in a most familiar way, and the wave of envy came crashing back upon her.

Did Katherine know him? She was pretty, to be sure, but could such a man really admire someone who was so . . . so negative and unpleasant? Why was she having such thoughts about a man she scarcely knew? It was most disconcerting.

The dance ended at last and she rushed to confer with Annabelle.

"Why Annabelle, you look flushed," began Francesca as she saw the heightened color in her fair cousin's cheeks.

"Oh my, Mr. Ambrose Doyle was just saying some very pretty things to me. It is enough to turn a girl's head!"

Though anxious to discuss her own matter, she said, "Do you like him then, Bella?"

"I rather think I do. He is not handsome, but then neither am I—" Francesca opened her mouth to object but Annabelle waved her hand to stop her. "It is true, but I think we look well together, and he is very amusing and kind *and* he owns acres and acres of land in Devonshire! I hope we can further our acquaintance in the coming weeks. I must talk to Papa about him . . ." She made to rush off until Francesca grabbed her arm to arrest her flight. For the first time since the conversation began, Annabelle took a proper look at Francesca's countenance. "My dear, whatever is the matter? Was your partner rude? Did he step on your toes? What can have caused such agitation in your angelic face?"

Francesca dipped her head, looking up at her cousin through lowered lashes like a naughty dog caught stealing food from the table. "Nothing of the kind, Bella. Mr. Bonnington-Smythe was politeness itself, though rather stuffy. No, I came to ask you if cousin Katherine is already acquainted with Mr. Ashbourne? They seem rather familiar. See, over there by the window."

Bella gave her cousin a knowing look and explained, "Yes, she passed through Bath while he was there, though I do not believe they are more than slight acquaintances. However, I own that the cozy portrait they currently present rather contradicts that notion."

"No matter, then," declared Francesca, determined not to let this unfamiliar, primal emotion take hold of her and ruin the best night of her life. "I must find my next partner." And she slipped off to the center of the room.

This time, Francesca determined to give full attention to her partner in order to avoid accidentally catching sight of the pair in the window. Her current dance partner owned much land and was regaling her with tales of pigs dying from a disease his farmers could not fathom. She was nodding in the correct places when halfway through the second dance, a figure tapped her partner on the shoulder and politely asked if he might steal Francesca from him.

Francesca stopped breathing as Mr. Ashbourne gently took her gloved hand in his and expertly spun her around the room, leaving her former partner in the center of the dance floor, spluttering at the lack of manners. She became dizzy at the realization that Mr. Ashbourne was actually dancing with her.

After several turns, he lowered his head and whispered into her ear, his nose tickling her skin and sending a thrill up her spine, causing a delicious sensation in her midriff.

"Are you unwell?" he asked. "You look faint."

She recovered herself and observed that he had a playful smile on his lips, fully aware of the power his presence had on young ladies. Not wanting to appear as inexperienced as she really was, she blurted out, "Oh no, you merely surprised me, that is all."

"Then I shall take pleasure in surprising you whenever I can, as it only serves to heighten your beauty!"

Francesca's cheeks burned under his scrutiny, and she bent her neck to avoid his piercing gaze and gather her confused thoughts. "It appears you are acquainted with my cousin, Katherine Townsend."

"I am indeed. We spent a little time together in Bath. I believe another cousin of yours, Annabelle, was there also. Katherine can play most divinely and has a passable voice. She and I sang together while she played. A very handsome girl, with grace and elegant manners."

Francesca felt her heart sinking and her girlish hopes dashing on the rocks of her fantasies. She searched for something else to say that would not betray her feelings, but Mr. Ashbourne spared her the trouble by telling her some amusing anecdotes about Annabelle's cousin William from their time together at Oxford. As he spoke and guided her smoothly around the dance floor, his soothing tones and friendly manner eased her anxieties. She was mesmerized by his mellow voice and consequently astonished when he released her from his arms; she had not noticed that the music had stopped. She clapped to cover her confusion and nodded toward the orchestra. The other couples followed suit. Then, with a grand bow, Mr. Ashbourne excused himself and swiftly exited the room.

Francesca felt like a candelabra that had lost all its flames in a large gust of wind, dark and empty. Her mother, noticing her apparent distress, came to her rescue and led her off the floor to get some punch.

"You look rather unwell, darling," soothed her mother. "It is near two in the morning. Perhaps you should retire."

"Oh no, Mama, I am quite well. But I believe you were right—I was in need of a drink."

"I think you have danced every dance! You must be exhausted. Are you enjoying the evening?"

"Oh, Mama, I think I might die of happiness! Would that it could go on forever."

"Well, by the looks of your dance card, it will go on for another two hours, at least! Come, let us return to the ball."

Try as she might, Francesca found the rest of the ball lacking. Her handsome consort did not return, and it appeared that he had left Haversham House for his lodgings. Francesca went through the motions of conversing and dancing with many more good-looking young men, but her heart was no longer in it as her heart had already been stolen.

Three

ITALY

Giorgio Giaccopazzi looked down at his hands, surprised to see that he was twisting the bed sheets just as his heart was twisting in his chest. It was not the way of nature. No parent should have to watch their child die. She was not yet forty. He examined his daughter's face as the eyelids fluttered and her breathing became ever more labored. Her raven mane of wild hair, wet with perspiration, stuck to her forehead in ringlets as her body exhausted itself, waging war against the fearsome enemy of fever—a battle it was losing, minute by minute. Her once olive skin was gray, the color of death. For the thousandth time, Giorgio bowed his head and pleaded with the heavens to save his only surviving child. A tear escaped and rolled down his wrinkled cheek, unheeded.

He raised his eyes from the prayer and cast them at the view from the window. A vast ocean of vines, pregnant with fleshy grapes, begging to be harvested. His *other* child. How much time had he devoted to *that* child when he should have spent it with this precious daughter of flesh and blood, now reaching out to touch death's gossamer veil? He caught a sob in his throat and groaned again to the God of heaven to save her, to give him more time.

A strange sound, barely there, caught his ear, and he shifted his gaze back to the invalid in the bed. Her eyes were barely open, but the expression in them was one of desperation and her lips were moving. He leaned close to place his ear by her lips.

"Papa."

He gently clasped her tiny, soft hand in his calloused one. "Si, my darling child. What do you need?"

"Papa, the end is near . . . must tell you something."

"Do not say such things—" He began to sweep aside the notion, but the dying woman imperceptibly shook her head,

"Si, Papa . . . You must be brave . . . let me go . . . I am not afraid . . . must tell . . . confession."

She swallowed hard and pain flitted across her features like a specter. He caressed her forehead delicately, sweeping the damp curls aside.

"Papa . . . lean closer . . . I *must* tell you."

How much longer would he have to stand in the door of the church and shake hands with people before he could go home and give in to the ache in his chest? How much longer need he pretend to be solid when in reality he was teetering on the precipice of despair? He must, it was his duty, but, oh, the pull of his own home and its privacy!

Giorgio pondered on the sober events just passed. The music and flowers had been all that he could have hoped for; the prayers and eulogy were heartfelt and intimate. This church, his church, familiar and comforting but, oh, the reason for his presence there today, unbearable! Death had been an all too familiar guest in his life. The threat of it an ever-present shadow. His dear wife taken twenty years before, still in her prime. The babies, one by one, until, at last, one had survived and patched their broken hearts with her love. Now, she also, taken by its cruel clutches to join the husband who had preceded her. He felt his shoulders bowing under the weight of his grief.

Blessedly, the last of the mourners finally exited the ancient church, and the bells began ringing the requiem, their somber tones matching his mood. He descended the slick marble steps, worn smooth over time by the faithful, and stepped into his carriage with relief.

The wheels bumped along the dirt path the short distance to the cemetery. He climbed out, shielding his eyes from the midday sun, whose brightness seemed to mock his misery. He had petitioned Father Addario to keep the burial private, and within moments, the tones of the Latin prayer were being repeated, their familiar cadence strangely soothing. He bent to pick up a handful of soil and as he let it slip through his fingers and onto her casket, a primal sob escaped from deep within.

The workman stepped forward and, knowing it would be too much to see his beloved shrouded in earth, Giorgio turned back to his carriage and collapsed, a broken man, into the soft cushions.

His hollow mansion echoed with each footstep, jeering at his desire for comfort and warmth. He shooed away the faithful housekeeper and flung wide the glass doors that looked onto his verdant kingdom. As far as the eye could see, his dominion lay, green, lush, and vibrant. Alive. He strode with strident step to seek peace in its quiet corridors.

As he paced, a great wail racked his breast, the emotions he had held at bay bursting forth, cracking the dam of resistance. Soon his thoughts turned back to his last moments with his beloved daughter. Could the confession that lay upon her dying lips be true? A confusion of thoughts seized his mind. How he had prayed that she would be blessed with children during the course of her marriage. A grandson to be heir to the vineyard. But the God of heaven had seen fit to withhold this benediction, and Giorgio had tried to accept and remain faithful. Then, when her husband, Alexander, had been thrown from his horse two years before and broken his neck, he had laid that prayer to rest. Yet this profession of a child, born long ago, unknown to all but the mother! How was it possible? The unanswered questions poured out as he sought to make sense of this new knowledge. His mind captured again upon the last scene with his daughter, Isabella, as she clutched at his hand, impressing upon him the truthfulness of her statement, and begging him to forgive her. Aghast at all it implied, he had sought to press her for details, however, before she could reply her wretched body was overcome with the cursed coughing and she had given up the ghost; at peace at last.

Finding one of the benches he had installed among the vineyards, he sank, holding his head in his hands, the tumult in his mind causing it to pound. He took a deep, shaking breath. Someone, someone must know something! But who?

Isabella had married at an older age than was customary. She had always rebuffed the suitors he had arranged for her. His friends had scolded him for his acquiescence on this—it was softhearted and indulgent, they mocked. Girls should marry whom their fathers chose for them; it was a contract forged to increase land and power.

However, Giorgio did not think like them. *He* had married for love, although his family had frowned upon the match. In spite of this, Concetta, his chosen wife, had woven her magic upon his parents and they had come to love her as a daughter. How could he then force an unwanted marriage upon his only child? He would not! He had contrived for many suitable young men to spend time at his estate in Florence but not until Alexander arrived had she paid any of them the slightest courtesy.

Alexander was older too, his first wife dying tragically in a carriage accident. For many years, Alexander would not even entertain the idea of marrying again, but at the age of thirty-five, he had had enough of loneliness and had accepted Giorgio's invitation at last. Isabella was twenty-three, and some thought she was past her prime, but not Giorgio. She had a maturity of feature that was enchanting and a fine figure. She no longer tittered and swooned like the younger girls and could hold a conversation about politics or the sciences that would engage any gentleman.

He thought back to the day Alexander and Isabella had first met. He had casually mentioned the visit some weeks before and had then been away on business, bringing Alexander back with him. As such, Isabella had not had time to prepare her studied indifference as she usually did around suitors and had burst into his study in the fullness of her natural beauty and character, ready to discuss with him the latest trouble among the workers, flushed from her recent ride.

Giorgio had indicated their visitor by casting his eyes to the side, and Isabella had stopped abruptly in mid-flow. Turning fully to face the gentleman in question, she had bobbed quickly in his direction, a crimson glow upon her olive cheek.

Giorgio had watched the man's face with intent as he read upon it an instant attraction to the ebullient woman who had thrust her presence upon them. Alexander had bowed in response, keeping his light-brown eyes firmly fixed on Isabella's dark ones. She had apologized for her intrusion and had prepared to leave when Alexander had contradicted her and insisted upon her staying. She, Giorgio noticed with satisfaction, had run her hand over her unruly locks to tame them and had sat primly on the edge of a chair and waited. Alexander had requested that she continue to detail the affair of the workers to her father, which she did reluctantly, after much persuasion. Alexander had proffered a solution, which had interested Isabella greatly, and Giorgio had fabricated a reason to find his land manager, leaving the two alone in his study.

As he returned, he was welcomed by the sound of sunny laughter from his daughter, and as he re-entered the study, it was obvious that the couple had found pleasure in the company of one another. Alexander, who had been invited to spend a week at the estate, instead stayed for a month, at the end of which the couple were engaged.

Giorgio managed a watery smile as he recalled the magnificent wedding day. A jewel in his life's crown. It had been magical and the marriage, by and large, had been a happy one but for the want of children.

His mind now surged forward as he recalled the confession on his dying daughter's lips. Did he think less of her? He examined his feelings. He was a man of staunch Catholic faith, but he was also a man of compassion, and he wept—not for the sin, but that the child had not been a part of his life, a solace in this time of mourning, a companion for his dotage. He wiped his eyes with his handkerchief. Yes, his mission was clear. He must find the child!

Four

ENGLAND

$\mathcal{S}$unlight flashed upon Francesca's face like a tongue of fire and woke her faster than any other means might have. She groaned and pulled the covers over her head to shield her eyes from the bright light. Almost simultaneously there was a pressure near the end of her bed and she heard Annabelle praising the day. Reluctantly she pushed the coverlet away, squinting into the bright room.

"I could barely sleep after the ball. My every thought was of Mr. Doyle, the memory of his flattery would not let me rest, and I—" Annabelle stopped abruptly as she finally laid her eyes upon her sleepy cousin. "Oh dear, were you not ready to arise? It is past twelve noon, and the day is so glorious and I could hardly bridle my impatience any longer—I just *had* to confer with you on the tone and meaning of his admiration. But I believe I have intruded upon your slumber and will take myself off this instant!"

Francesca sat up, shaking her head. "No, no. Do not trouble to leave now that I am awake, but do you not recall that we did not drop in to bed until four o'clock in the morning?" She sank back upon the downy pillows, her arm shielding her eyes against the noon day sun filling the room.

"What is sleep when there is romance to discuss?" replied her cousin with a smile lighting up her pale eyes. "I thought the memory of the gallant and handsome Mr. Ashbourne might have kept you from sleeping, but I see now that such is not the case. Oh darling, do you think

Mr. Doyle was using flattery as a way to pass the time, or do you believe him to be sincere in his attentions to me?"

"I am sure I cannot judge after so little time in his company and at such a public event as a ball, but he did appear to be most sincere from his expression as he danced with you. Have you spoken to your father about inviting him to Danbury Manor?"

"I tried to find Papa at breakfast but he did not appear. I think I will try again at luncheon and suggest that he include Mr. Doyle in the picnic we have planned next week. Do you think such a course is too forward?"

"I am sure it is not, since the picnic is to be a grand affair of fifty people rather than something very intimate. I think it is a splendid idea, Bella!"

Annabelle leaned forward to embrace her cousin and then flounced from the room.

Francesca fell back again in repose and was conscious of a throbbing in her temples, due, she was sure, to a lack of sleep. She closed her eyes against the light and reflected on the festivities of the previous evening but was soon troubled by the vision of her cousin Katherine's silhouette and that of Mr. Ashbourne in the open window. She was struck again by the impression of familiarity that existed in the pose. She shook her head to rid her mind of the troubling image. She succeeded in replacing it with the memory of Mr. Ashbourne dancing with her. Might not spectators have considered his attentions while dancing with her to be rather intimate? Perhaps it was just his way.

She replayed the manner in which he had leaned to whisper to her and the way it had made her spine sing as his nose brushed her ear. She shivered at the memory. She recalled the way her heart had skipped as he touched her gloved hand. She had felt attraction to young men before, to be sure, but this sudden, intense reaction was completely foreign. It was more than a little frightening that so small an acquaintance could elicit such a depth of passion. And what, really, did she know of him? Nothing. It was just the foolish fancy of a young girl. She would question her cousin Katherine about her acquaintance with him to ascertain the level of their friendship and to discover his character.

She dressed quickly and went in search of Katherine, who she found in the rose garden painting in water colors. She really was very gifted. Francesca could only hope for half her talent. "Good afternoon, Katherine. How you have captured the essence of this lovely day."

"I cannot agree. I seem unable to replicate the velvet of the rose petals. But it is no matter. It is a pleasant way to pass an afternoon while everyone is sleeping, even if I shall throw it in the fire later."

Why did she have to have such an unpleasant tone even after having been complimented? Francesca dismissed these thoughts and began again. "I had such a pleasant time with Mr. Ashbourne last evening. Annabelle tells me you are acquainted with him."

"Not really," she said quickly, brush in hand, squinting at the rose she was aiming to capture.

"Oh! I understood that you had met him while at Bath. I must be mistaken."

Katherine continued to paint without turning to face her cousin, "Yes, we did meet while in Bath and sang some songs together, but I would hardly call it an acquaintance."

Francesca could not help but notice the tinge of pink that appeared on her cousin's cheeks and the sudden stiffness of her spine. Could it be that she was withholding the truth of the matter from her? To what end? Francesca recovered herself and continued in the same falsely casual tone.

"I was hoping you could tell me about his character. He seems to be a charming and elegant young man with such good manners that I am wondering if it is all a great facade. Can anyone really be so pleasant?"

She had meant it as a lighthearted, comedic comment, but at her cousin's sharp intake of breath, she was dismayed to see that she may have hit upon a truth.

"Why Katherine, are you all right?"

"Yes, yes. I just caught my shoe on the edge of my easel and thought I might knock the whole painting to the floor," said Katherine.

"So, can you tell me of his character? Is he really so charming?" pushed Francesca.

"My dear cousin. I told you, I barely know the gentleman. However, I believe your Grandfather Haversham knows him. Why don't you go in search of him and ask after the gentleman?" Her tone was dismissive, and though Francesca dearly wanted to press the matter further, she thought better of it and went in search of her grandfather, Lord Haversham.

She found him in the library ostensibly reviewing some plans with her father. The two men were deep in a heated conversation that they hurriedly broke off as she entered. She glanced from her father to her grandfather and could not help but notice the heightened color in both men's cheeks.

"I must apologize for the interruption . . ."

"It is of no consequence," said her father a little too quickly, crossing the room to embrace his daughter. "We were just discussing some business." He threw his father a warning look. Curious.

"But I can come back if this is not a convenient time." The very air was thick with discomfort.

"Of course not, child," he said gently. "What is it you want?"

"I actually wanted to ask Grandfather a question," she said. "Grandfather, I was coming to inquire after Mr. Ashbourne. He was so polite and gentlemanly last evening, and I find I know very little of him. And then he left in such a mysterious fashion. I understand he is the grandson of friends of yours?" She raised her delicate brows in a query that was so touching that it melted her father's heart. Her grandfather's smile was less innocent.

"That is correct. His grandfather was a close friend of mine, though he died many years ago, and your grandmother is a friend of his grandmother. He is of marriageable age, and so we did propose that he attend your coming out ball. His father was not opposed to the idea. His family goes back to the time of Henry the VIII, and they own most of Shropshire, I believe. They are fine stock, my dear. And he will inherit his father's title. Eminently suitable."

Francesca could not account for why her grandfather's answer left her feeling unsatisfied, but there was no doubt that it did. Her father's forehead clouded, his lips set in a firm line.

Lord Haversham was a man of few emotions. Therefore, she wisely decided that since he had given her all the information he was likely to, she would take her leave. Perhaps Grandmama would know more. She kissed them both and left the room, wondering what could have led to such an intense discussion between father and son.

After tea, one of the maids announced the arrival of Phillip Waverley. Bella clapped her hands together in delight but Francesca experienced a sense of irritation. She tried to push the feeling away and arrange her features into a welcoming smile as he approached them both and kissed their outstretched hands.

"Wasn't it a wonderful ball, Phillip?" gushed Bella.

"Why yes, yes it was!" he agreed enthusiastically and looked eagerly into Francesca's face to see a confirmation.

"I never had such a wonderful time!" she replied truthfully.

"You seemed to dance with most every young man in the room," he laughed, "I expect you are frightfully tired today after all that exertion!"

"Yes, I am rather," she replied. "Though it was such a delightful evening that I wasn't at all sleepy until the last guests had left and Mary was helping me to get ready for bed. As soon as my head touched the pillow I was asleep and I didn't wake up until, well, until Bella woke me up." And she gave her cousin a dramatically petulant look.

"Phillip, did you meet anyone that you particularly liked?" asked Annabelle.

Phillip ducked his head quickly and coughed before answering.

"The room was full of pleasant girls bursting with youthful beauty. For a young man, it was a veritable paradise. And what about the two of you?"

"Bella dear is in love already!" exclaimed Francesca, and Annabelle opened her eyes wide and clasped her hands to her chest.

"It is true!" she admitted. "I met a Mr. Doyle who was utterly charming and made me feel as if I were the most beautiful girl in the room, which, of course, is poppycock, but it was so nice to hear it! Do you know him, Phillip?"

"As a matter of fact, I do. I was up at Oxford with him, and he invited me to spend time at his family's home in Surrey one year. He is an excellent chap and quite brilliant. Made me feel a bit of a dunce. He is the second son and has taken up the law. He was a year ahead of me and is gaining quite a good reputation for one who is still quite young."

"But what is he like? Do you think he is a flatterer in general, or was he sincere?"

Phillip leaned back in the chair and crossed his legs. "He is the genuine article, Annabelle. He was never anything but kind to everyone and was a favorite with the masters at Oxford. He was even courteous to the servants and the porters, truth be told, and I have never heard him be cross at all, now that I think about it. We spent quite a bit of time together in his last year at college and though he complimented everyone, I think you can be certain that he is not a flatterer and that he must, therefore, genuinely have a very high regard for you. In fact, I must disclose that we spent some time together last evening in conversation and he mentioned you to me as a very interesting and beautiful woman."

"Oh, he did not!"

"Annabelle, have you ever known me to tell a lie?" asked Phillip.

"Well no . . . oh, it is too exciting! I am going directly to have my father ask him to our picnic. Might you be able to join us, Phillip? Then there will be someone he is already acquainted with in attendance. Oh, say you will!"

"I can think of nothing I would rather do!"

He turned slightly in the chair to face Francesca and pet her dog. "What about you? Did you meet anyone who put a light in your step?"

"I did have the most marvelous evening, and I danced with so many charming young men. But there was one young man who did stand out above the others, I believe."

She paused and Phillip moved to the edge of the chair and gave her such a look, part encouragement, part desperation.

"He arrived late and left early and is an acquaintance of my grandparents. His name is Mr. Langley Ashbourne. Do you know of him, Phillip?"

Phillip tried to hide the disappointment he felt and replied in an even tone that he did not know the gentleman in question.

"Grandfather . . . well, you know how he is. He gave little evidence of his character, and Grandmama only knew his grandmother. Katherine keeps insisting that she does not know him well, though they met in Bath last year. I am quite at a loss."

"Did you not say that he mentioned my cousin William as an acquaintance?" Annabelle reminded her. "Can you not write to him?"

"It does not seem quite proper, though I would dearly love to."

"Then let me take on the task," said Phillip, impulsively. "I know your cousin William, and perhaps I can find others who are more acquainted with him and bring you back a report."

Francesca looked up and pierced him with her chocolate eyes. His heart skittered.

"Oh, would you?" she said passionately. "Phillip, I would be ever so grateful."

At that moment, her mother and grandmother entered the room, and the subject, not being considered quite appropriate, was changed quickly to talk of the weather and the food at the ball.

After the mandatory fifteen minutes of polite conversation, Phillip excused himself with a heavy heart and cursed himself for offering to help the opposition.

❧❦❧

The following day, Francesca and Annabelle walked into the village of Riverton St. Mary in search of ribbon for their summer hats. Bella was still twittering about Mr. Doyle and the fact that she had been able to persuade her father to send him an invitation to the picnic. Francesca was more taciturn, but Bella's exuberance meant that she did not notice.

Having found the perfect ribbons, they wandered along the streets in the pleasant, warming sunshine and came upon the very inn where Mr. Ashbourne had been said to be staying.

Francesca slapped her gloved hand to her mouth and looked pointedly at the inn's hanging sign. Bella, who had not been paying attention to anything other than her speculations on Mr. Doyle, stopped with a quizzical look on her face, then following her cousin's gaze, looked up. The connection dawned upon her, and she looked back at Francesca.

"Dearest, I do not think it would be quite proper for us to go into such an establishment unaccompanied. It is rather more of an ale house than a tea house."

"Of course, you are right. It was just such a happy coincidence and I entertained the idea that we might bump into him as he exited, if he is still here, of course."

They lingered on the road for as long as they dared and, disappointed, continued on their walk. Francesca could not resist a glance back over her shoulder before they crossed the bridge to go home and was just in time to see her cousin Katherine exiting the inn. She gasped which caused Annabelle to turn around but there was no one there by that time and indeed, Francesca wondered if her mind was not playing tricks on her. Why would a young woman of high birth risk being seen alone in an inn? She would surely lose her character. She must have been mistaken.

Upon their arrival home, they greeted Francesca's mother, Emily, and Annabelle's mother, who were working on their needlepoint. They showed their mothers the pretty ribbons they had bought in the village and discussed the weather and the people they had seen, as well-bred English people are wont to do.

As they were leaving Mrs. Haversham's sitting room, they heard the front door open and, looking over the banister, witnessed the entrance of Katherine. Francesca was seized with a sudden longing to know the truth of the matter and bounced down the stairs at a precipitous pace, leaving Annabelle at the top staring down in astonishment.

"Katherine," gasped Francesca. "Have you been out for a walk to the village? We have just returned. You should have told us and we could have gone together."

Her sudden presence had startled Katherine, who put her hand to her chest and looked up to see Annabelle looking down. She paused just long enough to gather her thoughts and look Francesca square in the eye. "No, I have just been walking in the meadows of the estate. It is such a fine day." She turned her shoulder to indicate that she wanted to pass by Francesca to go up the stairs to her room. However, Francesca was not done with her probing yet.

"In truth, then you must have a twin, for I could swear that we just saw you in the village!" Francesca clapped her hands together and kept her eyes on her cousin's face.

"I must, indeed, have a twin then," Katherine said cautiously. "For I have not been into the village today. Now, if you will excuse me, I must go and lay down as I rather feel a headache coming on."

Francesca watched her ascend the stairs with ever more questions whirling in her head. Katherine's manner had seemed defensive, and if she were innocent, why would that be necessary? On the other hand, it was so unlikely that Katherine would have compromised herself that Francesca decided to let the matter rest for the moment.

Five

ITALY

The estate manager, Mario, squinted in concentration. "Eighteen years ago, you say? Signore, you know I was a mere laborer back then."

Giorgio plucked at the corner of his waistcoat, wretched in anticipation. "Yes, yes I know. But do you remember anything from that time? My daughter may have taken a voyage of some sort . . ."

"Would that have been the summer of the hundred-year drought, Signore?"

Giorgio frowned, thinking, then said, "Yes! Yes, it was!"

"I remember very well that you were anxious that the crop not perish. You hired every man in the surrounding villages to bring water from the river to moisten the vines. We worked tirelessly to keep the vines from dying, and in the evenings the village laborers celebrated their good fortune. Oh yes, I remember it now."

"But Isabella, do you recall if she left at that time?"

"I do not, Signore, but Maria the cook was here then. Let us bring her here and ask."

With a flick of his head, Giorgio agreed, and Mario hurried down to the kitchens.

A rotund, hunched old woman entered the room, anxious about being hauled upstairs.

"Maria, you need have no fear," began Giorgio. "Do you remember my daughter as a young woman?"

The old cook's shoulders relaxed, and she looked up into the face of her employer. "Oh, to be sure, Signore. Such a beautiful girl, the beauty of all of Florence!"

"Yes, yes!" He sensed that his tone was impatient and mustered all his energy into rendering his voice as gentle and calm as possible. "I need to know if you remember the year my daughter returned from school. Do you recall whether she left on a journey that same year?"

The old woman lifted her eyes to the ceiling and pursed her lips in concentration.

"It was the year of the hundred-year drought," added the estate manager, helpfully.

"Was it? Let me think," she croaked. Giorgio held onto his fists tightly so that he would not drum his fingers on the desk. Waiting was an agony.

"I believe that was the year that a stable boy left without notice and the milking cow ran a fever and we could not get good milk to make cream. The whole kitchen was in an uproar as there was an important dinner to be held. We had to get our cream from afar that year and—"

"Yes, but did my daughter go away?"

He was failing this test of patience, and the look of distress reappeared in the lines of the old woman's face.

"I am sorry, forgive my impatience," he said softly. "But it is of vital importance that I know where my daughter made a journey to that year."

The look of concentration reappeared, but then her brow smoothed and her eyes lit up and Giorgio knew hope.

"Yes, yes!" she exclaimed. "You were so busy with the vines, and she told me that since she was not needed she was going to visit southern France with her maid. She said she was old enough to travel and had always wanted to see that part of the world. She told me because it meant that I did not have to provide her meals for a few months, and what with the problem with the dairy cow, it was a relief. Do you not remember it, Signore?"

France. Giorgio cast back in his mind, grasping at whispers of memories. He remembered the drought and the manpower he had hired in an effort to save his crops. They had worked night after night, day after day to water the vines and keep the grapes fleshy. His daughter had returned from finishing school, and though he had been happy to have her home, he had been consumed with the vines and the drought that had pushed him to the brink of financial ruin. He shook his head slowly. He had ignored his own daughter, neglected her, and it had forced her to find attention in another quarter. His regret was bitter indeed.

"What was the name of her maid, Maria?" he said gently. "Do you remember her? Does she still live?"

"She does! She lives with her sister in Sandicci. But she is very old, Signore, and I have heard that her mind has gone."

⚬❧❧❧⚬

The door of the tiny villa opened, and a white-haired woman wrapped in a shawl appeared. On seeing a gentleman, she dropped a curtsy. "What can a humble old milkmaid do for you, Signore?"

"I believe that your sister lives here with you? Luciana?"

"Yes, but what business can you have with her?" She closed the door and stood in front of it with arms crossed and leveled her gaze directly into Giorgio's eyes.

"She was my daughter Isabella's maid for many years, and my daughter has recently died. There is information your sister may have that is of the greatest import to me. Do you think she will give me an audience?"

The woman unfolded her arms and softened her gaze, her defensive demeanor relaxing.

"I am sorry that your daughter has died. She must have been young. Such a shame when the young are taken. It is true that my sister was a lady's maid, but I must warn you, Signore, her memory fails her. Sometimes she is here with us, and other times . . ." She flicked her hand toward the sky. "I will see if she is with us today. Please come inside my humble home and out of the blazing sun."

Giorgio told his driver to wait and entered the tiny dwelling. His nose was assaulted by the smell of urine and damp dog. As his eyes adjusted from the brightness outside, a tiny woman sitting in a rocking chair materialized. He looked hard to see if he recognized her at all, but she was silver haired, bent, and fragile and bore little resemblance to the woman who had lived under his roof almost two decades before. He now recalled that she had left their employ to take care of her ailing mother when Isabella had married.

"Luciana, here is someone to see you." The woman in the chair looked up at her sister, but her eyes were unfocused.

"Luciana, this is Isabella's father. He has come to ask you some questions, dear."

At the name *Isabella*, the dim eyes wandered back from the distance and locked onto her sister's. The sister turned to Giorgio and Luciana's eyes followed. There was no recognition in them, but in a faint, strained voice, she wheezed, "Ah, you knew Isabella? She was a beauty and no mistaking. She used to have such a temper as a teenager. I would try and dress her hair and she would give me a difficult time! But then she could be so sweet and gentle. Oh, how I miss her . . ." The voice faltered and stopped.

"I wonder, do you remember the summer you and Isabella went to France?" Giorgio encouraged her.

The woman slowly turned her head and looked directly into Giorgio's eyes. Hers were shadowed by cataracts and any color had long since faded away. She blinked and slowly put her finger to her lips.

"France . . . it is a secret."

Giorgio's heart rate quickened. "What is the secret?" he asked.

"It is a secret. Shh! We must not tell Papa."

Giorgio shot a look at the sister pleading for her help.

"Sister dear, it is no longer a secret. Come, tell us what happened. This man is a friend, and he needs to hear the story. Can you tell it?" The invalid shook her head and rocked the chair back and forth, slowly. "No. I made a promise. She made me promise. I cannot disappoint her. She was so lovely . . ."

Fearing that her vulnerable mind was wandering, Giorgio pressed on. "Isabella told me to tell you that you have fulfilled your promise and that she has given permission for you to speak of it."

"Ah, dearest Isabella. She was such a beauty . . ."

"Yes, we know that, dear. Now tell the gentleman about the journey."

"No, it is a secret." The elderly woman closed her eyes and began to hum, a smile creeping onto her lips as she rocked in the chair.

A stab of pain in his cheekbone alerted Giorgio to the fact that his jaw was clenched, and he attempted to relax and avoid letting panic consume him. He tried a different tack.

"I have the sad duty to inform you that Isabella has died."

The chalky eyes flew open and pinned him like daggers. "Isabella is dead?"

Without warning, the old woman threw back her head and howled in pain. Her sister thrust her arms around her in an attempt to console the fragile woman, who was shrieking like a distraught child.

"I am sorry, Signore," she bellowed over the wailing. "I think you must come back tomorrow and try again."

Giorgio nodded and made for the door. As he exited, he looked back on the tableau that formed a pseudo image of a mother comforting her small child. He sighed deeply with regret that he had caused the uproar and walked back out into the welcome sunshine.

He spent a restless night at an inn in Sandicci, filled with dreams of running from house to house in search of his infant grandchild and awoke in a great sweat before the sun was up.

Should I stay, or is the woman's mental state too unstable to yield the required memories? he debated with himself.

The inn provided a fine breakfast, and during it, a message arrived for him from the former maid's sister, which made the decision for him.

"Signore, my sister wept far into the night but then slept like a baby. This morning she is more alert than I have witnessed these many months. Please, make haste."

As he stood to knock on the now familiar cottage door, he checked his emotions and reined in his expectations.

He was quickly ushered inside. "Look, sister. Isabella's father has returned! He needs to know the secret." The old maid nodded and began to speak, and it was as if another woman entirely were before him. Yes, the eyes were still dimmed, but there was life in the expression and lines of the face.

"You are her father? I loved her as a mother would. I never had my own children, you know. Her own poor mother had died . . ." Her voice trailed off, and she sat lost in cloudy memories.

"You journeyed to France with her?" encouraged the sister.

"Yes, I remember that. Her father was busy . . . she was lonely. She loved horses. She spent too much time with the horses. I scolded her. She was drawn to the stables and would not mind me . . ." The old woman shook her head at the memory, and a smile tugged at her lips.

"And France?" pushed the sister.

"France? Ah, yes France. Poor Isabella was so neglected. We went to France to see her friends and then . . . she told me it was a secret. She will be angry with me for telling it . . ."

"No, no sister. She will not be angry. What happened in France?"

"She tried to tell her father . . . he was busy, always busy . . . too busy . . ." The old woman looked through him into the past. He felt a jolt of guilt, and he racked his memory for such an occasion. He had none. He wiped a tear from his eye.

"We traveled to Nice. She was quiet. Very quiet. Too quiet."

"Did you meet someone there?" asked the sister.

"Friends. We met friends from school. Good girls, happy girls. Isabella was sad. Why so sad? I combed her hair. Beautiful, thick hair. I'm going away."

"Isabella went away?"

"She left me . . . left me alone. Took another maid . . . I was her maid . . . she left me . . ."

"Where did Isabella go?"

"Isabella, she was kind . . . she gave me money, but I was alone . . . she left me . . . for four months. Four months. I cried when she left me."

"Do you know where she went?"

"It's a secret. Shh. Swear, Luciana. Swear you will not tell." The old maid frowned like a child caught disobeying.

"It is all right. Remember, she has given permission for you to share it with me," repeated Giorgio. Luciana quirked an eyebrow at him, still suspicious.

"She left. It was not proper. I told her it was not appropriate. For months and months. It is not proper . . ."

"You do not know where she went?" asked her sister.

"No. She would not tell me. I got letters. Short letters. She did love me. She wrote me letters."

"What happened when she returned?"

"She was ill. Gray and ill. Sad. Very sad. Her eyes—they were empty. Poor, pretty Isabella. She was so . . . broken . . ." Her cheeks glistened. "Where have you been? Who has hurt you? Do not ask, do not ask. We must go home . . . tomorrow we must go home . . . Luciana, this must be our secret." The muddled memories were tumbling out now.

"Did you suspect the cause of her sorrow, sister?"

"She was so pale, so tearful. She grieved . . ."

"Who did she grieve for?"

The old woman's eyes jumped from side to side then she whispered, "For the baby."

The sister looked to Giorgio with concern but he nodded. "She told you that she had a baby?" she asked Luciana.

"No, she would not tell me. I guessed. So much grief."

"Do you know who might have done that to her?" entreated Giorgio.

Her voice dropped to a whisper again, "That stable boy. He loved her. I should have known. I am to blame. I am guilty. When we got home, he was gone. Gone." She brushed away a tear. "But I kept her secret until today."

"You have done well!" said Giorgio. "Now that she is gone, it is right that you should have told me."

The old woman's expression clouded. "She is gone again? To France?"

Confused, Giorgio looked to the sister for direction.

"Yes, dear," she soothed. "She has gone away again."

"I hope that she does not fall ill again. I was so worried for her health," croaked the old maid. Sensing that the door to lucidity was closing, Giorgio pressed, "Do you recall the names of the friends she traveled with?"

The old woman's face crumpled as she strained to remember. ". . . Angeloni . . . from Rome."

He scribbled down the name. "I thank you from the bottom of my heart. You were an affectionate and devoted companion to my girl, and I am indebted to you."

He clasped her hands and turned to leave, pressing a leather bag of coins into the hand of the sister.

"Signore, that is not necessary—"

"I know, but this information is of great worth to me. I thank you for sending for me this morning."

He took one last glance at the maid rocking in the chair, lost in her memories, and with renewed confidence, entered his carriage.

Six

ENGLAND

Upon leaving Haversham House, Phillip ran his horse hard for a half a mile and then let it slow to a canter. He wiped his mouth with the back of his hand and cursed his new commission. Why had he offered to investigate another suitor's character when what he really wanted to do was declare his love for Francesca himself? He took off his hat and threw it as far as he could in frustration. Why not declare himself? The answer made him feel like a coward. The truth was that he was not sure that she cared for him in that way. She treated him well and fondly but more as a brother than a suitor, and now this infernal Ashbourne fellow had turned her head. Had he subconsciously offered to help in the hopes that he would discover him to be a cad, unworthy of Francesca's affections?

He jumped off his mare to retrieved his hat, mounted again, and took a more leisurely pace. This task would be a sore test of his integrity, for were he to find out that the man was a saint, could he be honest enough to relay a true portrait of him to Francesca? Worse, if the man proved to be a devil, would he be able to restrain himself from celebrating and showing his contempt for the man?

As he rode, he reflected on the change in his feelings over the last year. Though she was four years his junior, he and his older brother had played with Francesca and her cousins when they were children. She was like the little sister he never had, and they had had many adventures together among the fields and meadows of the two estates.

She had always been a pretty child with her wild, ebony hair, but it was her high spiritedness that he enjoyed so much. She was given to gesticulating with abandon when impassioned and had a fiery temper when crossed but not in such a way as to make anyone angry and her outbursts were all soon forgotten. She had a little dog whom she loved dearly and a horse whom she spoiled. Even as a young girl she had been an excellent equestrian. In fact, he had never met her match.

She hated to arise early and he had learned to avoid her before noon, and she dearly loved to dance; he had been chosen to be her dancing partner on many a wet afternoon.

When she turned twelve, it had been deemed unladylike to continue to wander about the grounds with young men, and he had missed the association very much. Other things had changed too, as she had been required to learn the art of becoming a refined young lady and her maid had had to learn to tame her wild locks into ringlets. There was less spontaneity and more needlepoint and music lessons, which she hated; less adventure and more history lessons. However, he was still invited to tea on occasion and to play croquet from time to time and their easy friendship had continued. She had still sought his company, and he hers.

Then he had left to go up to Oxford. He was to study the law, as he did not seem suited for the church or the military, and when it came time for the summer breaks, he was regularly invited to spend them with friends at their country estates or traveling abroad. And so it happened that three years passed where he did not see Francesca at all. Then, just before the start of trinity term of his final year, his mother had implored him to visit. He had arrived to great fanfare as he had done exceptionally well in his final exams of the previous year and his mother was all of a flutter with pride. She had brought him to Haversham House to parade like a peacock in front of the Havershams, which annoyed him immensely. He was feeling most uncomfortable with such praise being heaped on his head when the door to the drawing room opened and a vision of utter loveliness entered the room. He gasped before he could control his emotions and adjust to the comeliness that had developed in his absence. Francesca was quite unaware of her own metamorphosis or the effect that it had had on him and rushed to offer him her hand. She was eager to hear of his successes and peevish that he had stayed away for so long. He found himself tongue-tied and shy until her easy manner disarmed him and he relaxed in her company.

The hair that had been so wild was coiffed into a perfect crown and the play dresses had been replaced with fine muslin gowns that accentuated her womanly figure to perfection. The rosy, plump cheeks of childhood had been sculpted into prominent features that gave her a regal bearing of exquisite beauty, a beauty of which she seemed innocently unaware. Her entrance into the room had cast an enchantment upon him.

After that first renewed encounter, he had sought every opportunity to visit without appearing to be overly eager, and as the days passed, his heart had become more and more enslaved. For her part, she seemed to treat him as she had in the past, as a true and loyal friend. But he wanted to be more than friends. He had challenged himself to test the waters before returning to Oxford but had shrunk from the task for fear of damaging the comfortable relationship they enjoyed.

And so, the year had passed, and he had graduated, and yet he still lacked the courage to disclose his true feelings.

He trotted on miserably, wishing with all his heart that Ashbourne would prove to be a rake.

✢

Phillip's horse had stumbled and become lame, therefore he was not in the best of moods when he arrived at William's family home in Staffordshire. William and Phillip had played together as children when his family visited the Havershams and had attended the same boarding school. Though he and William were up at Oxford together, they had moved in very different circles for the most part, and his circle had not included the infernal Mr. Ashbourne. As old friends, Phillip had managed to wangle an invitation to William's home in pursuit of information.

"Phillip, my, but it is good to see you! How was your journey?" William welcomed.

"I would have been here hours earlier but my horse fell lame in Stoke. It took me an age to find a decent horse for hire. But I am here now. It is good to see you again, William!"

"How are your parents? And your brother?"

"My parents are both well, and my brother is enjoying life as a married man. Did you know that he is about to become a father?"

"Well, well. I still think of him in short trousers trying to fish in the stream on your estate. Can he really be old enough to have a child?"

"Come, come, *we* are both old enough, are we not?"

William shuddered involuntarily. "The thought of having a wife and child at the present moment fills me with fear and trepidation. I want to get settled in my regiment and establish myself. Who knows but that I will be flung into the middle of a war soon?" He chuckled.

"Ah, but you have just not met the right girl yet," Phillip teased. "Then you will think of nothing else but making her your wife."

"You sound as though you speak from experience. Who is she then?" asked William.

"Oh, no. I speak in theory only," Phillip countered, hoping that the heat he felt creeping to his face would not give him away.

At that moment, the door opened, saving him from further denials, and William allowed his mother to welcome their guest.

❧❧

William's family had been invited to dine with their neighbors, the Fairweathers. They had four daughters and were a very merry family. As they took the barouche to the appointment, Phillip used the opportunity to pry into the character of the irksome Mr. Ashbourne.

"Langley? Yes, I know him quite well. But do not you? I was often with him in the dining hall. Splendid fellow! Always good for some fun."

"No, I did not have the fortune of meeting him. What of his family?"

"He is the only son of a baronet. So, it was of no account if he failed his exams, you see. I believe his father is an older man, more like a grandfather, really, and I understand that his mother died while he was yet a child."

Harrumph. A sympathetic character then, thought Phillip with disdain.

"Why do you ask?" said William.

"Oh, he appeared at Francesca's coming out ball and I was intrigued. He came late and left early. Very mysterious."

"Ha ha, yes, that sounds about right. He is devilishly handsome and has the young ladies fairly fainting over him."

So far, the report was not in Phillip's favor. He must find some flaw.

"Would he, perhaps, compromise the young women, then?"

"Far from it! As far as I can tell, he seems to have the greatest respect for the fairer sex. I would suggest that he has merely not yet found his equal."

"He appeared to give Francesca quite a bit of his time," noted Phillip.

"Did he now? Well, she is a beauty, isn't she? Can you believe how she has improved in the last twelve months? Yes, now that you mention it, I do believe she *is* his equal in looks. Perhaps she has piqued his interest after all?"

He turned to look at Phillip and remarked, "Is that it? Are you in love with her yourself, then?"

"No, no not at all," he protested. "Francesca and I have been friends since childhood. I was simply interested," he said and looked out of the window to escape further scrutiny.

"Hmm, methinks you do protest too much! But in all seriousness, Francesca and Langley. Yes, I can see them together. Did she appear to be beguiled?"

"I do not know," he lied. Then he hurried to change the subject.

The Fairweather daughters were very congenial. They were all in the first bloom of womanhood and were each very pretty, but none of them was yet married. Their mother had made the invitation to William's family after learning of their house guest, with a view to Phillip being bewitched by one of them. Her manner was obsequious, and it grated on Phillip's nerves, but their father was a very agreeable man who loved to read and fish.

Very little time had passed when it became apparent that the oldest Miss Fairweather, Miss Verity, had set her cap at Phillip. He found her to be intelligent and charming and had his heart not already been taken he would have found her company delightful. She was very slight with curly blond hair and pale blue eyes that made him think of starling eggs. She was quite short and looked up into his face in a most appealing manner, and he found himself quite flattered by her attentions.

Phillip in turn acted in a most gentlemanly way and gave her his full attention. She talked of her schooling in Switzerland and her visit to Scotland to see an aunt.

After dinner, she announced that she would play for them all and asked Phillip quietly if he might change the pages for her. He knew enough of music to do a fair job and agreed to accompany her to the piano. He looked up to study the rest of the company as he turned the music. The third Miss Fairweather was obviously well acquainted with William and they were discussing some of the local families. It was clear to an observer that she very much admired William, but it was equally obvious that he was oblivious of her sentiments.

Phillip glanced at the other inhabitants of the room. He caught Mrs. Fairweather staring at him, whereupon she hastily turned her head. He felt a smile coming. Mrs. Fairweather was sitting on the edge of her chair, twisting a handkerchief in an attitude of great agitation. It really was a trial for a woman to have so many grown daughters who were still single. Mr. Fairweather was conversing with William's father and William's mother was persuading the other two sisters of the virtues of Bath.

As the evening was ending, the Fairweather family invited Phillip and William to attend a ball with them two days hence. They declined, having not received a formal invitation, but Mrs. Fairweather explained that they could attend as their guests, since the hosts were a very generous family.

Phillip went to bed that night feeling that he had made some delightful new acquaintances and looking forward to the ball. He did not fall asleep quickly, though, as his errand had not yet been completed and Ashbourne's character had not been thoroughly proved.

◦◦◦

On the day of the ball, Phillip could not help but notice, with some humor, that the women required much more preparation than the men. Phillip had spent a very pleasant afternoon with Mr. Fairweather fishing in his pond and he had told Phillip that the young ladies had begun their preparations as soon as breakfast was finished. He, on the other hand, had spent the day in sport with Mr. Fairweather and would begin to prepare for the ball barely an hour before.

While fishing, Phillip had discovered that Mr. Fairweather was an effortless man to converse with and that he had an encyclopedic knowledge of many things due to his love of reading.

"You know that my wife has her eyes set on you for our oldest daughter, do you?" said Mr. Fairweather during the course of the afternoon.

"I believe I did notice that, sir," replied Phillip.

"Well, what do you think of it? Verity is fairly taken with you. She is a sensible girl, and you seem to be a fine fellow. You could do worse!" he added with a chuckle.

"Your daughter is one of the most amiable young women I have had the good fortune to meet, but I must confess that I am about to embark on a career in the law and am not in a position to marry at present."

"Bosh! She comes with a generous dowry. She could help you set up in the law and she is an intelligent girl, you know."

"I do not doubt it, sir, but I am really not in the market for marriage at the present time." He hoped his words were not hurtful, but the reality of his deep feelings for Francesca meant that he could not in good faith mislead this worthy man and his family with false hopes of a future matrimony.

"She'll be disappointed. She has taken a real liking to you. Ah well, these things cannot be forced, I suppose. You will continue to visit, though? We all greatly enjoy your company."

"Perhaps if I am in the county and you are willing to receive me?" said Phillip.

"Of course, boy, and she may succeed in turning your head yet!"

⊸๑ ๑๑๑

At the ball that night, it was plain to see that Mr. Fairweather had shared none of their conversation with his oldest daughter. Her face lit up when she espied Phillip enter the ballroom. His heart sank in turn. Mr. Fairweather grabbed his sleeve and whispered in his ear,

"No sense spoiling an evening's entertainment, lad. You can still ensure that she has an agreeable time!"

Phillip swallowed deeply and pasted a smile on his face. He greeted them all affably and then, at their insistence, added his name to all the sisters' dance cards. Pushing down the uncomfortable notion that he was going to prove a great disappointment to the oldest Miss Fairweather, he danced his way through the first half of the evening.

At supper, a young lady from the county sang and played, and as he let the beauty of her voice entrance him, he noticed someone enter the dining area. Langley Ashbourne! His senses stood suddenly to attention, and he paid particular notice to the young man's conduct. He was impeccably dressed and leaned lazily against the door frame, examining the occupants of the room just as he had done at the Haversham's ball. His manner was again aloof and arrogant.

After a moment, an older woman noticed Ashbourne and leaped to her feet to join him. Phillip watched as his manner changed from cool to warm, and his face broke into a most charming smile. Déjà vu. Phillip felt more irritated than charmed by it. The woman was obviously an old acquaintance, and she led him back to her table, where a very fine young woman was seated. Phillip had noticed her earlier as she had a haughtiness in her bearing and danced in a very guarded, stiff fashion. Her clothes were of the finest quality, and her hair was pulled into a rather severe style, garnished with an exquisite tiara. She raised her gloved hand to Mr. Ashbourne, and he kissed it, never letting his eyes stray from hers. Then a very curious thing happened. Her icy stiffness seemed to melt in his presence, and she became like putty in his hands! Infernal man! Were all the women in England powerless to resist his magic?

William observed Phillip studying someone and followed his gaze to see who had captured his attention.

"Well, if it isn't old Langley!" he said. "What a coincidence! He's a bit out of his stomping grounds. We'll have to meet up for cards later."

Phillip murmured a response and continued to scrutinize the young man's behavior. There was nothing in his manner at the table that could be called into question; he was all politeness and manners. It grated on Phillip to no end.

Miss Verity Fairweather had earlier made it abundantly clear that she desired to dance the entire evening with Phillip, but he had cautioned her that it would be impolitic to be a last-minute guest and not spread his attentions around. It was beginning to get rather awkward when William, thankfully, pulled him aside and told him that there was a card game in progress in the library. Phillip was not really one for cards, he found gambling in general a waste of time and money, but it was the perfect excuse to extricate himself from the persistent Miss Fairweather. He left her with a very pretty little pout on her lips, wondering why her charms had so little effect on him.

The library was smoky and dark, and the game appeared to have been going on for some time. As Phillip's eyes adjusted, he noticed Langley Ashbourne on the opposite side of the table with a large pile of money in front of him. He was obviously enjoying a successful night. The men at the table looked up and made room for William and Phillip. The stakes were quite high, and Phillip decided that he would only play for an hour, during which time he would watch Langley closely.

Langley seemed to play honestly and displayed the camaraderie that might be expected around a card table. Phillip's mood plummeted. He, himself, was playing fairly well and had only lost a modest amount of money.

The hour had passed, and he was watching for the right moment to excuse himself when Langley shocked the table by pushing the entirety of his winnings into the center, challenging the other players with his eyes. The mood in the room shifted, and the other men sat up, tensely.

Phillip took this moment to exit the game, but remained in the room, wanting to discover how the round would play out. Two other men also excused themselves, which left William, Langley, and two older men. Each player was attempting to read the other players' eyes to deduce who was bluffing and who looked confident. William and an older gentleman were soon out but Langley and the other man continued on. Langley laid down a full house with a flourish and went to grab the money, but the other gentleman slowly laid his cards on the table. It was a royal flush.

Phillip regarded Langley's expression. The color briefly drained from his face, but in an instant, the sour look was replaced with a genuine smile. He then stood and shook hands with the winner, all grace and sincerity.

Langley crossed the room to shake hands with William, who introduced him to Phillip. Langley grabbed his hand, and his face split into a good-natured smile, totally unlike the one he bestowed on the ladies. Phillip couldn't help but feel drawn to him. His charisma was strong.

"That was jolly bad luck, Langley," commiserated William.

"Ah. Sometimes you win, sometimes you lose. It is of no consequence. Come, let us go back to the ladies."

Phillip considered the amount that Langley had lost to be of great consequence. He estimated it to have been 500 pounds.

Langley followed William and Phillip to the little clutch of Fairweathers and was introduced. Three of the sisters were immediately hypnotized by Langley's smile and general manner but Verity, Phillip noticed, seemed immune. He watched them all with interest. Langley danced with each of the younger Miss Fairweathers and gave the impression that he was genuinely interested in their conversation. He pointedly avoided asking Miss Verity Fairweather to dance, so Phillip finally took pity on her.

While they were dancing, he asked what she thought of the dashing Mr. Ashbourne. She looked up into Phillip's face with the gentlest of expressions and said, "I cannot see his appeal, sir, when compared to a truly handsome gentleman," and dropped her lashes modestly onto her rosy cheeks in such a way that it pulled at his heart.

It was time to leave Staffordshire before he cruelly hurt this admirable young woman.

Seven

ITALY

$\mathcal{A}$ ntonio, there is someone here to see you!"
The horse turned her head and flicked her mane. Antonio was struggling to keep her hoof between his knees as he used a tool to extract a thorn that was making her lame.

"I am busy. I will be there in a little while," he replied and returned to the task. A shadow fell across the stall and he said tersely, "Luigi, I said I would be there in a moment."

"I am not Luigi."

At the familiar baritone, Antonio dropped the hoof and wiped his brow, turning slowly to face the man from his past, unsure of how he should receive his former employer. A thousand memories crowded his mind; a scent, the silken touch of hair across his arm, a laugh, a touch, rejection. He bent his head in deference and then looked Giorgio Giaccopazzi in the eye.

"I am Signore Giaccopazzi, I—"

"I know well who you are, Signore."

"I have been searching for you for many months."

Antonio remained silent and kept his gaze steady.

"Do you not wish to know why? Are you not curious?"

"Indeed, sir, I am at a loss to understand your visit. I have not worked for you in over eighteen years. Tell me, to what do I owe this honor?"

"I am sorry to have to tell you that my Isabella is dead. She died of the fever six months ago."

Antonio wiped his brow again to hide his dismay and give himself time to recover from the freshly unearthed emotions, long buried. "I am sorry to hear this, Signore. She was a beautiful person inside and out, but I still fail to see why you should seek out a former stable boy to tell him this news in person."

Giorgio looked around for somewhere to sit in the oppressive heat and stench of the stable and, seeing a saddle stand, leaned against it. "There was a child."

The whispered phrase hung in the air like dandelion seeds caught on the breeze.

Antonio's defensive demeanor melted away at the staggering news, and he crouched to the floor beneath Giorgio to look up earnestly into his face. "There was a child? Oh, it all makes sense now . . ." He looked down, ashamed to admit what was already understood, unsure of the motivations of the man before him.

"You did not know?" Giorgio murmured. "Tell me what happened. I wish you no ill. I seek no vengeance. I am a broken man. At one time, I may have whipped you, but I am too old and lonely now.

"Isabella did marry, but she did not have any children. Her mother, as you will recall, died when she was young, and Isabella's husband died in an accident, and I am now left, a lone man with only my vineyards for company. As Isabella lay dying, she confessed her sin but died before she could tell me any more. I have spent much time and money trying, unsuccessfully, to find the child. And now at last I have found you, only to discover that you did not know."

Antonio pulled up another saddle stand and looked into the distance, seeing not the fields beyond the stable door but the past. A young maiden his own age, bored, lonely, spirited, and beautiful beyond description, interested in the horses and the people who cared for them.

"She married then? Did he deserve her?"

"He was a good man, a very good man."

Antonio nodded and gripped his chin for courage. "It all began after she returned from finishing school, Signore. You were much consumed with the vines and the drought, and she came to the stables seeking companionship in the horses, but after I helped her and we spent more time together, we . . ." His voice trailed off as his mind replayed the memory of the day the line was crossed between servant and served, of returning from a ride and helping Isabella down from her favorite horse. He had held her waist for just a fraction too long, and they had stood too close, breathing, wanting, still, until the magnetism of her drew him in and their lips touched and changed their relationship from that day forth.

He continued after a moment. "She would seek out my company in the stables and would insist that I ride with her. For safety. We would stop in fields full of poppies and talk for hours. She was captivating, and I was merely a man. A young and weak man. She would play the coquette with me, and I would feel anxious about her being so familiar with me, a mere servant, but she seemed genuinely to enjoy my company. I was flattered, I confess.

"And then one day I realized that I had fallen in love with her, and the next time we were alone, it was as though a barrier had broken down and I succumbed. I tried to feel guilty, but I was so full of love for her and so happy. I thought not of the morrow but lived only for the moment.

"Then one day she came and she was different. Something had changed. She told me that she was going to travel to see her school friends and that when she returned I must be gone. I was devastated at the rejection and became impassioned, but she stood still and waited until my anger was exhausted and then calmly bade me goodbye. Of course, in the days to come, I had to admit that it was a love always destined to end, our stations being so different. I thought perhaps you had discovered us and demanded she break with me. I left the next morning and ventured far north.

"I should tell you, Signore, that I have never really stopped loving her. She was the mate of my soul. I never found her equal." He stopped, exhausted by the memories and the passion. A silence gathered and the sun shone on the dust, forming cones of swirling light. "You have not found the child?"

Giorgio looked down at the floor, sighing, knowing now that his quest was far from over.

"Alas, no. I was hoping that you knew where the child was, but I see clearly now that you do not. I am an aged man, and I desire only to see my grandchild before I die and pass down my legacy, my vineyards. It is clear that I must continue my searching until I find the child or die in the attempt." He struggled to his feet and Antonio leaped to his assistance.

"Signore, when—if, you succeed in your quest, I would very much like to meet my child. Please, remember me."

Giorgio nodded and patted Antonio's hand tenderly. "Do you want for anything?"

"I want for nothing, Signore, except for the love of a woman and a family. I came here as an inexperienced boy and am now the manager of all the horses. I have done well financially, but my life is empty. I am familiar with the loneliness you speak of. Remember me, please, Signore."

✣

Antonio watched the broken man leave and enter his carriage, then sat upon the saddle stand, deep in thought. He had been eighteen that summer when she returned from finishing school. Life was just beginning, and he was popular among the maids in the village and the servant girls in the house. As he worked the horses, he was aware that his muscles were developing, and he enjoyed the looks of admiration from the girls.

Isabella had surprised him a few weeks after her return from school by asking him to ride with her. He had been shocked. He had noticed her beauty from afar. Of course, who would not? But he knew his place, and besides, there were so many young maidens accessible to him.

She had entered the stable in full riding gear and a veil across her face to keep off the dust. Her presence was tangible, her manner haughty, and authority rippled off her. The attraction he felt was real and dangerous.

He remembered declining and pointing out that it was not fitting, but she had laughed at him; he was a servant and posed no threat to her honor. She explained that she wanted to follow a new trail that might be dangerous and that she would need a companion for safety. He could follow some distance behind to keep things appropriate. She barely gave him a look and spoke most of what she said with her back to him.

They had begun the journey with a good distance between them, and the discomfort he had felt at first soon evaporated away. She was right and he was a fool. He was no more than a hireling to her, existing only to serve and protect.

After an hour, she took a sudden sharp turn up into the foothills of Fiesole, where the way for a horse was narrow. He had never attempted such a trail and pulled closer to advise her of the risk of such a venture. She had thrown back her head and laughed, calling him a coward and urging her horse on faster. He had followed more closely and as the trail twisted and turned, his concern rose. This was no easy way for a lady and her mare.

After thirty more minutes, he began to relax as it was evident that she was a fine equestrian and more than equal to the task. He began to worry less and enjoy the scenery more.

He was just beginning to wish that he had brought something to drink when he heard a sharp cry. He looked up to see that Isabella's horse was no longer in his field of vision and urged his own horse onward. As he reached the summit of a small hillock, he looked down upon Isabella, who had been thrown by her horse, which was now eating grass not far from her. He stopped his own horse and jumped off in some anxiety as he knelt to assess the damage. Isabella rolled onto her back with a grimace and told him that she had landed on her shoulder. He slid his hands behind her back, gently lifting her to a sitting position, and leaned her against the hillside. She took off her riding hat and veil with her good arm and shielded her eyes from the sun. He ripped the fabric from his sleeve and fashioned a sling for her arm. As he slid the cloth around her back and tied the sling at her neck, she looked at him, as though seeing him properly for the first time, and her eyes widened in appreciation. He moved back onto his haunches so as not to appear to be too intimate and looked at her cautiously. Her color was heightened from the ride and her carefully coiffed hair had dislodged in the fall and fell in ringlets around her face and shoulders. Her ebony eyes were squinted slightly in pain and her rosy mouth was in a pout. He took a sharp intake of breath and moved further away, alarmed by the uncontrolled passion rising in his breast.

She had laughed then at his discomfort and asked his name. She had rolled the syllables around on her tongue like a sugared fruit, and it had caused a frisson down his backbone. Then she asked how long he had worked for her father and about his family with genuine interest. As he explained that his mother had died in childbirth and his father soon after, her expression had turned to compassion and they had shared their feelings about being motherless. In that moment, she had become dangerously real and surprisingly equal.

At length, the difficulty of their situation bore down upon him and he asked if she could ride. She moved her shoulder in experimentation only to cry out in pain, and it was clear that she could not. The only solution appeared to be that he should put her back on her horse and walk it down to the bottom of the hilly trail, then ride back to her home for a carriage.

He bent and scooped her into his arms, their faces too close. As her honeyed breath danced against his cheek he had trouble concentrating and she was uncharacteristically quiet. The air between them was thick with tension.

He delicately placed her on the mare who, fortunately, was of a docile temperament, and slowly descended the hill leading both horses. At intervals, a little squeak of pain would escape her lips but no further conversation was had. They were clearly each dealing with a surprise mix of emotions.

When they reached flatter land, he helped her descend, being careful not to clip her shoulder, and positioned her comfortably, before galloping off to alert the household.

As he rode, he relived the moment her breath had grazed his cheek, over and over again, and at each revision the tender sensation in his heart increased in intensity. He argued with himself about the folly and impropriety of such thoughts but the memory was so delicious that it became a treasure to be taken out and enjoyed with just a hint of guilt; an innocent fantasy that would never be realized.

Isabella was rescued by the head groom who berated Antonio the whole way there and back on the idiocy of such an adventure and the impropriety. Antonio took the scolding because the joy of the intimate moment was the best reward, the memory of which could never be taken from him.

Upon their return, Isabella was whisked away to her rooms and he returned to the stables. The young maid servants who continued to smile and wave at him had, somehow, lost their luster when compared to the prized jewel. Life returned to its normal rhythm.

After a week of convalescence, she reappeared, unannounced, a perfect silhouette, at the doorway to the stables. Seeing his surprise, she demanded that he accompany her again. He knew it was madness, but he was powerless to resist. He made her promise that she would not take such risks again and inquired about a chaperone. She downplayed the notion with a laugh saying that she had told her maid she would be with a stable boy and that the idea of danger or compromise with a servant was so foreign that the maid had found the arrangement acceptable. Her eyebrow arched on one side. and her lips matched it in an enticing invitation. He could not have denied her had he tried.

And so began an addicting habit. Most mornings they would ride and then let the horses graze and sit among the wild flowers and talk of their hopes and dreams. It was startling to both that they could be from such different spheres and yet have so much in common.

Over time, the very air would hum with attraction, and he trembled for fear that he would make a mistake, crossing an unseen line that would shatter forever the idyllic rhythm of this illicit paradise.

Then came that fateful day that he had held her a fraction too long as he helped her dismount and the gravitational pull, which began with man in the Garden of Eden, inevitably drew them together, their lips had touched, and they were never the same again.

Passion had ignited their relationship, but the recklessness of stealing private moments and the need for subterfuge fueled it. Stolen moments, charged looks, desperate kisses. Two young, unbridled, vital humans thrown together by circumstance and kept together by a reckless disregard for standards and a lack of supervision. Once the forbidden fruit had been tasted, there was no going back, so sweet and addictive was its savor.

He well remembered the day when she had boldly declared that she loved him. It was a moment never to be forgotten and, indeed, it had spoiled all other romances for him.

The day she came to inform him of her immediate departure and order that he be gone when she returned came as unexpectedly as a bolt of lightning. He raged, demanding an explanation; she waited in silence for his anger to dissipate and then quietly but firmly insisted that he leave. She would entertain no debate on the subject and left as abruptly as she had arrived.

He had sunk to the stable floor in shocked despair and confusion, and after a restless night of questioning, his depression and heartbreak had turned to sadness at the age-old class distinctions that he blamed for the savage end to their affair. His pride was bruised and beaten, his heart in pieces, but he realized that he would never stop loving her and that she was right. He had to leave. He left before dawn, never to return.

Now to learn that she had borne his child! He had never suspected, not once.

Eight

ENGLAND

Cather, you are such a snob!" cried Francesca's father, John Haversham.

"There is nothing wrong with desiring to keep the regal bloodlines pure! Do you then favor diluting the blue blood of our nation? Surely not!"

It was an old bone of contention between them but his father had taken it up with renewed energy of late.

"Of course, I believe in the separation of the classes, but you are taking it too far, Father. Relationships cannot be calculated to engineer pure bloodlines at the expense of people's real feelings."

"Bosh! Of course they can. What do you think the royal family has been doing for generations? Exactly that."

"And marital felicity is sacrificed. A heavy price! Cannot merely socializing with those of your own class bring about happy unions? Such manipulation of matrimony on the basis of wealth, power, and blood can only lead to misery. What is the purpose of life if it is not about trying to find happiness?"

"For shame, John, are you insinuating that your mother and I make each other miserable?"

"Of course not, Father. But it is a happy accident that you are contented now. Can you honestly say that at the beginning of your marriage it was so?"

His father paused to drink from the tumbler on the table at his side.

"You see, your hesitation is tantamount to a confession! You and mother are fortunate to have been able to carve out some degree of satisfaction from an arranged marriage. Can you say that all your friends have been so lucky?"

"That is beside the point. Purity of the bloodlines is essential to maintain Britain's position as the driving force of the whole world. Would you have us lose that title to the likes of the French or the Prussians?"

"So, your position is that the only way to maintain our standing in the world is to arrange marriages for all the gentry in England, thus forfeiting their desires and inclinations? I cannot agree, sir!"

"That is the problem with your generation—no sense of duty. My generation, we knew what was expected of us and we did not shrink. No, sir, we did not! We have made this country great. Country before self; that is our motto. If I were Francesca's father I would guide her into the right houses and be very careful of the company she kept."

"Father, I will not force my daughter to marry someone she does not like. I was fortunate that Emily was both compatible and of a high-ranking family. I truly loved her before our marriage. I feel most fortunate that there were no machinations—"

His father laughed, "Ha! You think there were no machinations! Do you know your mother? She schemed and plotted for a full year to ensure a meeting between you and Emily."

John raised his eyebrows in surprise but merely said, "Then I was most fortunate that I was a willing pawn in her schemes. How would it have gone if I had not liked her? Would you have insisted, then?"

"The past is the past, and it has all worked out and kept our bloodline a remarkable shade of blue. Let us not argue about it."

John looked out the window, his jaws clenched. "I refuse to force anyone upon Francesca, Father, and I would appreciate it if you would not meddle either." John was quickly losing patience, and rather than precipitate a falling out with his father, he continued, "I must go and see to the horses. If you will excuse me, Father."

As he hastened through the door and out into the grounds, he thought about his father's admission. Had his mother really engineered his meeting with Emily so that he would be marrying *her* choice? Had his parents actually discussed the options and decided that Emily, with her fortune and breeding, was the perfect match to ensure a pure blood-line and transfer of wealth? He shuddered at the thought.

He remembered clearly the day he had met Emily. He had thought it was by chance, but given his father's statement, it appeared to have been the result of a carefully crafted plan. He felt sick to his stomach. How fortunate for all concerned that he and Emily had been instantly attracted to each other. Her family's position and wealth meant that she could marry for love and not for more practical concerns.

He arrived at the stables and instructed the servant boy to ready his horse. He felt a great need to run off his fury with his father's old-fashioned and harmful philosophies.

As he galloped through the estate, he reflected again on the first time he had had met Emily. He had not considered himself ready for marriage and had attended that dinner with his parents at their particular request. Upon their arrival, they had been welcomed by their hosts, slight acquaintances of his parents, and visited with them while awaiting the dinner gong. He remembered that he had had his back to the door and as it opened the hostess had said, "Ah, here is my niece, Miss Emily Davenport, lately arrived from Surrey for a visit."

He recollected how his world had been instantly thrown into sharper focus as he had set eyes upon the most lovely young woman he had ever beheld. Their eyes had met and held, improper on a first acquaintance. Her power to command his attention was like a magnet, and he was unable to drag his gaze away until the hostess had coughed in distress at the awkward situation and broken the spell.

As he moved and severed the electric connection, he became aware of his every breath, every blink of his eyes, every pulse of his heart. He risked a look again at Emily, and it appeared as though she were bathed in a spotlight, everything surrounding her blurry in contrast. He imagined this disorientation must be what it felt like to be struck by lightning, only this was a lightning that filled him with awe, not pain. It was like an injection of pure spiritual enlightenment.

Emily, he noticed, had skin like porcelain and high cheekbones. Her nose, though delicate and feminine, had a slight bump on the bridge, which, rather than detracting from her beauty, lent her countenance some charming character. But it was her eyes and hair that hypnotized him. Her almond eyes were of an arresting, vibrant blue whose equal could only be found in nature and were emphasized by the contrast to her ebony, gleaming hair. As she spoke to the guests, her fine eyebrows arched playfully and he stopped breathing.

His mother approached as he continued to stare in utter admiration, and she tactfully asked if he would help her into a chair. He transferred his gaze to his mother, trying to register the words that came from her mouth, but his mind was totally engaged by Emily's radiance, and she had to repeat the question before he recovered himself and assisted her to a chair.

At dinner, he was delighted to find himself seated next to Emily and was gratified to learn that she was not an empty shell, as so many refined, young ladies were, but that she had a sense of humor and a keen intelligence. As they talked, every movement of her slender fingers sent thrills through him, each turn of her graceful neck was poetry. He was bewitched both body and soul. In truth, he knew from that very night that she was the woman he wanted to make a life with and that to continue living without her would be misery.

To discover that this seemingly natural course of events was actually the result of a scheme of his mother left him feeling outraged. How fortunate for him that he had loved their choice.

His thoughts turned to his daughter. He had seen the wretchedness of other people's children who had been forced to marry against their own hearts but in their parents' interests. They led separate lives in hollow mansions, only eating together for appearances. He would never impose such a life upon his daughter for the approval of society. Indeed, he rejected a society that sacrificed its children upon the altar of power, money, or title. Deep love and true companionship were his own lucky lot and he wanted that and more for his beloved Francesca.

He looked up to see that he had ridden further than he had intended and turned the horse around so as not to be late for dinner. The hard ride had succeeded in blowing away the majority of his anger, and he headed for home, subdued.

⟋⟋⟋

"He is intent on allowing Francesca to make her own choice," said Lord Haversham.

"Indeed, that is unfortunate," said Lady Augusta. "You have placed us in a position that will necessitate that *we* take action to ensure the continued well-being of our estate. John and Emily have sufficient resources for their own needs from Emily's dowry, but it is not ample enough for both houses.

"We must act! Our standing in society may depend upon it! I would rather die than be snubbed by our friends. Do you know how long it has taken me to rise to the top? The shame of a fall from grace would kill me. I have orchestrated the social ruin of many who tried to climb the social ladder without the proper qualifications. They would delight in my fall. I could not bear to be mocked and sneered at by *them*. The humiliation would not be borne." Augusta huffed and turned away.

"This is your fault, John!" she suddenly cried, whirling back to point at him. "We will have to move abroad if we do not do something to save ourselves!"

Her eyes shone with tears, and her husband came to lay his hand upon her shoulder. She shook it off as if it were a hot coal.

"Augusta, I know the stakes are high, believe me! All is not lost. We will maneuver some more, and all will end as it should."

"Will it, John? If things are as bad as they say in America . . . I cannot, I will not, live with the shame and degradation of bankruptcy."

"The journalists are exaggerating the situation. They write shocking headlines to sell more papers. I will write to my plantation manager and you will see that is not as bad as they would have us believe."

"That does not help our lack of funds here! Surely you have not really plowed all our available cash into the scheme?"

"It was necessary to shore up the operation. It is just a temporary setback. I have things in hand, and as soon as the next crop is harvested, the money will flow back into our coffers." He placed his hand back on his wife's shoulder, and this time she did not shrug it away. "In the meantime, if we can tap into the Ashbournes' fortune, our immediate needs can be relieved. Our plan is already in motion and moving forward satisfactorily. Francesca seemed to be captivated at the ball, so I arranged that Langley be invited to Annabelle's picnic. Furthermore, I believe Francesca is to make a journey to Brighton with one of her mother's sisters, perhaps a little bird can suggest he make a visit there too. Our darling granddaughter will surely marry our choice but believe it to be her own. We have succeeded before. I have no doubt we shall succeed again!"

Nine

ITALY

Giorgio pushed his hands through his white hair in desperation. Every lead led to a dead end. He had spent a great deal of time and many resources attempting to run down each piece of new information only to find an impenetrable wall at the end of every journey.

Unfortunately, the man he had just left, Antonio, had shown genuine astonishment that Isabella had had a child. No one was that good an actor. He smiled as he imagined the thoughts that would now be running through Antonio's mind. A lonely man had just discovered he was a father. His experience would somewhat mirror his own, he surmised.

He explored his memories to see if he had any recollection of Antonio as a youth, but alas, he did not. As the master of a vast estate, he was not in the habit of associating with stable boys.

Antonio was a fine-looking man now; lithe, muscular, handsome, and energetic. He could well suppose that as a youth he had been very appealing. A definite temptation for a beautiful young woman whose father did not give her enough attention. He felt a stab of remorse. Oh, that he could relive that summer and be a better father. She had deserved more. Regrets such as these were like specters that haunted his days.

He wiped his face with his hand, pulled his leather pouch around, and opened it. The next name on his list was the Contessa Tomaselli of Rome, the former Allessandra Angeloni. He sent up an urgent prayer that the contessa would at last hold a key to his grandchild's whereabouts.

The Villa Tomaselli was a grand affair with its Grecian architecture and landscaped gardens. He was welcomed at the door by an officious looking maggiordomo who looked irritated that Giorgio had not sent word in advance of his arrival.

"I can easily find lodging nearby and return tomorrow if it is more convenient," wheezed Giorgio.

"That might be preferable, Signore. The contessa is very busy and involved in many charities. Send me word of your lodging, and I will send a messenger to tell you when she will be available."

Giorgio nodded slowly and turned to leave, the very image of a downtrodden man. Serendipitously, a door just adjacent to the top of the grand staircase opened, and a woman holding a small white dog exited and glanced down the steps. At the pitiful figure Giorgio portrayed, her curiosity was piqued, and she sent a maid to discover the gentleman's identity.

As Giorgio was about to enter his carriage, the maid ran out of the villa and importuned him to return and tell his business. With renewed hope, he slowly stepped down from the carriage steps and made his way, leaning heavily on his cane.

To his surprise, the contessa herself was standing in the hall and approached him upon his entry. "Good Signore, may I ask your errand? You appear so downcast that I fear it is bad news." She held the dog up to her lips and kissed him, worry lines prominent on her forehead.

"Fear not, good Signora. It is not bad news for you that I bring. I am Giorgio Giaccopazzi of Florence. I believe you were at school with my poor daughter, Isabella."

The contessa brought her hand quickly to her mouth, gasping, her eyebrows raised in apprehension. "Do you mean that she is dead, Signore?"

"Yes, she died of the fever over six months ago, and I—"

The contessa had raised her hand to stop him and glanced at the inquisitive expressions of the maggiodormo and the maid.

"Signore Giaccopazzi, let us repair to the drawing room, where we will enjoy complete privacy." She motioned to a door with her hand.

The maggiodormo threw his head back and lifted his nose high in the air, deeply offended at the insinuation, and the maid's countenance fell.

After they were seated in the room, the contessa explained, "The servants are my husband's, and they are continually spying on me to report to him my many offenses. My marriage is not a happy one, Signore, though I lack for no comforts or entertainment. My father's power has increased fourfold through this alliance, it is true, but there is no love for me in it and my husband takes great delight in abusing me with the gossip of the servants. But enough of me, why have you come to visit to tell me that poor Isabella has passed away?" She stroked the tiny head of the white dog and looked at him expectantly.

"I understand that you traveled to France with my Isabella sometime after you completed your schooling in Switzerland?"

"Indeed, I did," she answered cautiously.

"I beg you to tell me what transpired during the course of your travels, Contessa."

"I do not know that I understand your meaning, Signore?"

He cleared his throat. "As she lay dying, Isabella confessed to having given birth to a child that year, but before I could press her for more details, she was gone."

The contessa relaxed back into her chair and a look of resignation crossed her features, but she offered no conversation, so Giorgio pressed on.

"I am left alone with no family to brighten my days and with an impressive empire that no heir will enjoy. I am desperate, Contessa. Please tell me if you know of what I speak."

Warring emotions waged a battle across her dark features as she appeared to argue within herself as how best to handle the situation that had been thrust upon her. "I divined that something had occurred to make her melancholy, but Isabella gave no hint as to what it was and, at first, I did not press her on it. She joined our group in Nice and appeared to be forcing herself to be merry. I do not know if the others noticed, but we were close at school, she and I, and I could tell that she was deeply sad to the very core of her being. At length, I ventured to address her on the subject but she would simply laugh and ask me what could possibly be wrong. We were young and rich and enjoying the delights of Nice, she said. What was there to be woeful about? But woeful she was.

"After the others retired each evening, I would attempt to engage her in conversation, but she would always feign a headache and retreat to her room with her maid. After several weeks of indolence, she shocked me by announcing that she was urgently needed by a cousin in Grasse, though she told the rest of the group that the need was back in Italy. She explained that she was leaving her maid at the pensionne and had hired a maid who came highly recommended by the concierge.

"I protested at her traveling alone and insisted on accompanying her but she said that the matter of her cousin was delicate and needed the utmost confidentiality, and though I entreated her for more details, she would not give any.

"The next morning, she left before we arose. I asked her maid if she knew why the urgency and secrecy, but she seemed as bemused as I.

"That afternoon, my cousin Michaelangelo Morretti of Milan arrived. I had been so anxious for Isabella to meet him as he was a fine match for any lady. It was most vexing. However, in time my cousin succeeded in distracting me from my reveries concerning poor Isabella and introduced us to some of his acquaintances, very exciting people who took us to see many places of interest and many operas and such like. In fact, I fell in love with one of my cousin's friends and from then on, all my energies were caught up in those tender emotions so that I forgot about Isabella, who had, after all, been gone now for such a long time.

"We were beginning the work of packing up to repair to Rome for the Christmas season when Isabella unexpectedly reappeared and declared her intention of leaving for Florence, post haste. I cannot tell you how much she was changed. She had gained weight, and her once lively countenance was much downcast; her usually vibrant complexion was gray, and I asked her if she was ill. She protested that she was not ill but that her cousin's situation had taxed her to the very utmost and she was in need of seeking refuge at home to recover her spirits. I grasped her hands, attempting to peer into her soul, and asked what terrible calamity had befallen her cousin that would cause such distress. She explained that her cousin's reputation had been irrevocably compromised and that she, Isabella, had worked hard to repair the damage from false accounts of the events. She protested that her cousin was innocent of the false accusations leveled at her but that she had allowed herself to succumb to the overtures of a very powerful, older man who was seeking vengeance for the alleged humiliation. As I pinned her with my gaze, she seemed to crumple and collapsed into a chair. I summoned her maid who took her upstairs to rest. When I inquired after her the next morning, they were gone." The contessa leaned forward and fixed her gaze on Giorgio's face before continuing.

"I believed her story for I had no reason to doubt it but your tale has illuminated my memory, and as I reexamine the events of that time, I can see that indeed the distress was not her cousin's but her own. It explains the haste and secrecy and leaving her maid behind in Nice. Indeed, she was more womanly in her build when she first arrived in Nice than when we had parted at school, but that I attributed to the fine fare of your cook, whose praises she would often sing. It all makes sense if I consider that she was actually with child. The shame would have been too great to admit even to one's closest friend." She reached forward and clasped Giorgio's hand. "I am ashamed to admit that had she confessed to me her situation, I may have thrown her off. We are so quick to judge in our youth, are we not?"

She leaned back, deep in thought and reflection. "Yes, yes I see now that it was so," she said softly, stroking the dog again, who delighted in the attention.

"You say that she went to Grasse?" He pounced on the new information like a cat on a mouse.

"That is what she said, yes. But this calls into question all that she told me, does it not, Signore?"

Giorgio's face fell at the truth of what she said. Age and sadness settled into the wrinkles of his face like a death mask. "Do you perhaps at least remember the name of the pensionne in Nice, Contessa?"

"Indeed, for it is the shrine to my first and only true love," she smiled.

Ten

ENGLAND

Francesca was dozing in the warmth of the sun when the wheels of the carriage hit a hole in the road and jerked her awake. A smile still played on her lips and her mother suggested that she had been having a most interesting dream. She had in fact and her eyes widened and she pretended to cough into her handkerchief to cover her embarrassment. She had been dreaming that she had been riding with Mr. Langley Ashbourne, but not on her own horse; scandalously, she was riding with him on *his* horse and holding him around the waist to stay on as he galloped the horse along the meadows. She tried to grasp at the memory as the dream disappeared like wisps of smoke from her consciousness. She sighed and leaned her head against the carriage window.

Annabelle and her family had left a week earlier, and Francesca and her family were now on their way to Annabelle's family home to participate in the picnic. Bella had already sent her two letters full to the brim about Mr. Doyle. Francesca was beginning to be bored by the poor man already, and she had scarcely met him.

As they arrived, the servants were bringing the wicker baskets of food into an empty carriage and the dogs were barking all around them. Mr. Pike, the butler, was sweating profusely and shooing the dogs away, directing the servants and mopping his brow. His face was flushed and his wig askew. All seemed in a pleasant pandemonium.

"Careful, now, careful," Pike directed. "Oh Sally, you will break the china! Have a care, have a care!"

Annabelle glided down the staircase looking bubbly and eager and came to embrace the Havershams affectionately. "Mr. Doyle arrived an hour ago and Phillip Waverley about a half an hour ago, and the Dillworths and the Ashdowns and Edwardses arrived just before you. We shall make such a merry party!"

"Phillip is here, then?" said Francesca, happy to know she would have a friend to distract her from Annabelle and the vexatious Mr. Doyle.

"Oh yes, and I forgot to tell you that cousin William has invited Mr. Fine!"

Francesca's stomach leaped up like a carnival dog at the unexpected but welcome news. She swallowed and cleared her throat so as to appear nonchalant. "You mean Mr. Ashbourne?"

"Yes, yes of course! Isn't that fun?"

Francesca became instantly critical of her choice of dress for the occasion. She had chosen a simple dress since a picnic seemed to warrant it but she was horrified to confess that had she known Mr. Ashbourne would be there she would have been much more careful in her selection. It was an infuriating admission.

As she turned to face the door of the great house, Phillip, William, and Mr. Ashbourne appeared at the top of the staircase to join the party. Phillip had a friendly, open, pleasant face, but oddly, the close comparison with Mr. Ashbourne left him appearing wanting.

She now faced a social dilemma. Should she run up the stairs to greet Phillip and in the process be reintroduced to Mr. Ashbourne, or should she wait at the bottom of the staircase for them to come to her? Which would be the more dignified way to behave?

As she pondered this, Phillip noticed her and made the decision for her by running down the stairs to greet her and her parents. Mr. Ashbourne remained at the top of the stairs, Francesca noticed, surveying the guests as if he were watching an operatic production. How maddening that he did not come down with Phillip for an easy introduction.

After the greetings were accomplished, she was grateful that Phillip turned and called up the stairs, "Come, Langley, let me make the introductions."

In truth, Phillip had been more than dismayed to arrive and find Mr. Langley Ashbourne one of the party invited to the picnic. He had hoped to find some private time to talk to Francesca and tell her of his discoveries, but upon encountering the subject of her interest, it became clear to Phillip that he would only be of secondary interest today. His spirits flagged, but he took courage and mustered up a good humor.

Unfortunately for him, he turned just in time to see the angelic anticipation upon Francesca's lovely face as Ashbourne finally descended.

Ashbourne descended slowly and gave his attention first to Francesca's mother. He made a great theater of lifting her gloved hand to his lips and saying, "But of course I remember the beautiful Mrs. Haversham, hostess of the memorable ball in Wiltshire. How could I forget?"

He then turned his attentions to her husband, and they spent a good while talking of the upcoming picnic.

Phillip kept his gaze trained on Francesca, who was failing in her attempts to appear calm and patient, shuffling from foot to foot and putting her hand to her neck compulsively. He had to hand it to Langley; he certainly knew how to play hard to get.

At length, Ashbourne recognized Francesca, repeating the same theatrical kissing of the hand and saying what a pleasure it was to meet the debutante again and how fine she looked. Francesca was just opening her mouth to respond to his greeting when he hastily turned and explained that he had promised the hostess that he would help her into her carriage. Francesca was left with her mouth open, her hand still raised in the greeting and a look of bewilderment on her face. It was comic indeed. As Ashbourne retreated, Francesca came to herself and let her hand drop to her side to smooth her dress.

"Well, what an extraordinary fellow!" chuckled her father, noticing the smudge of color upon his daughter's cheek. "He appears to relish playing the mysterious character, does he not?"

"Oh, Father, you do love to exaggerate so!" she said, then hurried to greet Annabelle.

The picnic was to be at a hill, some five miles distant. The caravan of carriages, some covered and some not, made its merry way at walking pace so as not to upset the food hampers. Francesca had seated herself in her cousin Annabelle's carriage with her aunt and uncle. Her parents were in their own carriage with Phillip and Mr. Doyle, who had arrived on horseback and had been looking for a seat in the caravan. Mr. Doyle was effusive in his praise. "What a fine family this is! I am honored to be invited to such an auspicious event. I remember fondly the ball I attended at your house. Most gracious hosts as I recall, and meeting dear Annabelle will burn it into my memory for evermore!" He smiled benevolently upon the occupants of the carriage, and the Havershams exchanged a look of mirth.

"Are your affections returned, sir?" asked Mr. Haversham pleasantly.

"I believe they are, I believe they are! In very fact, the invitation to this little party has given me courage to approach her father for his permission to profess my feelings to the lady this very day. I believe she will make me a very happy man!"

"Upon such a short acquaintance, how can you be so sure?" asked Emily Haversham in her gentle way. Mr. Doyle puffed out his chest and put his hands on his knees, "My dear lady, when feelings are this passionate, I believe one must act upon them as soon as may be! Life is short, and 'carpe diem' is my motto! I have not been long engaged in the law, but I can offer Miss Haversham, Annabelle, a comfortable home and a good income. She will want for nothing."

"Then let us be the first to congratulate you," said Mrs. Haversham, smiling. "You could not have chosen a better companion than my niece. She is the kindest child and will be an affectionate wife."

Phillip shook his hand in congratulations.

"What of you, Phillip?" asked Mr. Haversham. "Have any young ladies turned your head?"

Phillip scrutinized John Haverham's features to see if there was any hint of suspicion on his face, but his gaze was without guile. He decided to tell the truth. "I have recently met a very pleasant young lady, but I must confess there is another that may have already stolen my heart."

Emily Haversham leaned forward in excitement. "My dear Phillip, do we know her? Pray tell us who she is."

"I am not sure of the young lady's affections, indeed I fear that she has given her heart in another direction, so it would be impolitic of me to name the lady."

"Pooh! I admire your honor, and yet it is so irksome!" Emily laughed. "I hope you will discover her true feelings soon. Are you in an agony?"

"Yes, truly I am," he confessed with full candor.

"Then I pray that you will be put out of your misery sooner rather than later," she said, patting his arm. "Any woman would be blessed to call you husband."

The picnic hill was a gently undulating meadow with shade trees at convenient locations and a brook at the bottom. The servants placed the picnic blankets under the canopies of leaves and all was very agreeable. Mr. Doyle had brought a yo-yo and was unusually proficient at it, which made for great entertainment and disposed Francesca to think a little better of him.

Francesca, Annabelle, Annabelle's parents, and Mr. Doyle shared a blanket, though Annabelle's parents sat on chairs brought for the occasion. Although he was clever with the yo-yo, Francesca soon began to find Mr. Doyle's conversation rather tedious and she found his person unattractive with his receding hair line and hooked nose.

Annabelle, on the other hand, was hanging on his every word and laughing at all his rather pointless jokes. Francesca considered the possibility of them marrying and shuddered at the thought of having to endure his breakfast conversation whenever she visited. Still, she loved Annabelle like a sister, and she had never, in truth, seen her so happy and alive.

After the chicken and bread had been eaten, Phillip came to ask whether anyone would care for a stroll along the brook. Francesca jumped at the chance to escape the vapid comedian and lifted her hand to Phillip so that he might help her from the ground.

As soon as she alighted, straightened her dress, and opened her parasol, she approached Mr. Ashbourne and asked if he might like to join them. Phillip pulled at his ear in irritation and looked away, praying that the invitation might be refused.

"I fear I am a dashed lazy fellow who is rather in need of some slumber after such a sumptuous repast," Ashbourne said, nodding in the direction of the hosts, who nodded back in appreciation.

Frustration flickered across Francesca's features, and she turned abruptly for fear of giving herself away. Phillip offered up a silent prayer of thanks.

The two of them wandered down to the brook, bantering and reminiscing about childhood. When they were well out of earshot, Francesca touched his arm and looked earnestly into his face. "Have you discovered anything about our mysterious Mr. Ashbourne, other than that he likes his sleep?"

Phillip took a deep breath. "He is the only son of an aging Baronet, whose younger mother died while he was yet a boy."

"Oh, the poor motherless man!" she gasped.

Phillip refrained from commenting. He continued, "He has admirers wherever he goes and enjoys being aloof and mystical. He considers young women a pleasant distraction, no more."

"Oh." She looked into the distance, pensive. Crestfallen.

"According to William, he was not a terribly serious student but hates to be idle, so he went up to college just for the fun of it."

"Then he really must not like me since he made the pretense of being tired just now."

"Do you really like him so very much?" asked Phillip.

"I cannot really like a man I do not know, but he presents an intrigue. And he cuts a very fine figure, don't you think?"

"Alas, I am a poor judge of what a young lady might find attractive, Francesca."

She glanced at him and then looked back at the picnic party. "I suppose I am annoyed that he does not pay me more attention, if I am to be totally honest. Perhaps I am not pretty enough to interest him."

"That is most certainly not the reason," he replied quietly.

"Are you in earnest, Phillip? Do you think me greatly improved? I am not sure of my beauty. Mother is so beautiful that I feel I am a mere shadow in comparison."

Her honesty caught him off guard. Could this vision of loveliness really not see her own comeliness in the looking glass? She outshone her mother as the sun outshines the moon. Was it possible that she could be blind to it? He peered into her eyes to gauge her sincerity. What he saw were pools of liquid hope, devoid of guile. "I am in great earnest! You are greatly improved and can be confident in your own handsomeness, Francesca. Do not allow someone like Langley Ashbourne to steal your confidence."

The intensity of his tone and stare were new to her, and she returned his gaze in search of something, but he turned his head quickly and resumed his walk along the brook's edge, recommencing the light banter, and the moment passed. She reached up to put her hand through his arm, and they continued their gentle stroll. He asked her all kinds of mundane questions but did not repeat the earlier intensity of conversation, all the while, her mind questioning what, if anything, had just happened.

Of a sudden, a bird let out its sweet song, and she turned to catch a glimpse of it. As she did so, she saw Mr. Ashbourne approaching them. All previous musings fled in an instant, and she turned to Phillip. "Look! Mr. Ashbourne has come to join us!" They broke apart to make room for the newcomer.

"Enjoy your nap, Ashbourne?" said Phillip as pleasantly as he could.

"Too much jibber-jabbering from the ladies for a poor soul to get any sleep! I thought they would never stop! This looked to be the more relaxing pursuit, so I decided to join you."

Phillip noticed that Langley looked deep into Francesca's eyes and then, pointedly, at her lips. Subconsciously his hands clenched into fists.

"Indeed, you are most welcome!" gushed Francesca.

"What fun we had in Staffordshire, Waverley, did we not?" said Ashbourne.

"We did indeed."

"I believe that you were particularly interested in a certain young lady there, a Miss Fairweather?"

Astonished, Francesca glanced at Phillip to gauge his reaction.

"The Fairweathers are a very pleasant family with delightful daughters, but I fear you are wrong in supposing that I was interested in one more than any other."

"Oh, indeed I am sorry if I am mistaken, but Miss Verity Fairweather told William of her high regard for you, and I assumed the regard was mutual."

"I do hold her in the highest regard, but then so do I all her sisters. They are very beautiful and accomplished and would be a jewel in any man's crown."

"Why Phillip, you have never mentioned them to me," exclaimed Francesca before turning to Mr. Ashbourne. "Do tell me what she is like. It is high time Phillip found a wife, and perhaps I can play cupid if you think she is worthy of him." She gave Phillip such a loving and agreeable smile that he died a little at the irony.

"Verity Fairweather can sing and play like an angel. She has recently returned from finishing school in Switzerland and can speak excellent French, or so I believe as my own French is 'affreux!' She can paint worthy of any London gallery and her needlework is exquisite."

"I wonder that *you* are not interested in her, Mr. Ashbourne, such an accomplished young woman as that!"

"She is not my type, Miss Haversham. She is very short and remarkably fair of complexion with sunshine-colored ringlets. A fair Madonna to be sure, but, alas, my fancies tend to darker hair and a more olive complexion," he said as he laid his gaze directly upon Francesca, who bowed her head under the weight of his gaze.

Phillip groaned.

To cover her confusion, Francesca said, "Phillip, did you not like Miss Fairweather? Are you not in search of a wife to share your life?"

Could she not know what torture her words were?

"I am focused, for the present, on establishing myself in the law so that I might have a stable home and income to offer a future bride. Who knows how long it will take to arrive at such a desirable situation."

"But I understand that Miss Fairweather is blessed with a substantial dowry," responded Mr. Ashbourne.

"It is true, but my fancies tend in another direction too. As lovely and accomplished as she is, Miss Fairweather is not my type either."

"Then what is your 'type' Phillip?" demanded Francesca.

Phillip prayed for forgiveness as he boldly lied, "Auburn hair and a fair complexion are my preference."

"Then I shall try to find you a wife," said Francesca. "For I think you are very much in need of one."

Eleven

ENGLAND

The elderly waiter looked nervously down upon the stately gentleman, slumped in slumber, his white head leaning against the wing of the leather chair. He was not a favorite of the staff at the exclusive London gentleman's club, but he was certainly one of its most venerable members. Apprehensively, the waiter cleared his throat. "Excuse me, Sir John."

The sleeping man stirred, temporarily disoriented. The waiter tried to shield the moment from other members of the club and give Lord Haversham, Francesca's grandfather, a modicum of privacy. "Sir John, I have some correspondence for you from the directors of the club that is of a delicate nature and rather urgent."

He leaned over and presented the letter on a silver salver. Sir John, recovering himself, shifted in the chair and sat up, ramrod straight. He cast a stern eye upon the messenger—whose stomach clenched in anticipation of a reprimand—then reached for the note and dismissed the waiter with a slight nod. The waiter withdrew, breathing a sigh of relief.

Lord Haversham paused, looking down at the letter with disdain. Without opening it, he ripped the paper into pieces and threw it into the open fire to his right. It was so undignified to mention fiscal matters in a public place, and besides, he was a Peer of the Realm, and as such, he commanded a certain respect that was utterly lacking. It was a disgrace that this club, where his father and grandfather were founding members, should be so indelicate. He would have to seriously consider taking his membership elsewhere.

He unfolded the newspaper and turned to the international pages. After reading for some time, he leaned his august head against the chair back and groaned.

"Sir John, how do you do this fine morning?"

Lord Haversham looked up into the face of Lord Petersham, a friend of many decades. He was a man whom some called Midas; it seemed that everything he touched did, indeed, turn to gold. It rendered his current situation even more bitter. "Albert Petersham, how good it is to see you! When did you arrive in town?"

"I have just arrived, sir. My wife came down to prepare the town house a week ago, and I was summoned to appear tomorrow. Thought I would spend a night at the club before the festivities begin."

The old friends conversed about family and other acquaintances.

"Did you hear about old Cusworth?" asked Lord Petersham. "They say he has lost everything in that South American mine venture of his! His family goes back generations at Cusworth Hall but the bailiffs are banging at the doors. What are things coming to when one of the oldest families in the land is turned out of their family estate? There is no respect for breeding from the lower classes anymore. If that was not bad enough, it appears that his son did not marry the young heiress his father had chosen for him and instead eloped with a near pauper and has kept it a secret these twelve months! The shame of it! Cusworth's wife is being rebuffed by her oldest and closest friends—your wife is one, come to think of it—and shunned by society. She is suffering wretchedly, or so they tell me. The heiress has married someone else, and so the money that was to rescue them is no more."

Sir John coughed and drank from the tumbler at his side.

"And how go your American ventures? Tobacco, isn't it?" said Lord Petersham.

"Splendidly!" Sir John lied. "I am planning a voyage in the spring when the weather improves."

"Really, I thought I heard of some kind of blight to the crops out there? I must be mistaken."

⚬⚬⚬

Sir John stood in the doorway looking at his wife, Augusta, for some minutes before she noticed him. Though their marriage had been arranged, they had come to respect each other over the years and had become a formidable team. She had cast a blind eye over his pursuits, and he had allowed her to blossom in the best of society. Society, it seemed, was her natural environment, and she had risen like cream to the top of it, deciding who was worthy to be accepted and who was not. Her opinion was to be valued over almost all others. A new friend could not be welcomed into the inner circle without her prior approval.

Her once chestnut hair was now a distinguished pearl gray. Her skin, though no longer tight, was not the skin of an old woman, and her cheekbones were still prominent, which gave her a regal bearing. She was reading, head bowed, and petting her little dog. He hated to disturb the scene, but it must be done.

കുള ഉപ

Lady Augusta Haversham rolled over, her arm across her forehead, the pulse in her temples beating a tattoo. The full weight of the reality of the situation pressed heavily against her mind. Never did she ever imagine finding herself in such a state of affairs! In the world she had created, it was she who led the charge in humiliating those whose fortunes had turned. Now the shoe appeared to be in danger of transferring to the other foot and she was terrified. The crows would all come home to roost. How would she bear it?

The rage she had felt toward her husband had burned down to embers of resentment at some time in the long night. How could he have mismanaged things so poorly? Surely, they had friends who would help them, but, oh, the shame in having to go cap in hand like the dregs of society when she was its queen.

She sat up to drink from the cup on the nightstand, but the ache in her head forced her back to the pillow. She reflected upon the man she had married. Forced by her parents, who were in want of a title, to marry John Haversham II, she had gone for the week of hunting against her will, stubborn, petulant, and determined to dislike the man they had chosen for her suitor. She had omitted to pack her newest gowns to spite her mother and mount her rebellion. What a shrieking match they had waged in her bedchamber upon arrival at Haversham Hall.

She remembered how, despite her prejudice and her resolve to hate him, he had presented an excellent first impression, and she had been frustrated by feeling some affection for him against her will.

As the week had progressed, she had discovered that he was a snob of the first order who was obsessed with pure bloodlines, fiercely loyal to king and country, and reasonably intelligent, all traits she admired in a man. She could not say she loved him, but she esteemed him highly and, weighing things in the balance, realized that she could do worse. There were few guarantees in marriage anyway, and there was the title to consider, which would elevate her above her peers and even her mother. They were married six months later.

In the first few months of marriage, she discovered that, in addition to the characteristics she knew of, he was arrogant, dismissive, vain, indifferent, and, at times, ill-tempered. He was not, however, cruel or abusive in any way, and she was content with that. She made it her mission to tame him and induce him to fall in love with her with an aim to carving out a tolerable life for herself.

She was quick to master the management of the house and learned to orchestrate social events where influential people came to make things happen. It was not long before everyone who was anyone desired to see and be seen at one of Lady Augusta's parties. Over time, she successfully built a social empire with a sophisticated hierarchy that flattered Lord Haversham's prideful nature. He soon came to appreciate her talents and to view her as his greatest asset in manipulating society to his advantage. It was never a marriage of great romance, but it did develop into one of mutual approbation.

Now, this life she had carefully crafted was all in peril. Their scheming to have Francesca meet and marry Langley Ashbourne was all the more crucial. Francesca must be brought to bend to their will for it was the only way to save them.

Twelve

FRANCE

*G*iorgio had endured the arduous journey to Nice in the south of France to find that the previous owner had died and that the new proprietor had only been in his position for five years. Witnessing the crestfallen expression of the gentleman, the proprietor had offered one small breadcrumb: his housekeeper had been a maid with the previous proprietor and she may have some recollection. Would the gentleman wait while he fetched her?

Giorgio looked around the vestibule, seeing everything but seeing nothing. After the passage of some ten minutes, a woman appeared dressed in black from head to toe. She had a pleasant face but wore a nervous expression. She approached Giorgio slowly. "Monsieur?"

Giorgio raised his head as though it weighed as much as a mill-stone but his eyes were alight with hope. In faltering French, he said, "Madame, thank you for seeing me. Please sit down."

He noticed her hesitate as she took in his fine clothes and opened his hand to offer her the seat next to him.

"I am interested in the autumn of eighteen years ago. My daughter had come here from Italy with her maid to meet some friends from school." The woman's expression was blank. He continued, "After a few weeks I understand that she left her maid here, alone for several months and visited Grasse with a hired maid."

The woman's eyebrows raised in recognition and Giorgio took courage.

"Yes, Monsieur, now I remember it well. I was but a house maid at the time, and I would go in to see to the room of the young lady and that of her maid. When your daughter left, the maid would speak to me at length every morning and every evening. I recall that at first, she was anxious that her young charge had gone off without her, but after a few days, she seemed to adjust. The mademoiselle had left her a very generous allowance that enabled her to go on excursions and to little performances. Your daughter was very particular about sending her maid letters every week, as I recollect, which went a long way to easing her maid's mind."

"What happened when the young lady returned?"

"Can I ask your interest in the case, Monsieur? It was so very long ago."

"My daughter died recently, and on her death bed began to tell me of that journey. She died before she could complete her tale. I am anxious to know what happened in Grasse."

The austerely dressed woman nodded. "I do remember her return as it was in such haste and they were gone before I came to their rooms the next morning."

"Did you by chance see her?" Giorgio asked.

"I was the one that opened the door to her as the proprietor and the porters were engaged at that hour. She looked ill and as though she might faint. She dismissed her hired maid and begged me to help her up to her room. She leaned on me heavily as we ascended the main staircase and asked me to help her into her bed. Then she bid me leave her. I entreated her to let me get her maid as I was afraid for her, but she was determined to be alone. I was so worried that I waited outside her room for a full half an hour in case she should need further assistance. I believe she sent me for one of her friends at last, and then I went back downstairs to my duties.

"The next morning, I arose early to check on her but she and her maid were gone. I have wondered to this day what became of her."

"She came home in time for Christmas," Giorgio said. "And though she was quiet at first, I did not notice anything very wrong. She later married and was very happy until her husband died. She herself succumbed to the fever seven months ago."

"I am sorry to hear that, Monsieur. Her maid was very fond of her. She was an amiable and considerate mistress by her account."

Giorgio weighed his options and decided to trust the woman. "Would it surprise you to know that she had given birth to an illegitimate baby in her absence from this hotel?"

The woman's hand flew to her mouth, and she brought her head down with resolve, engaging Giorgio with her eyes,

"Indeed, sir! It would make sense of a puzzle. The morning she left, the cook was outside very early meeting with the butcher, and she happened to catch sight of the mademoiselle, your daughter. The cook was a gossipy old woman, and later that morning she was telling anyone who would listen that she had a niece who had had a baby on the wrong side of the sheets that she had been forced to give it away and that the look on your daughter's face was the very same look she had seen on her niece. The housekeeper scolded her for smearing a refined young lady's character and told her that if she mentioned it again she would see the cook to the door. It didn't stop her though. She would just talk about it when the housekeeper was out of the kitchen. It made me ponder on it though, Monsieur. Your sweet young lady did look haunted by something when she returned so ill, and she was as pale as a wraith."

The light shone on the moist cheek of Giorgio and he took her hand. "Please, do you call to mind where she stayed in Grasse?"

"I do. We sent her trunks after her at her request. It was L'Hotel de Sainte Marguerite."

Thirteen

ENGLAND

Mr. and Mrs. Barrington, Francesca's uncle and aunt on her mother's side, had sent an invitation to Francesca to tour the south with them, now that she was officially "out." The couple were set to visit with Francesca's mother for a week and then they would begin their holidays. This would be the first trip Francesca had ever taken unaccompanied by her parents and she was excited beyond measure.

Her parents had allowed her to purchase several new dresses and had even agreed to have them made in the London fashion. She had two new head dresses, one of which consisted of a huge white plume. She felt very fashionable wearing it.

She endured the week as best she could, reigning in her impatience with little success until the day finally arrived for departure. She kissed her parents a fond farewell and settled into the comfortable carriage, ready for adventure. Alas, the journey was so long that ere half a day had passed, she was already bored by the monotony.

They stopped for lunch at an inn in Surrey, and she was allowed to order for herself, which she felt was a little accomplishment. Brighton, their first destination, was yet six hours hence, and her uncle and aunt, hunger satisfied, dropped into a comfortable sleep. Francesca was left to occupy herself and allowed herself the luxury of remembering all her interactions with Mr. Ashbourne. Her heart gave a little leap as his perfect face swam into view. She imagined him leaning at the door to supper at her ball and his imperious studying of all present. She had thought him very proud in that instant, but then her mind replayed his change of countenance as her grandmother had approached. The pride had softened into a gentle benevolence that suited him very well. She imagined that even the Saints could not have produced a more tender expression.

The stage of her mind changed to her own introduction to the gentleman. His magnetism had been strong, and she had felt so drawn to him as she had never felt drawn to any other in such a manner that she had felt confused and agitated, impatient at her own lack of experience. Did she fancy that he had shown her any special consideration? In truth, at that moment, she did not.

The image altered to the intimate picture of Mr. Ashbourne in the window with cousin Katherine. She quickly wiped that vision away as it still made her unaccountably jealous.

She moved the memories forward to the unexpected dance he bestowed upon her and the way his nose had tickled her ear. Surely that was proof of his special regard, was it not? However, this portrait was pushed aside by his sudden departure. Truly, her head was beginning to spin.

She changed the performance in her mind to the walk by the brook at the picnic and his penetrating gaze as he spoke of his preferences in beauty. He had been very deliberate in his particular choices, and she remembered the way he had held her eyes, hypnotized by his own, imbued with hidden meaning. She was certain he had been hinting at his partiality for her, but again he had left abruptly and indeed, soon after, had left the whole party when they returned to Annabelle's home, insisting that he was needed at his estate. His conduct was very bewildering.

She toyed with the idea of painting his likeness to hide in a little locket to bring out when fancy prodded, but, alas, she was not adept enough at the art and she could hardly ask Katherine to paint one for that would not appear appropriate, and she still was not satisfied as to her cousin's own feelings for the man in question.

She leaned her head dreamily against the carriage window and presently fell into a very pleasant state of slumber.

Brighton was everything she could have hoped for with its white-tipped waves, screaming gulls, and enchanting promenades. It was her first view of the ocean, and the water, if not blue in color, was a pleasing jade. She felt as excited as a child and could barely stop herself from ripping off her shoes and stockings and plunging her toes into the icy, refreshing water.

The smell of the salty air was heaven, and she was intrigued by the bathing machines with their brightly colored red-and-white fabric, though the idea of plunging her whole person into the murky water was not one she relished.

They were staying in a very respectable boarding house on the front and spent most afternoons walking along one of the closer promenades. The bright sunshine and coastal vistas lifted Francesca's spirits to an almost celestial level.

On one such afternoon, she had left her aunt and uncle sitting on a bench along the beach front and had walked a little way off to lean against the railing and raise her face to the sun, eyes closed. The warmth kissed her skin, and she basked in its glow, allowing her mind to empty.

"Why, I believe it is Miss Haversham."

Her eyes flew open and proved that she was not dreaming. Mr. Langley Ashbourne was standing right beside her. He bowed. "I must apologize for not warning you of my presence," he said as he studied the look of astonishment on her face.

She quickly recovered. "What an unexpected surprise!"

"Unexpected, though not undesirable, I hope." His eyes were alight with mirth and warmth, so unlike the coldness he had shown when she first espied him at her ball.

"Indeed not! But what are you doing in Brighton, Mr. Ashbourne?"

"I have an aunt here that my father visits each summer. She came first at the exhortation of her doctor but found such a circle of new friends that she has never moved away! Truth be told, she is a little eccentric, and the society here suits her. Where are you staying?"

"Marine Parade at the White Heart boarding house."

"But I know it well! Is Mr. Higgins still the proprietor with the wife who has the lazy eye and the pesky cat?"

"You paint them very accurately," she replied with a wry grin. "I should hate to be the target of your description to strangers. I tremble to think what a caricature you would paint."

"In your case, Miss Haversham, I would have no need to resort to wit," he said, much more seriously. Francesca felt color creep to her cheeks. Seeing the redness, he continued, "Why, Miss Haversham, I appear to have discomforted you! It was certainly not my intention. I would never disparage the virtues of a young woman of high birth. Indeed, I described you to some of my acquaintances just yesterday and sang the praises of your beauty and talents."

"For shame, Mr. Ashbourne. You flatter me too much!" She raised her fan and batted it near her face while her reticule hung from her wrist. She looked over his shoulder in some confusion, searching for her aunt and uncle. Why did this man so undo her composure?

On seeing her distress, he said, "Shall we take a walk? Where are your companions? Are your parents here or perhaps your maid?"

She was grateful that the attention was now no longer focused on herself as it made her vaguely uncomfortable, and she replied hastily, "I am here with my aunt and uncle. They are just yonder. Pray, walk with me, and I will make the introductions." She proceeded to walk along the front, and he fell in beside her until they reached the bench whereupon sat her relatives.

"Aunt, Uncle, may I present Mr. Langley Ashbourne? He is an acquaintance of Grandmother and a friend of cousin William and was a participant at my ball."

Langley bowed to her companions and took her aunt's hand with the same theatrical flourish as she recalled from the picnic. The expression of delight on her aunt's face proved that he had quickly made a convert. "Why Mr. Ashbourne, it is delightful to make your acquaintance," she purred.

"I was just asking your delightful niece if she would honor me with a stroll along the promenade. Would you care to join us?"

"Indeed, we would, sir!" said her uncle and they rose from their bench to accompany the pair.

After some pleasantries, the older couple tactfully fell back to allow the young couple the opportunity to talk in some degree of privacy.

Francesca, while trying to listen to the unusually talkative Mr. Ashbourne, examined her feelings. Here was the man she had been thinking of for months. She shrank at the thought. She had desired his attentions for some time now and here he was, with no distractions. Why did she feel a faint sense of foreboding? She shook her head to dispel the ugly notion and enjoy the moment.

"Do you not agree?" asked Mr. Ashbourne.

Abruptly, she was pulled from her reverie to realize that she had absolutely no idea upon which subject Mr. Ashbourne had been speaking. To cover her blunder, she made a pretense of dropping her reticule which Mr. Ashbourne immediately recovered. As he handed it back, his fingers brushed her own and a jolt of electricity surged up her arm. Her eyes flew to his face, and she was caught off guard again as she met the intensity of his gaze.

Modestly dropping her eyes, she thanked him for rescuing her property and proceeded to continue their walk along the promenade. "I am so sorry, what were we talking about again? I seem to have forgotten." And she bestowed upon him a very pretty smile.

"I was asking you your opinion of the quality of sound between a harpsichord and a pianoforte."

"Oh, I cannot say as I do not play either."

"Do you not? Then what do you like to do with your time?" he asked.

"I sincerely love to sing. My mother and I often sing duets as she plays the pianoforte."

"Then I should very much like to hear you!"

"I did not say I was very good!" She laughed.

"I am sure you are too modest, Miss Haversham."

"No indeed! I know for a fact that you have heard my cousin Katherine sing, and her voice is that of an angel. Mine is nothing by comparison, but I do love to sing."

Langley hesitated slightly. "Ah, yes, I do recall. Your cousin *is* blessed with a pure and clear voice, to be sure."

"Aha, so you *did* spend time with my cousin! How do you like her? She is a fine girl, is she not?"

Langley's tone became more guarded. "I did sing with her at an evening of cards in Bath for the entertainment of those present, but we did not associate other than that evening, so I cannot say anything as to her character. She appeared to be a very pleasant young lady."

His chiseled profile had become taut, and, though intrigued again at the denial and the paradigm shift in his personality, Francesca decided to let the matter drop. She looked out at the sea and noticed another bathing machine. "Have you ever used a bathing machine, Mr. Ashbourne? I should so like to use one, but my aunt and uncle say they are too old for such frivolities. What say you?"

"I did use one several years ago, and I have to inform you that it is not as fun as you might imagine, Miss Haversham. The bottom of the sea is very sharp with lots of pebbles, and the water itself is glacial. Add to that the very unpleasant feeling of the seaweed wrapping around your ankles and you should be very glad that you have not had the misfortune to attempt it!"

She looked at him in earnestness, but on seeing the amusement in his face, she realized that he was hoodwinking her. She clapped her hands in delight, the earlier uneasiness swept away. "No, really Mr. Ashbourne."

"It is certainly cold and wet, and I have not tried it since. I prefer swimming in the lake on our estate. It would damage your curls Miss Haversham. Honestly, I would advise you against it."

As they reached the end of the promenade, they came upon a little puppet theater where a spirited performance of Punch and Judy was under way. Francesca stopped to regard the puppets and enjoy the countenances of the enthralled children. After several minutes, she became aware that Mr. Ashbourne was looking out at the sea and back along the path they had traversed. His expression was one of impatience, and it occurred to Francesca that there were many sides to Langley Ashbourne and that she was not yet sure which was the genuine and which the mask.

"Are you not diverted, Mr. Ashbourne?"

"Oh, to be sure, to be sure," he said weakly.

"Perhaps you would prefer to take tea in a tea house?"

"Yes, I am a little thirsty." Turning, he asked Francesca's aunt and uncle if they would enjoy a beverage, to which they assented.

Upon finding a suitable establishment, they had a very pleasant half hour together before Mr. Ashbourne begged their pardon and left to return to his aunt, who was expecting him.

"What a charming young man!" exclaimed Francesca's aunt. "He was most agreeable and paid prodigious attention to me. Not many young men would do the same. And to favor his aunt with his company shows an uprightness of character, do you not think, Francesca?"

"Yes, Aunt, he was all manners and politeness but, I confess, I have witnessed other moods which cause me some degree of concern. I want very much for him to be as good as I hope, but I am never quite sure which Mr. Ashbourne will make its appearance!"

Fourteen

ENGLAND

Phillip dropped his head into his hands and groaned. As he lifted his head, he came face to face with the calendar in his father's office. He was to begin his law career on September seventeenth, which gave him only two months to try for Francesca. If he failed, he would dive into his career and hope one day to meet someone who might not fade by comparison with her and with whom he could whittle out a tolerable life. He would settle, as many of his friends and acquaintances had done.

There were really so few happy marriages in his experience. His brother had been fortunate, and Phillip loved to spend time at their home with its palpable aura of happiness. Francesca's parents were another example of what he truly desired. Unfortunately, his own parents did not have passion in their marriage so much as friendship, and although their house was not unhappy, he wanted more for his future home. But without Francesca, he feared that was not possible. Verity Fairweather with her blond ringlets? Perhaps.

He pushed back in the chair and his hand touched his father's dog, Hermes, and he began to stroke its head. He let his own head fall back until he was looking up at the ceiling. He still had not found anything to impugn in Langley Ashbourne's character so his attempt for Francesca would begin with a serious disadvantage. How could he seriously compete against such a paragon of masculinity? He conjured up the image of Francesca's expression as she caught sight of Ashbourne at the top of the stone stairs at Annabelle's house the day of the picnic. Would that she looked at him in such a way! He tried to remember how she had seemed when he had begun to hint at his feelings by the stream that day. She had peered into his soul with—was it incredulity? Had he imagined a connection as her face softened in realization that he found her beautiful? Or did she turn to see Langley approach because the thought that he had feelings for her was appalling? Five more minutes would have solved the mystery, but alas, the wretched Ashbourne had chosen to make his appearance at the critical moment.

He kicked the leg of the desk in frustration and caused the dog to jump up. "Sorry old boy. Come here." He let the dog's velvety ear slide between his fingers. The dog settled down again and grunted with pleasure.

How to move forward? He was too honorable to invent a story about Langley, though he was sorely tempted, and besides, he respected Francesca too much for that and honored the code that the best man should win. However, could a man really be that flawless? His gut told him that men who appeared perfect were displaying a carefully crafted facade. But how to find out? William had been very little help as it turned out and only knew of Langley in a vague, distant sort of way. What he needed was to find someone who was more intimately connected with Langley's family. Where was the man from? Hampshire? He needed to find an acquaintance in the area. He decided it was time to pick his mother's brain.

Lady Waverley sat in the bay window in her private parlor, enjoying the warmth of the sun and working on her needlepoint. Her cap made a sort of halo, highlighted as it was by the sun's rays. His parents may not have the kind of marriage he desired, but he had no complaints about their parenting. His mother was devoted to her children and a true friend. He noticed, for the first time, that her cheeks were slightly wrinkled and her hair more peppered with gray. He smiled at the picture she formed and went to sit by her.

"Phillip! My dear boy, how nice it is to see you this fine morning." She laid down her needlework and gave him her full attention.

"Mother, I feel that I would like to do some traveling before I start practicing law. I don't know when I might have the chance again for some time. I would like to visit an area I have not been to before. Do you have any friends in Hampshire?"

"Hampshire? Why, that is a very good plan! Perhaps your father and I could come along and make it into a holiday? It is too long since I went on an adventure."

"I should like that very much, Mother."

"Let me see . . . I do believe that your father has a friend from his days at Oxford with whom he has kept in contact and whom he has not seen in far too long. I believe he hails from Hampshire. Let me make some inquiries and see if your father is willing." She clapped her hands together in delight. "On the way back, perhaps we can stop in and see your brother and my dear grandson. How I do miss him!"

As fate would have it, the old college chum was celebrating his six-tieth birthday and had mentioned mounting a small hunting party to celebrate the occasion to Phillip's father. He had wondered whether he had the energy for such a journey, but on hearing that his son wanted to do some traveling, decided to accept the invitation.

Charles Gray had turned to the church for his career, as he was the fourth son of a gentleman. He had been awarded a comfortable living by an uncle on his mother's side in Hampshire and had enjoyed ministering to his flock in the village of Thanet for the last thirty years. He was beloved by his parish and led a quiet life with his wife, and an unmarried daughter. Four sons were married but lived close by.

As the Waverleys approached the vicarage, they beheld a solid brick house of quite regular architecture bursting with clematis on the front wall. Flower boxes under every window gave the home a very merry appearance.

Charles and his wife came out to greet them and were most wel-coming. Behind them, hanging in the shadow of the doorway was a woman whose beauty was without parallel. Phillip regarded the par-ents and then looked again at the shadow in the hall and could hardly believe that they were kin. He admitted to himself that when he had heard of an unmarried clergyman's daughter, he had imagined to him-self a plain little wisp of a woman who was neither suited to romance by countenance or disposition. How far from the truth he had been, at least in view of her appearance.

The Grays led them into the vestibule, and the young woman fell further and further back, shrinking into the wall. Phillip was intrigued.

They were shown to their rooms and then invited to the drawing room to socialize before dinner should be served. Phillip's father was soon in deep reminiscence with Charles, and his wife and Phillip's mother found much to talk about and were becoming fast friends.

The daughter, whose name was Anne, played very quietly at the piano. Phillip could watch her without feeling that he was prying since there was no one else to talk to at present, and she was performing an entertainment of sorts. Her skin was the color of marble, he supposed a testament to her staying indoors much of the time, her hair twisted up in a very plain manner as though in an attempt to disguise her beauty. Her dress, too, was very plain and a light gray rather than the usual white muslin. Her eyes whispered of sadness, and he noticed that she did not smile. However, her attempts to diminish her comeliness had failed.

As she finished a piece, her eyes met Phillip's accidentally, and she immediately dipped her head to avoid his gaze, embarrassed—or was it ashamed?—at his attentions. Gallantly, he moved to sit by his father on the other side of the room so as not to give the young woman any more discomfort.

Just before dinner, several other couples arrived who had been friends with the Grays for many years. When they sat at dinner, Phillip found himself placed next to a Mrs. Waterman. She was very good company, had traveled much abroad with her husband, and had some very humorous tales.

After several stories, she quietened, letting others share the limelight. Phillip noticed her looking at Anne with sympathy as the next guest shared an anecdote. Mrs. Waterman turned her head to take a sip from her glass and caught Phillip looking from her to Anne. She lowered her voice so that only Phillip would hear and said, "It is such a shame about Anne. Would you believe me, sir, if I told you that she was once the belle of the county?"

"Actually, I can readily believe it. Though she goes to great lengths to disguise it, her fairness is without match!" said Phillip.

"She is a mere shadow of her former self. Such a crime. She is one of life's random beauties that sometimes grace a household not otherwise blessed with it. Oh, sir, if you had met her just four years ago you would have seen the spell she could cast on a room. All the young men were in love with her, with no coquetries on her part. It was not purely her physical appearance that appealed; she was such a lively soul with a zest for life and all it could offer. It makes me want to weep seeing her now, so dry, brittle, and broken."

"Pray, what could have befallen her that would merit such a change?"

Sotto voce, Mrs. Waterman replied. "She lost her character."

Phillip could not help but glance in Anne's direction at this shocking news. "How could it be?"

"Oh, sir, it is a very sorry story, one I take no delight in sharing. Four years ago, she met a very fascinating young man at a ball in the next county. They were well matched in looks, and by all appearances he was a young man from a good family, though no one quite knew all the details. He was quite taken with Anne and pursued her aggressively. He was all manners and good breeding, and her family welcomed him readily into their bosom. His conduct could not be criticized in the slightest, but alas, in that, they were deceived.

"He suggested that she visit her cousin in Hertfordshire with only her brother as companion. He had relations in the area, he claimed, and it would enable them to visit each other with more privacy. He emphasized that this should be a journey she took without her parents.

"At first, he was as good as his word and continued to act in an honorable manner befitting a gentleman, but after a few days he encouraged her to stroll alone in the estate to facilitate a private rendezvous. She was young, and he exploited her inexperience shamefully.

"They fell into a pattern of meeting in a clandestine way each afternoon, unaccompanied."

She gave Phillip a knowing look and glanced down the table to where Anne sat quietly staring at the tablecloth in front of her, a hollow statue.

"I am very sad to hear it," said Phillip. "I would never think to put a young lady in such a compromising position. He perhaps, had other motives?"

She nodded. "He obviously was not the gentleman he had presented himself to be and valued her virtue but little. His manners and breeding soon left him and were replaced by more . . . base emotions. He pressured her to become more intimate than is acceptable for a lady without a chaperone."

Phillip shook his head in disbelief. Mrs. Waterman appeared to be finished with her account, but he felt compelled to know the end and urged her to continue.

"By and by they were exposed by a manservant returning from the village, where his mother lay ill. He was shocked to find a lady alone with a gentleman in a deep embrace and uttered a small cry that alerted the couple to his presence. He ran and told the housekeeper, who alerted Anne's uncle.

"By the time the uncle found the place, the young man had escaped, leaving Anne sobbing in the glade. Her reputation was in shreds, and it was all the uncle could do to contain the damage. The manservant was threatened to within an inch of his life that he should never reveal what he had seen. Nonetheless, there were rumors.

"Her parents were devastated, of course, and as the full realization of the ramifications dawned upon Anne, she withdrew from life and shrank into the person you see today. Her dear parents never prosecuted the fellow as they did not desire to bring down any more disgrace upon their daughter. Despite that, the secret spread. She lives daily with the guilt and the shame."

"That is a truly mournful tale. I imagined that some adversity had befallen her, but I did not imagine it to be anything of this sort," said Phillip.

"Please, never disclose that you know the account. It is just so hard to see her this way. She was such a light and that wretch extinguished it. She is broken, quite broken."

Phillip felt a subtle shift in his reasoning and a puzzle piece dropped into place, causing an ugly thought to wander into his consciousness. His stomach rolled and he broke out in a cold sweat.

"Do you, by chance, recall the name of the scoundrel?" asked Phillip.

"I do indeed, sir. His name was Langley Ashbourne."

Fifteen

FRANCE

The sun was casting its tangerine glow on the white stucco as it fell to its slumber. Giorgio felt more as though he was in Morocco than the south of France. His bones ached, his head ached, his eyes ached. Would that *this* journey prove fruitful! He put one foot on the steps and braced his body with his arm on the wall, head hung low, struggling for the next breath. He felt a cool breeze touch his brow and looking up saw that the door to the little hotel was open.

"Monsieur, Monsieur, are you unwell? Here, let me help you into the foyer and get you some refreshment," said a young woman.

He smiled, unable to speak for the present and allowed the young woman to guide him up the last of the stone steps.

Once inside, he slumped onto the simple wooden bench, closed his eyes and took a deep, shuddering breath.

The return of the young woman surprised him from a slumber he had unwittingly fallen into. She pressed the glass of cool, clear water into his hand. The water sloshed as he took it, and the glass wobbled all the way to his mouth, only stopping when it was pressed to his lips. The chilled liquid slid pleasantly down his throat. He smiled at the young woman, and as his consciousness returned, he noticed for the first time that her gown protruded beneath her chest.

The disorientation ebbed, and he asked in his broken French, "Madame, would you be so kind as to find the manager of this hotel for me. I fear I must rest a little more."

"Of course, of course," she replied and hurried off.

Giorgio loosened the kerchief at his neck and took another sip.

Within a few minutes, an old, white-haired woman appeared wearing a helpful expression. A couple of young gentlewomen, who appeared to be in the last stages of imminent motherhood, descended the stairs behind her.

"Monsieur, I am the manager of this establishment. I understand that you have asked to see me?"

"Indeed, dear Madame. I have traveled far to get here and feel confident that you are in possession of facts that will make my journey worthwhile."

The woman frowned, stepped back, and crossed her arms. "We do not give out information, Monsieur. I regret to inform you that you have wasted your time!" She turned to leave.

Giorgio struggled to stand, but his knees gave way and he sunk back onto the bench causing the wood to groan. The woman turned back in alarm. He raised his arm and spoke in a small voice, "Madame this is concerning something that happened more than eighteen years ago."

The walls of the hotel seemed to lean in with interest. The woman paused and then decided to walk back and sit next to Giorgio.

"Even so, Signore," she said in Italian. "My records are confidential. But let us say that you have piqued my interest. Tell me your story." At Giorgio's surprise, she added, "My mother was Italian, and I am fluent in both languages."

Giorgio nodded and began his tale. "It would have been in the autumn eighteen years ago. My daughter came here, unbeknownst to me. She had left Italy to stay with friends in Nice, but I have since learned that she left them for the space of some months and came here with a hired maid."

"Tell me about her."

"She was full of life, slight of build, and had magnificent hair that was wild and thick unless trained very well. She spoke French very well with but a slight accent."

"Was? Is she no more?"

"Alas, she is not. However, with her last breath, she confessed that she had birthed a child. But death triumphed before I was able to learn more. You know not how far I have traveled, seeking clues hither and thither, and I fear it has taken a toll on my health."

The good proprietress nodded in acknowledgment. "You understand what kind of establishment this is, Monsieur?" Her eyebrows raised slowly and a wry grin appeared on her lips.

"I do, now, Madame. I come not to condemn. I come merely to seek for the babe. I am old and aging every day, and I have no one left. I have so much to share. I am a wine maker of some repute, the emperor of a grand kingdom, and I seek the child in order to bestow it upon them. If not . . ."

"Monsieur, there are many girls who come here who can answer the description you gave. Can you not give me more details?"

"Her name was Isabella Giaccopazzi. She was sweet and kind and had a laugh like a melody."

"It is not enough, the young mothers come to us under assumed names . . ."

"She had a strawberry birth mark upon her neck. Just like the one her mother had."

The woman grabbed his arm. "I remember that girl! It was such an unusual blemish, and she took great care to cover it when she had her hair dressed. The baby had it too, I recall. Wait here, Monsieur. I was undermanager in those days, and I kept the records. I will search in the cellar for the record book."

She left at a great pace, and Giorgio leaned his head against the cool brick wall and closed his eyes. Fatigue hit him like a glacier.

He awoke as the madame gently shook his arm, exclaiming, "I have found it, Monsieur!"

He struggled to open his eyes and gradually focused on a large leather-bound book with shiny parchment pages. The proprietress's finger was under a name written in fine script: Imelda Grimaldi.

"See here, there is a notation at the side: baby shares mother's strawberry birthmark."

Giorgio shuddered with relief. "Is there an indication of where the baby was placed?"

"No."

Giorgio slumped again.

"But I was there, I remember now because of the commotion she caused. Our custom is to find peasant farmers to take the babies or send them to the Sisters of Grace orphanage, but your daughter bonded with the baby and seemed to become attached to it. She would take it out in a carriage, and we thought she might decide to keep the babe. But then one afternoon she returned in some distress with an empty carriage, looking as though death had visited her. We feared that someone had stolen the baby, but in great gasping tears, she told us that she had found a couple worthy to take her baby, and that no child of hers would end up in an orphanage. Most of the girls did not care. They were happy to be rid of the problem, but not your daughter. She truly cared for the little girl and found a home for her, but it tore her apart."

Giorgio looked up sharply. "The baby was a girl?" He smote his chest. "Do you know to whom she gave the child?" he asked, his tone pleading.

"I know only that they were English and that they were staying in the villa Normandie."

Sixteen

ENGLAND

*D*oes Miss Haversham suspect that you have followed her here to Brighton?" the older gentleman asked.

"I would wager she does not, Father," said Langley.

"What good fortune that her grandmother let that little treasure of information slip. Do you have further plans to gain her confidence?"

"We have arranged to go for a little adventure to Lewes Castle tomorrow."

"Well played, my boy. Though it is very tiresome to be continually on the lookout for funds, I am rather enjoying my stay here in Brighton. I haven't been for years. What ruse did you use?"

"An old one. I told her that you have an eccentric elderly sister who lives here whom we have come to visit."

"Well, at least you refrain from describing me that way! Is this one handsome at least?"

"Oh, Father, this one is perhaps the prettiest of them all, though it really matters little to me. Are you entirely sure, this time, that she is to inherit?"

"Well, her mother has a fortune of her own, though not enough to run Haversham House alone. But her father stands to inherit from his father, and he has an enormous rambling estate up in north Wiltshire, so they must be worth a large fortune, though I cannot seem to find anyone who can accurately detail it. Importantly, neither estate is entailed, so the granddaughter will inherit after her father dies. If you can reel in this fish, you will save us and live as a wealthy man the rest of your days. Do you think she is someone you could learn to care for?"

"I have found that I really care for no one other than myself, Father, but she is pleasant enough and will make a tolerable partner in life. She is quite young and exceptionally naïve—I can easily train her to expect that many husbands live their lives quite apart from their wives, most of the time, leaving me free to pursue my own interests while maintaining a very pretty wife at home. Yes, she will look decidedly well on my arm as we visit all the best houses in society. I do believe, Father, that she is the one to save us."

"Do you think you are yet a favorite of hers?"

"I have paid her very little attention until today as, in my experience, the ladies seem to thrive on a little mystery. After our stroll, and tea on the front, I am reasonably sure that she has bitten my lure. I will enjoy the game of reeling her in, as you so aptly put it!"

"What about the other one?"

"Katherine? Well, there again fate has not been so good to us. Would you believe she is Francesca Haversham's cousin? She keeps asking me how well I know Katherine, and I am obliged to maintain a pretense of not knowing her. Dashed awkward, really. Had you not learned that Katherine is to receive nothing and that she will have to depend on the largesse of her brother, I should probably be married to her already! A lucky escape! Where did you hear that she would inherit a large fortune of her own, anyway?"

"Sir William Benchley. I should have known he was a doddering old fool and did not know his facts. How did she take your breaking off the engagement? You did break it off, I suppose?"

"I did broach the subject, but the girl is more determined than I thought. She would not accept it and has threatened to expose me if I do not honor my promise. It may be a bluff, though, as her cousin Francesca certainly knows nothing of it. However, we do have insurance; by exposing me, she will expose herself as a lady compromised. Not something a young lady would do before careful consideration."

"Well, that is a complication! Will she not eventually tell her cousin?"

"No, I am sure if it. As I said, she has too much to lose. We agreed that the engagement should be kept a secret because of my supposed, previously arranged, engagement. Indeed, she has allowed herself to be in several compromising situations with me that a true lady would never want to come to light for fear of damaging her reputation. You see, I always hold the trump card!"

The older man laughed, a deep menacing guffaw. "My dear son, you have learned your lessons well. She would no more talk of it than she would confess to seeing a vision! You have done well. Now, let us secure the real prize forthwith."

❧❧ ❀❧❧

"Does my bonnet sit correctly, Aunt? It feels as though something is amiss."

"My dear Francesca, it is most becoming and sits quite well on your head. You are taking prodigious care of your appearance today. Are we to assume that you do, in fact, favor Mr. Ashbourne?"

"Oh Aunt, I hardly know! I fall quite to pieces when he is near and feel very young and immature. Until recently, he appeared not to even notice my existence, and I own I was rather hurt by it. Yesterday, however, has given me hope that he might like to pursue me."

"Have your parents met him?"

"He came to my ball and then he was at the grand picnic at Bella's and he introduced himself. Grandmama knows of him and greeted him at the ball, and Bella's cousin William knows him from Oxford."

"Well, that sounds like some worthy recommendations, for your grandmama appears to bestow her favor rather sparingly. What did your mama think?"

"To be honest, he did not stay long enough in Mama's company for her to form an opinion, but I think she would like him very much on further acquaintance. You liked Mr. Ashbourne, did you not, Aunt?"

"I did! He has very proper manners. He is a fine example of gentlemanly behavior and is very pleasing to behold. Yes, I think I rather do like him. What do we know of his character?"

"Grandfather did not seem to know anything of value about his character, so I have put Phillip Waverley on the task. Do you think that is very wrong of me?"

"Perhaps a little forward. Now, Phillip Waverley, there is a fine young man in need of a wife! Do you not consider him, Francesca?"

"Phillip? He is the nicest, kindest man I know but he is more of a brother to me. And anyway, I am told there is a young lady whom he is courting. Mr. Ashbourne spoke of it in Phillip's presence, and he did not really deny it!"

"Oh well, more is the pity! We know exactly the depth of dear Phillip's character. Never matter. Perhaps the outing today will reveal more about Mr. Ashbourne and we can form our own opinion."

"What a fine day for a ride!" Francesca looked out of the window of the barouche at Mr. Ashbourne, who was riding a fine horse alongside.

"Yes, it is a fine day!" He trotted up to the coachman and pointed to an area up ahead that was a good place to stop to obtain a good aspect of the castle. As soon as the barouche stopped, he ran with haste to alight from his horse and hand down the ladies from the carriage.

Francesca's heart fluttered as she placed her gloved hand in his. Her aunt was beaming at Mr. Ashbourne and nodding favorably.

The castle dated from the eleventh century, and Mr. Ashbourne was a veritable fount of knowledge concerning its history. He explained that it was built by the first Earl of Surrey in 1069, a close friend of William the Conqueror, and that it was an example of Motte and Bailey architecture. He further detailed how it was part of William the Conqueror's power structure after conquering England. Francesca's uncle was enthralled by the history lesson, but Francesca tired of the facts and hung back with her aunt to look at the scenery.

"He is very knowledgeable is he not, my dear?" asked her aunt sympathetically.

"Very, but I find my mind is wandering . . . I never was particularly interested in history. I much prefer looking at this view. Quite makes me want to paint a picture!"

After several minutes, Mr. Ashbourne noticed that his quarry had lost interest and stopped to turn around and walk back to the ladies. Francesca's uncle's brow furrowed in disappointment at the abrupt end to the history lesson.

"Not a historian, Miss Haversham?"

She dropped her eyelashes and dipped her head. "I must confess, Mr. Ashbourne, that I am not, though I do admire the structure and am very impressed with the views."

"Then let us take a walk around the grounds and I will try to impress you no more." He smiled at her pleasantly without the least trace of impatience. "What was your favorite subject to study, then, if not history?"

"French was my favorite subject. I seem to have a gift for languages, and it came rather easily. Do you not agree that we prefer subjects we are good at?"

"Indeed, but French is not my forte. Therefore I will not attempt to converse with you in that language and embarrass myself! To your point, I seem to be able to remember dates and events very easily and therefore have always loved history. Even as a boy, my father would tell me tales of war, and I would be engrossed, afterward playacting them with my tin soldiers."

"That sounds rather fun. My governess had no gift for teaching history. She never talked about the people as if they had actually lived. Instead, she gave me long lists of dates and events that I had to learn by rote. I did not merely dislike history, I detested it!" She flung her arms in a wild gesticulation, accidentally knocking Mr. Ashbourne and causing him to stumble in surprise.

Before Francesca could apologize, Langley laughed. "Well, well, Miss Haversham! I did not realize you wanted to roleplay the battles this moment! En garde!" He posed as if holding an imaginary sword.

She readily joined in the game and mirrored his pose, and for several minutes they danced the dance of warriors engaged in a skirmish. Upon finishing, her aunt and uncle gave them a round of applause. They both bowed.

"I believe there is a very nice spot for a short repose around the bend. Does that suit everyone?" Langley asked.

"Why, yes!" exclaimed Francesca's aunt. "For I confess, I am feeling rather hot and in need of some shade."

"Then follow me," he said as he offered the good lady his arm. She beamed at the gesture and took it. Francesca fell back to accompany her uncle.

"Your young man certainly knows how to flatter, my dear."

"Uncle! He is not *my* young man, as you well know!" The corners of her mouth curved in a very pretty smile.

Her uncle patted her arm good-naturedly. "It is such sport for those of us in middle age to tease the young about romance. You must not mind me. He is rather fine, though, is he not?"

Francesca smiled at the remembrance of Annabelle's nickname for Mr. Ashbourne.

"Yes, he is rather fine," she agreed.

"Are you not interested in pursuing a relationship of a romantic nature with him then, my dear?"

"I did not say that, Uncle. I just said he is not *my* young man *at present*." She gave her uncle a knowing look.

As they walked, she watched fondly as Langley Ashbourne bestowed attention upon her aunt and admitted to herself that her feelings for him were growing. He was a young man who was not only of a pleasant appearance but whose heart seemed to radiate goodness too. At least most of the time. And he had sought her out, at last. The future held much promise!

Seventeen

ENGLAND

*P*hillip threw the sheets from off his legs and stared at the ceiling. It was unusually hot, and he had been tossing and turning for endless hours, his mind feeding on the new evidence of Mr. Ashbourne's callous disregard for the virtue of young women. He debated whether to just be done with it and arise for the day just as the grandfather clock in the hall struck four. *Too early*, he thought.

Restless, he felt the burden of the facts he had uncovered. He must not only tell Francesca that Mr. Ashbourne was a disreputable man of corrupt moral values, he also felt a further, immediate need to actively protect her from him. This was an odd thought, as he had no reason to believe that they were currently even in the same county. However, as the hours ticked by, the seriousness of the situation crystallized in his mind. Had Langley, even now, designs on Francesca's maidenhood? Was he actively stalking her? He shuddered at the thought. Anne's countenance swam before his eyes and the shadow of what she had once been filled him with sadness. He felt an exigent wish to be on the road, to be doing something constructive. He rolled over again and his arm hung over the side of the bed, his night shirt falling off his shoulder.

Should he not simply write the details in a letter? He vaguely remembered his mother mentioning that she was traveling with relatives in Brighton but had no knowledge of the address where they were staying. No, as illogical as it seemed, he felt an overwhelming urgency to ride to Brighton in haste and search her out. His impatience to be on the road was like a bitter herb in his mouth, and he wrestled with it, rolling it around till it burned.

The clock struck the half hour and he could stand it no more. He arose and penned a note to excuse his absence to his parents and his hosts. It felt so much better to be up and doing. He dressed in haste and quietly ran down the stairs, shoes in hand, anxious not to rouse the household. As he entered the main hall a maid looked up from sweeping the hearth in the parlor in surprise. He bowed to her and ran out the door, stopping only to drag on his confounded boots.

The crunch of his shoes on the gravel echoed noisily around the courtyard as he went in search of his mount. It was too early for stable boys to be up, so he saddled his own horse and leaped upon it, urging it forward.

An early morning mist hung over the lawn of the vicarage, like a veil. He plunged through it, desirous to shorten the distance between himself and Francesca as quickly as possible.

⁂

FRANCE

"It is so many years ago, Monsieur. I am not sure we still have our records from that year." The voice floated out of an open closet door.

Giorgio gazed out of the office that looked onto the village square. The weekly market was in full force, and the vendors were calling out their prices as women with baskets danced a Viennese waltz through the maze of stalls. It was noon and Giorgio's handkerchief was already damp.

"Voila!" said the property manager, flourishing a piece of paper in his hands.

Giorgio made an effort to stand, but the manager, seeing his distress, hurried over to stand by him.

"Spring of 18 . . . the villa Normandie was rented to a . . . let me see . . . ah, a Mr. and Mrs. John Haversham of Wiltshire, England."

He looked over in triumph just in time to witness Giorgio clutch his chest and slip ungracefully to the cold stone floor.

៚៚

BRIGHTON

After several days of hard riding, Phillip finally glimpsed the sea. It was nearing nine o' clock in the evening, and the sun was beginning its descent, throwing a celestial footpath along the water, inviting him to step upon it. He pulled up his mount and removed his hat, relishing the view.

He continued at a trot until he reached a boarding house on the outskirts of the town and, leaving his horse in the stables, went to seek a room for the night before beginning his investigation on the morrow.

Having secured a room, he described Francesca to the desk clerk but discovered that there was no one of that description staying at that hostelry. He turned to mount the stairs, head bowed, and as he did so, bumped into an elderly gentleman of high rank. He made his apologies and ascended the staircase, being much occupied in his mind about Francesca, and failed to notice the man's son approach from the other side of the establishment. In turn, the young man was so self-absorbed that he did not catch sight of anything but the young man's coattails, as his father recovered from the entanglement.

៚៚

After a hearty breakfast, Phillip began a long morning of canvassing every hotel and boarding house in search of Francesca and her relations. It was quite astonishing how many places one could stay at to enjoy the seaside air! By luncheon, he had had no success and repaired to the inn for some sustenance.

៚៚

It was the third day of their holidays, and Langley felt convinced that he could orchestrate time alone with Francesca. He knew that she trusted him and was confident that she had fallen in love with him. He had decided to repeat his modus operandi, though it had twice failed to bring about the desired outcome. He would stalk his wealthy prey and persuade them to commit some indiscretion, using the threat of exposure to blackmail them into an engagement. Of course, in execution, it was much less mercenary than it sounded, and the dear little flies had no idea that they were being invited into the spider's parlor. Luring them in had proved successful, but securing the marriage to a tidy fortune had not yet come to pass. There had been unforeseen complications. And Anne Gray was merely for sport. This time, however, he felt certain of success.

He had invited Francesca to visit with his fictional aunt and suggested that, since it was so close (he had provided the address of her rooms), and she was a respectable woman with a maid, that it was not necessary for her aunt and uncle to chaperone them, for they would be chaperoned momentarily after her departure from their care. Francesca's aunt had hesitated and looked to her husband for direction, but Langley, seeing the aunt's hesitation, had gathered her hand in his and placed upon it such a delicate kiss that she was quite a flutter and gave her permission without really meaning to.

Mrs. Barrington stood at the entrance to the boarding house and waved goodbye with her handkerchief, an uneasy feeling of apprehension biting at her heels as the couple flew by in an open carriage.

⁂

"What a beautiful day it is to be with such an elegant and fashionable young lady!" Ashbourne began. Francesca could hardly believe his words. He did care for her, then? All her anxieties and misgivings dissolved away, and she allowed herself to relax and soak in the pleasure of his attentions. She fluttered her fan and peeked over it in a flirting kind of way. Langley relaxed too; he had but to open the parlor door.

"What did you think of the opera last evening?" he asked.

"It was simply divine!" she replied and described her favorite scenes with many gesticulations.

She leaned back and closed her eyes to relive the magnificence of the previous evening. "I was rather surprised how much I enjoyed it. I have only heard German opera before and always find it rather dreary. Niccolo Piccini is so different, and I was quite transported!"

She sat up after a while, looking around, in confusion. "We seem to have been driving for some time. I thought you said your aunt lived close by."

⊷⊙⊱ ⊶⊙⊰

Balding on top like an eagle, with rheumy eyes that sparkled devilishly, the aged gentleman Phillip had bumped into the previous evening regaled him with tales of his son's conquests. Distasteful as it was to listen to the tipsy fellow, Phillip felt obliged to give him a little of his time since he had been in the wrong the night before and had seemingly hurt the old man's pride.

His eyes were faithfully on the storyteller while his mind was busy worrying about Francesca, when part of the tale sunk in and he said, "Pray, can you repeat what you just said?"

"I said that my son is, at this very moment, securing the hand of a wealthy young debutante to ease our pecuniary woes." The crinkled man cackled with delight.

This commanded Phillip's full attention. He proceeded with casual caution. "I suppose that the young woman is a willing participant in the betrothal?" His fingers dug into the upholstery as he leaned forward to catch the answer.

"I suppose it depends on your definition of 'willing!'" the old rogue snorted.

Phillip closed his eyes, took a calming breath, and spoke in a clipped manner. "Is it not dishonorable to ensnare a vulnerable, young woman into an engagement? But I am sure I misrepresent your son's intentions?"

The extra drink was rendering the nobleman defenseless to withhold the truth as he replied, "You have summed up the situation admirably, sir. Desperate times push us to use bold measures. There is no real harm done."

Phillip's head tilted in disbelief and he nudged down a swelling fear as he forced himself to ask, "Who is this poor, unfortunate female?"

The brute put his finger to his nose. "Oh sir, you cannot betray me into revealing such details, but this much I will own, she is a dark beauty from Wiltshire."

An invisible energy punched Phillip in his gut. He jumped to the edge of the armchair, shoulders tight, face taut. "Where is this drama being acted out?"

The fiend's eyes were drooping as he experienced the effects of the liquor and he was powerless to suppress. "Lighthouse Cove..." he mumbled even as he slumped against the back of his chair.

⁂

"My aunt? She is in the habit of taking an afternoon siesta," beamed Langley. "I used her as an excuse. I thought perhaps you might prefer a picnic with me in a very pretty cove I know. I have been searching for a way to have you all to myself. Hence, the small fib. Can you forgive me?"

He dipped his head and looked up at her with an expression full of apology, smiling delightfully.

Her previous concerns waned at his confession, and, in spite of her former reservations, she was flattered by his attentions. To date, his conduct had been beyond reproach, and she justified his small deception on the grounds that he appeared to be an honorable gentleman.

She sat back in the carriage and endeavored to be pleased that he was favoring her, but, alas, the unease she had attempted to ignore returned as the unscheduled and illicit journey lengthened. Two conflicting emotions began to war with each other: reckless excitement and adherence to propriety. One did not throw off a lifetime of indoctrination that dictated that a young woman should never be alone with a young man in a solitary place. Propriety cut a thrust and started to win the battle of her conscience. She edged away from Langley imperceptibly, mounting concern forming a knot in her stomach. They had left the busyness of the town. She now had no one to appeal to.

⁂

With no backward glance, Phillip rushed to the reception desk to ask directions to Lighthouse Cove. The desk clerk was helping another patron and Phillip's toe tapped uncontrollably as he failed to rein in his impatience.

⁂

"How far is the cove?" Francesca asked, her voice having lost some of its energy.

"Oh, not far now!" Langley hollered as he whipped the horse onward, seemingly unaware of the heightened anxiety in his young companion.

"Will we be meeting a party there?" she asked in desperation, hoping to find a way out of her current dilemma.

"Why, no! I want you all to myself," he said. Then in a gentler tone, he added, "Don't you want to be with me, Francesca? I thought you felt about me the way that I feel about you. Come, you cannot pretend to be ignorant of my feelings! I prefer you to any young woman of my acquaintance. Do you not feel the same?"

She looked at him, worry etched on every feature, a pitiful look that would have halted a more decent man, but it did not break him. He was on a mission to save his own hide and she would be a necessary casualty. And besides, she *was* very lovely. Life with her would have certain advantages, to be sure.

"I would much rather spend time with you in a public place," she said quietly.

"Ah, but we could not speak so openly in a public place, my darling."

Her breath caught on the intimate word and impropriety shot a lunge back in the battle. Had he really called her, "my darling?" Was this term of endearment not clear evidence of his deep feelings for her?

He slowed the horse and took her hand. "Do you not trust me, little thing? I promise to be very good. Look, it is just yonder."

She looked over and saw a very secluded little cove with golden sand. She glowered back at him with a deep line between her eyes. He appeared entirely untouched by her fragility; indeed, he seemed to be enjoying the sight of her dangling from his web.

"Yes, yes, it is very pretty," she said with even less energy.

⁓⊙℘ ℘⊙⁓

When at last the vital intelligence had been obtained, Phillip spared no time in fetching his horse. The youth in the stable jerked his head up in surprise as Phillip skidded into the stables.

"I have not finished seeing to your horse, sir."

"It does not matter, it is of the greatest importance that I leave immediately, there is no time to lose!" He thrust a handsome tip into the young man's hand, pulling himself up into the saddle with ease. "Do you ride well? I need you to come with me."

"Now, sir?"

"Yes, this instant! It is absolutely essential, and I will take responsibility if this causes trouble with your employer. Make haste! We must leave without delay."

Now that he knew where to find Langley, speed was of the essence.

⚬⚬⚬ ⚬⚬⚬

Langley had the horse trot close to the cove and jumped down, lifting his hand to help Francesca down with such a benevolent air that she felt a momentary lull in her anxiety. As she placed her hand in his, she looked from right to left to discern whether there were any other people in the isolated spot. Her heart sank to see that there was no one. When she hesitated, he placed his hands firmly around her waist and lifted her down. In other circumstances, pleasure would have flowed through her at his masculine touch but in her present state of affairs she felt a searing panic rise in her chest.

The more she hesitated, the rougher he became, taking her hand and almost pulling her down the path to the beach. In his other hand, he held a picnic basket. She felt compelled to be led along, but the hollow feeling inside continued to grow and she could not prevent herself from constantly looking behind her in search of rescuers, while Langley made meaningless banter.

Upon reaching the sand he relinquished her hand and laid out a blanket. He opened the basket and revealed some cold meats, fruit, and bread. On the one hand, she was delighted with his thoughtfulness, but on the other she was very alarmed that they were alone and unchaperoned. Her parents would be very dismayed. Her eyes began to sting.

⚬⚬⚬ ⚬⚬⚬

Fewer and fewer dwellings graced the roads, and Phillip wondered at Langley's audacity in taking Francesca to so remote a location. He pushed his horse as fast as he dared, looking behind sporadically to ensure that the youth from the stables was keeping pace.

The faint roar of the waves sounded in his ears, and he knew he was close. He prayed that he was not too late.

Langley sat down and patted the blanket next to him, smiling all the while. He felt a certain ecstasy at seeing her unease. It fed something inside him, leaving him feeling acutely satisfied. She looked so pretty when she was vulnerable. He reached up for her hand and gently pulled her down to the blanket, his heart beating louder as he took pleasure in her obvious agitation. His passions were strangely aroused and he wanted very much to kiss her but knew that he must tread carefully so as not to frighten her and jeopardize his plan.

As they broke through the trees, Phillip pulled sharply on the reins. The coastline was spread out before him like a cloth, gritty sand and frothy surf. He looked to his left and then to his right and saw in the distance an empty open carriage. Kicking his mount again, he sped forward.

Francesca sat on the blanket as far from Langley as she could. Voices in her head were screaming at her to leave immediately, but to where? She was trapped with no means of retreat and no other persons to entreat for help. Desperation was threatening to overcome her, and she pushed down a sob, biting her lip in distress. This action seemed to heighten Langley's attraction, and he inched over to her side of the blanket and began stroking her hair, then trailed his finger along her cheek to her chin. This both electrified and terrified her, and she flinched.

"You do trust me don't you, my darling? I would never hurt you."

He was leaning so close she could feel his breath on her skin and she braced, holding her breath. He began talking nonsense and she felt his lips touch hers in a hint of a kiss. She reared back.

"Mr. Ashbourne, you are making me very uncomfortable. Won't you please take me home?"

"I thought you liked me, Francesca. You have given every indication that you do. You have teased me and now it is natural for us to kiss. That is what sweethearts do. I know that you have little experience with men but trust me. No one will think less of you."

He traced her lips with his finger in a silken touch, and she gulped, a single tear escaping and tracking down to her chin. He lifted the tear off her chin and licked it from his finger. She stiffened in revulsion, but he leaned forward grabbing her shoulders to place a more passionate kiss upon her mouth. As their lips touched and she knew all hope was lost, a masculine shout was heard in the distance. Rescue!

She reared back once more and jumped up, almost faint with relief as she saw Phillip running toward them. She raced to him, unable now to stem the tide of tears. Phillip clasped her in his arms, and she laid her head against his coat in great racking sobs. He looked up and fixed Langley with an icy glare. Langley returned it with defiance. "I do not believe you were invited," Langley spat acidly.

"And I do not believe it is either virtuous or honorable to take an artless, innocent girl and compromise her character," shot back Phillip.

"I was doing nothing of the sort! Had you not interrupted, I was going to make a proposal of marriage to her!"

"You have disqualified yourself as a suitor by this and past conduct! Oh yes, I have found you out, Langley! I have come to deliver Francesca from your snare and take her back to the protection of her relatives."

Without further discourse, he pivoted around with Francesca under his arm and escorted her back to his horse, where the stable boy was waiting upon another horse.

"Oh, you have proclaimed yourself her protector now, have you?" yelled Langley after the retreating couple. Phillip did not dignify him with a reply.

He helped Francesca onto his horse and led it by the reins back along the coastal path as she whimpered in distress. He kept his own counsel as he knew that if he opened his mouth, just then, it would explode with accusations against Ashbourne. The fury he felt throbbed in his head and his nails cut into his hands as he balled his fists.

After they had traveled some distance, giving him time to reign in his emotions so that he could speak without his voice trembling with anger, he attempted to draw Francesca into conversation to assess her condition.

"Francesca, did he . . . did he hurt you?"

She shook her head, still looking down fixedly at the horse's back.

He was fearful of the answers but felt that it was of vital importance to ask them. "Did he . . . force himself upon you in any way?"

She shook her head again and wiped her nose, still hanging her head. He breathed a sigh of relief. All was not lost. "Did he attempt to kiss you?" He waited in anguish for her reply. At length, she slowly nodded.

"The cad! I should challenge him to duel!" he roared, unable to conceal his emotions anymore. This outburst initiated another bout of sobs and he carefully bridled his fervor to save her from more distress.

They walked along in silence for several minutes and at length her weeping subsided.

"How did you find us?" squeaked a broken, watery voice.

He seized upon the opportunity to tell her the whole story in detail, in order to allow her sufficient time to recover her composure. "I returned to my lodgings after a morning spent trying to find you. Having traveled long the day before I was in need of a little respite. As I entered the establishment to retrieve the key to my room I happened upon an older gentleman, whom I had bumped into the evening before. I had apologized at the time, but on seeing me, he renewed his grievance that I had jostled him. Given his advanced age I again renewed my apologies and offered to buy him a drink, which he accepted.

"We began a pleasant conversation during which he boasted that his son was, at that moment, wooing a young lady of considerable fortune and that he dearly hoped that he was successful in securing her hand in marriage as they had fallen upon hard times. I experienced a sense of foreboding and asked after the young lady in question, who eerily resembled you."

Francesca gave a little gasp.

"I calmed myself to inquire as to where the fellow had taken his lady for the proposal as the villain was now succumbing to the effects of the liquor he had consumed. He told me as he drifted off to sleep. I quickly sought directions to the cove from the innkeeper.

"Thank goodness he told you," she whispered.

"Yes! I promptly fetched my horse and paid this youth here to accompany me. Every furlong was an agony to me as I had very recently learned in Hampshire that Langley had compromised a respectable young lady—"

A gulping cry came forth from the direction of the horse but, Phillip pressed on, "—and ruined her character and thereby her spirit. I felt very unsettled after I heard her story and could not rest until I started out on a journey to find you and warn you. That was, in fact, the very reason that I came into the area, for fear that he had designs on your virtue, but I did not suspect that he had followed you to Brighton!" He chanced a glance at her and saw that she had lifted her head somewhat. "What was her name?"

"Miss Anne Gray."

"Is she very changed?"

"Her friends tell me that she is, and I can attest that she is a mere shadow of a woman. By all accounts, she has altered from a vivacious young girl of great beauty and opportunities to a slinking figure who hides in the corners of rooms and seems close to tears at all times. She has no chance of marrying."

Francesca nodded and wiped her nose again. They walked on in silence, some more.

"Do you . . . think . . . this will . . . ruin *my* character?" she whispered.

"From what you have told me, I appeared before he had time to dishonor you, and I am a witness, as is this fellow behind us. If he dares to mention the incident, I will confront him about Miss Gray and make sure all of society knows about his misconduct regarding her. Did he force you to come here or did you come willingly?"

"Oh, Phillip! He grievously deceived me and my aunt and uncle by telling us we were going nearby to visit with his aunt but he never had any intention of taking me there and brought me here by deception. I was so uncomfortable as soon as I realized his deceit, but what could I do? There were no strangers around to turn to. Oh, I am ruined and I have brought disgrace to my poor parents!"

"Hush, hush you are not ruined," he said gently. "I am your witness."

"I was flattered by his attentions, Phillip—in that I am guilty. I am a stupid, stupid, silly girl. What must you think of me?"

"He took shameful advantage of your lack of experience and youth. The fault is all his!" he said with emotion. "And Miss Gray is evidence that he is a serial predator of the worst kind!"

After several more moments Francesca cleared her throat. "I fear that he may have compromised cousin Katherine."

Phillip whipped his head around. "Pray, tell me why you suspect this?"

Francesca recounted their intimate conversation at her ball and admitted that she had seen Katherine leaving the inn where Langley was staying, in the village. She explained that she had tried to broach the topic but that Katherine repeatedly denied any association.

"I fear that you are right then, but I sincerely hope that you are wrong."

Eighteen

ITALY

Giorgio swatted the doctor away. "I am well! Stop this fussing!"

"You are not well, Signore. You have suffered several small heart attacks over the last month. You are very lucky that you did not die in France."

Giorgio tutted in disgust.

"I plead with you not to take what I have said lightly, Giorgio. You must rest. It is rest or death. I cannot state it any plainer than that. I could, perhaps, find you a nurse?"

"I have plenty of servants who can minister to me without hiring a nurse like an invalid!"

The doctor, who had been a close friend of Giorgio's for thirty years, paused as he put his equipment back in his bag and turned his head, "You *are* an invalid, my old friend, and if you do not obey my orders I will no longer be able to enjoy a leisurely drink with you. Instead, I will be giving the eulogy at your funeral."

"Bah, what nonsense! I am fit as a fiddle."

"Come, you know that you are not. You *must* rest; your heart is in a delicate state, and it needs time to recover."

He had finished packing his bag and sat down in an arm chair. "Now, tell me what you have learned on your travels."

Giorgio's drooping countenance lifted, and he leaned back in his chair and smiled like a cat, making a tent of his fingers, elbows on the arms of the chair. He recounted in detail all his journeys, the dead ends and frustrations and finally discovering what had happened to the baby. The doctor made the appropriate noises of interest and surprise. "What will you do now?"

"I would have traveled to England as soon as possible"—the doctor shook his head in alarm—"but I see that such a journey would be too risky." The doctor's lined face relaxed. "Therefore, I will send my estate manager, Mario, as there is no one else I trust as much, except you, my old friend, and you cannot possibly go. Mario will travel to England and make inquiries as to where this Haversham House is situated and then present the facts to the family. I will request that the child come to me in haste as I am on death's door"—he winked at the doctor, who shook his head again, but smiled—"and am unable to travel and he will explain that she is my heir."

"What if she will not come?"

"What nonsense, of course she will come! She is the heiress to a vast vineyard. I know the English. They like money!"

"She may not need money. Have you considered that she may not know she was adopted? The English may be fond of money, but I believe they put blood, blue blood, above all else. You may stir up a hornet's nest, the consequences of which you cannot possibly foresee. Her parents may even prevent their daughter from ever hearing the news."

"Ever playing devil's advocate, Alberto. In that case, I will send my manager with a prayer and pray continually while he is gone, that God may bless him that she may learn her true heritage."

The doctor did not respond but merely stared at the wall in contemplation.

"I must see her, Alberto. I am so lonely, and it distresses me that this," and he pointed outside to his property with a sweep of his arm, "should fall into the hands of strangers after I am gone. This is my legacy, and I have been torn with emotion that it would never be passed down to any heirs and now God has seen fit to present me with a granddaughter. I do not believe that He would taunt me with knowledge of her only to snatch her away. God is not cruel. I believe that I have found her for a purpose, and it gives me such joy, such hope!"

The doctor smiled. "Then rest, Giorgio, if not for me, then for her, my friend."

c⊛⊷ ⊷⊛ɔ

Mario Lombardi looked up at his employer with surprise. "You want me to travel to England to find your granddaughter? But the vineyard, my wife . . ."

"I will make it worth your while, Mario, and there is no one I trust more to fulfill this commission. And you speak some English. You know that if it were not for this infernal weak heart, I would travel there myself. But alas, the good doctor has forbidden it. He thinks I may be facing my own mortality, so speed is critical."

He looked into the eyes of his estate manager with a pleading expression. "I must find her to tell her of her legacy . . . before I die."

"Of course, Signore, of course, you are right. I will instruct Angelo on running the vineyard while I am away and promise my wife a big gift from my travels."

"You are a good man, Mario. Now here are my instructions and the travel plan."

Nineteen

ENGLAND

The rest of the slow journey passed in silence as Francesca vainly attempted to recover. Phillip directed the horse to the first hostelry they encountered. "I think you need some refreshment to aid with the shock. See, you are shivering, and it is a very hot day. Come, let us take refreshment here, for you cannot return to your aunt and uncle in such a state. We also need to discuss how you prefer to deal with this unfortunate incident."

Tears sprang to her eyes again but she bit her lip and nodded and allowed herself to be lead into the establishment. It was not a very fashionable place, and thus there were not many people to witness her distress.

Phillip guided her to a table in the rear and allowed her to sit with her back to the rest of the customers. He ordered tea and some hot cakes and then patiently waited for her to gather her wits.

"I have been such a fool!" she whispered.

"You are young, Francesca. You could not have suspected that he had evil intentions. I believe that this was a carefully orchestrated plan. Remember, his father supposed me a disinterested stranger and as such confessed to me that they were in dire need of funds. You presented the perfect solution: beautiful, rich, and the sole heir of an unentailed fortune. And let us not forget that you are not the first young woman to be caught in his web."

"Why do you think he did not marry this Anne you speak of?"

"I see two obvious reasons but they are mere conjecture. First, I would suggest that he enjoys dallying with beautiful woman for the pure thrill of the chase for he is apparently uninhibited by any sort of moral code. And second, she had no fortune. Katherine, we know, will not inherit, and the need for funds must have become critical. Goodness knows if there are any other young women he has ruined . . ."

A whimper escaped from deep within Francesca, and Phillip, realizing his tactless remark, quickly corrected himself. "Not you, Francesca. God helped me to find you before you were compromised. I spoke thoughtlessly. Forgive me. No, I was thinking of Anne, who was not so fortunate." He sent her a timid smile of apology and tenderly touched her hand. She could not meet his eyes for the shame that burned in her own.

The tea and cakes arrived but Francesca could not eat. Only after excessive encouragement from Phillip did she drink a little.

When he noticed that her trembling had subsided, he broached the subject of her aunt and uncle. "Do you want to tell the Barringtons?"

"I cannot bear to tell them the truth," she gasped.

"I was not suggesting that you had to tell them everything. We do, however, need to decide whether to hold the scoundrel accountable. Is it moral to allow him to escape judgment out of fear, and permit him to inflict the same fate on other innocent, young women? If his finances are as desperate as I suspect, then he will soon choose another victim out of sheer necessity. I saw him playing cards with a reckless abandon at a party that only now makes sense."

Francesca looked sharply into his eyes with misery and alarm. "Phillip, if he anticipates exposure, I am ruined for he will surely drag my name through the dirt with his!"

She stopped, aware that her voice had become a panic-filled crescendo. Continuing in a tight whisper, she said, "I peered into the window of his soul today, and it is dark and vile. He is utterly without scruple! He will think nothing of spreading false rumors about my character if he feels threatened."

"I would deem it an honor to defend you against any concocted accusations by that libertine!"

"I am not so naive as to imagine that the gossips would not relish such a story, be it truth or fiction! I cannot bear to bring such shame on my family!"

Phillip pondered this for a while and nodded. "You make a valid observation. I think I must write to him privately and warn him that if he breathes one word of this or if he tries to take advantage of another young woman, I will make him pay dearly. If his financial situation is as dire as I believe, such a threat may be enough to prevent him spreading malicious falsehoods. He must, after all, maintain his semblance of good character in order to seek out another heiress."

"So, he will go unpunished," Francesca murmured.

"Anne's family have not pursued him at her request. If you want to protect other girls, you will need to bring him to justice by going public—"

"No!" Fear flashed across her features. "Oh, Phillip, I cannot. Please do not make me. I cannot bear for my parents to ever know of this."

She was shaking again, and he realized that he could push her no further at this time.

"I must confess, I would delight in beating the scoundrel till he begged for mercy!" he continued, which comment produced the merest hint of a smile from Francesca.

"How about this for now, and we can consider further action in the future when you feel stronger? I will tell your aunt that you were just leaving with Langley when you felt a little faint and I happened upon you. We can say that, though he was very solicitous about your health, he had received a message from his father's estate manager to call him to an urgent meeting, and I assured him that I would see you safely back to your aunt and uncle so that he might leave that instant. You can say that you feel unwell again after your arrival—"

"In truth, I do!"

"—and that will allow you to lay low for a few days until you have recovered your spirits. I think to insist going back home early will only raise suspicions."

She nodded, miserably.

"Then let us be off. You have been gone a long while already, and we are several miles from the town."

Gently, he helped her to her feet and took her elbow to guide her back to the stables. On seeing a carriage for hire, he ordered it and helped Francesca inside, hiring a maid to accompany them.

Her aunt accepted their story without reservation and bundled Francesca up the stairs to bed, clucking like a mother hen.

As he took the carriage back to get his horse, he allowed himself to surrender to the strong feelings of protection, relief, and anger that he had suppressed. He shuddered to think what might have happened to Francesca had he not arrived when he did and thanked Providence for the strong impression to go in search of her.

At last he had found the flaw in Langley's character for which he had been hunting but he took no pleasure in it. The cost had been almost eternally too high.

Twenty

WILTSHIRE, ENGLAND

*D*elicato, delicato! I have, how do you say, treasure, in the bags!"
Mario had been on the road for three weeks and had experienced many setbacks and frustrations. He had finally arrived in London, made inquiries, and at last discovered the location of Haversham House. He had also found a most beautiful vase for his wife while in London and was now watching a porter throw his bags onto the back of the post carriage with no care for its contents.

After rescuing the bag, he settled himself into the carriage that was headed to Wiltshire. It was crowded, which necessitated holding the bag on his knees and being crushed into the side of the compartment. It was most inconvenient. And cold. He reflected on the huge sum that he was being paid for this commission and how much he cared for his employer, which helped improve his feelings about the situation somewhat.

Giorgio Giaccopazzi had rescued him as a boy. Left an orphan at age twelve, he had resorted to stealing food because he was starving. Giorgio happened to be in town on business the day Mario had been caught and was being dragged before the magistrate. He was small for his age and emaciated and for some reason Giorgio had taken pity on him, telling the magistrate that he would give the boy a job and be responsible if the boy was ever caught stealing again. From that day forth, Giorgio had provided for him and even sent him to school to learn basic reading and math.

Mario had begun working at the vineyard in the lowliest of positions, and Giorgio had personally overseen his training, mentoring and molding him. In return, Mario revered Giorgio as a father figure, and indeed, no father could have done more. He had fought hard to win his respect by working harder than anyone else and excelling in his studies and had risen from position to position until, at age thirty, he had been awarded the position of estate manager. It was a proud day, and he had been choked with emotion when Giorgio had announced that he would replace the deceased manager. He had proposed to his sweetheart that very day, and they were married the following week. Given this history, Mario would happily walk through fire for Giorgio if that were what he required.

After several hours, the carriage had emptied, having made two stops. Mario was able to spread out and even sleep a little. He was awoken from a fitful slumber by knocking on the roof of the carriage. He jerked awake, stretched the crick in his neck, and opened the door to find himself in the middle of the English countryside in the dawn mist. The sun was just peeking above the horizon like a reluctant debutante, making the mist glow. He looked at the driver who was retrieving his valise and shrugged his shoulders while showing his palms, eyebrows raised. It was a very Latin gesture and made the carriage driver smile.

"That way," the driver said, pointing up a lane. "One mile that way. Can't miss it!"

Mario touched his cap, bowed his head in thanks, picked up his bags, then watched as the carriage was swallowed up in the mist. He turned with resignation and began to walk up the lane.

It was chilly and damp and he shivered. He was beginning to appreciate England, but he did not enjoy the climate and missed the warmth of his homeland. As he walked, the birds accompanied his steps and several rabbits turned tail, exposing their white hither parts. His bags became heavier and heavier, and he was just considering taking a rest when the house rose out of the haze like a dryad.

It had a ghostly appearance because of the dewy fog but was, unarguably, of very fine architecture. It was large, but not ostentatiously so, and was very regular in appearance, with well-tended gardens and a pond in the forecourt. His footsteps crunched on the gravel drive, sounding louder than usual in the early morning quiet.

He looked at the big front door and decided to find a tradesman's entrance. It would not be good manners to arrive unexpected at the front door at this early hour. He walked around to the side and found a stairwell that lead down to a basement. As he descended, he saw movement in the kitchen, dropped his bag, and knocked sharply.

A harried-looking woman with disheveled hair opened the door with an inquisitive look. "Can I help you, sir?"

"May I enter?" he said in heavily accented English. The woman cocked her head to one side. He tried again, this time pointing to the interior of the building. "May I come in?"

He extended a letter for the woman to see his reference. She took it and read and then stood aside for him to enter. "You have come at a very early hour, sir." Her tone was annoyed.

He scrunched his eyes and peered at her in incomprehension as her own country accent was very pronounced. She pointed to the clock on the wall.

"Oh yes, mi scusi. I came by the post. I traveled all night."

"Well, you better come in to the kitchen then and have some tea." She pushed him into the room and bade him sit at a large table that was empty.

The kitchen was functional rather than decorative and had several large iron ovens. A very young maid was cleaning out the ashes while a woman he assumed was a cook was pinning up her hair under a white cap. The first woman pulled out a chair and motioned for him to sit.

"Who have we here?" asked the cook.

"I don't rightly know yet," replied the other woman. "He has a letter but it is written in very poor English. Here, have a look and see if you can understand it."

"Where are you from?" said the cook loudly and in an exaggerated tone as though the man were deaf and stupid.

"Italia. Italy."

The cook looked at the other woman and formed a silent "oh" with her lips. She took the letter and read the characters written upon it. "It says he has come from Italy at the request of a Signore Giaccopazzi of Florence with very important information for Mr. and Mrs. Haversham. What on earth? What kind of information?" She looked at Mario suspiciously.

"I have information about a journey they make to France eighteen years ago."

The two women looked at each other and then at the visitor, distrust rippling off them.

The first woman said, "Sir, as you must realize, you are very early and will have to wait on Mr. Philmore, our butler. He will decide whether you will get an audience with the master of the house."

Mario nodded.

"In the meantime, I will make you some tea and toast. Whoever you are, you must be hungry."

The clock struck five and several more maids appeared with cleaning utensils, looking at the swarthy visitor with unfeigned interest. Mario ate the toast hungrily but with careful manners. As he partook, more and more servants entered the kitchen area, and the downstairs of the big house came to life. By the stroke of six, it was a veritable bustle with footman buttoning up their livery and lady's maids primping their hair. Mario watched the worker bees with the same interest they showed in him.

Apart from the paler skin and different style of clothing, he could have been back in Giorgio's kitchens. The servants performed a well-orchestrated ballet as cooks kneaded dough and servants walked through, carrying clothes to mend and shoes to shine.

As the clock struck seven, everyone gathered to the kitchen table and a man Mario assumed to be the butler strode in. He was tall, thin, impeccably dressed, and held his nose as though there were an unpleasant smell in the air. At his signal the servants sat down and the cooks put a bountiful, if plain, breakfast in front of them.

After a moment, Mr. Philmore noticed the stranger. "Who, may I ask, are you?"

"This is Mr. Lombardi," said the plain woman in black. "He claims to have an important message for the master. He has a letter."

She pointed at the letter on the table and Mario stood and handed it to the butler, who read it, with every line on his face furrowed. "What is your information?" he demanded.

"I must not tell it to anyone but your master," he said firmly.

"I cannot just let any stranger who claims to have 'information' have an audience with Mr. Haversham. You will need to give me more details or I will have to show you to the door."

He stood and looked imperiously down his nose at Mario.

"Audience? I do not know this word. I say only that it is about their visit to France, eighteen years past. Mr. Haversham, he will want to see me. I know this."

Mr. Philmore straightened his waistcoat and put his glasses in a little pocket, shaking his head. "This is most irregular, most irregular!"

"Please, signore. I have traveled so far. Please, the date. Tell him. My master, he is a very sick man. Please—"

Mr. Philmore was immune to sorry tales and raised his hand to stop the man speaking. He was tempted to throw the foreigner out on his ear but feared that Mr. Haversham might be angry that he was not informed about the man, given the rather unusual circumstances. "Stay here!"

Mr. Philmore approached the breakfast room with some trepidation about whether he had made the right choice. He took a deep breath and entered the room.

Mr. Haversham was an early riser and was reading the newspaper, relaxed and refreshed. Philmore came to stand by him and gave a delicate cough. Without looking up, John Haversham said, "What do you need, Philmore?"

"It may be a matter of some delicacy, sir."

John Haversham closed the paper and leaned back in his chair, an expectant expression on his face.

"There is a foreigner in the kitchen who will only deliver his message to you. He said that it is concerning your sojourn in France eighteen years ago . . ."

John Haversham's shoulders stiffened immediately and the color drained from his face, stopping the butler in his tracks.

"Did I do the right thing, sir?"

John Haversham recovered his composure with some difficulty and with a rasp in his voice declared, "Bring him to the library in ten minutes, Philmore," Then he roughly stood and strode from the room, leaving the butler to stare after him in awe, wondering what could have so rattled his employer.

Twenty-One

ENGLAND

Mario followed the butler through the grand house to the library. As Philmore opened the door, Mario entered and came face to face with a gentleman of middle age whose every feature was etched with anxiety. He had light hair peppered with gray and eyes brimming with concern.

The man stood abruptly, dismissed the butler and stood in front of Mario, his back to the fireplace, fight in his stance. "Who are you? What is it that you want—money?"

"Money? No, no sir, I have news. Great news for your family!"

"News, news? Explain yourself!"

It was evident that Mr. Haversham was in a challenging position, ready to engage in battle. Mario felt the need to put the gentleman at ease.

Mario resumed his narrative. "You lived in the villa Normandie in Grasse some eighteen years ago, no?

"You seem to know already that I did!" barked John Haversham in desperate agitation.

Mario raised his arms in defense. "Signore, please. My message. You meet a woman, a woman big with child, yes? She give you her baby."

The look in John Haversham's eyes shifted from anger to fear. Mario, noting the change quickly continued, "It is good, she give you baby. No problem. I here for the grandfather."

John Haversham sank into the other chair, gripping the arms tightly, eyes squinted in apprehension. "Her grandfather . . . ?"

"Yes, yes, I start story. Grandfather, he not know about baby all these years. The mother, she get sick, very sick. As she die, she tell him. She say she had baby. No other babies. Her father lonely man. His wife die, his children die, and now his, how you say, daughter, she die. Her father very sad.

"His name is Giorgio Giaccopazzi. He hear about baby and he say, 'I must find this baby.' He rich man, very rich. Much land, vineyards. He want to share with baby. He search for baby, make many travels. Now his heart, it weak. He send me to find the baby."

"But what does he want of her?" said John in a weak voice.

Mario leaned forward in earnestness. "He want to meet her. Share with her. Love her."

John Haversham moved in his chair, the look of fear replaced by panic.

"Is this not good news, Signore?" said Mario, perplexed.

John's emotions had just taken a journey that left him drained and afraid. The man's very presence was evidence enough of the validity of his claims, but he needed more evidence.

"How do I know that my daughter is one and the same child?"

"His granddaughter, she have a mark, here," and Mario pointed to the nape of his neck.

John Haversham's eyes opened slightly wider, a telltale sign that the comment had hit its mark, then closed them with a sigh of resignation. "No one here knows that she is adopted, not even the child herself," he croaked, piercing the Italian with hooded eyes.

"Ah."

The comment was loaded with comprehension. Mario began to fathom why his news had not been greeted with overtures of joy.

"I will need time to think through the ramifications before taking any action. You cannot in any way understand the English attitude toward bloodlines." Then almost to himself, "I must give this a great deal of thought."

Having made an immediate decision about Mario, he looked up and said, "Please, give me some time by leaving and stay at the Kings Arms Inn in the village at my expense—"

Mario sought to interrupt. "I need no money, Signore—"

"I insist, I insist, but I will ask this one thing of you; that you swear to tell no one the true reason for your presence until I have had time to discuss this with my wife. Do you understand? There is so much at stake, and I confess I do not know which course to take at this time. I had never considered this ever being discovered and am quite unprepared. Do I have your word that you will keep this to yourself? Can I trust you?"

Mario had not understood everything John said but his agitation spoke volumes and Mario placed his hand over his heart. "I promise, Signore. Tell no one."

⊙⦿⊙

Having shown Mario to the door himself, John Haversham returned to the library to deliberate. Never in their wildest dreams had they foreseen a relative coming to lay claim on the child. He sat back in one of the armchairs and allowed his mind to drift back to the past.

Emily had been determined in her belief that the child had been given to them from God and that all the rest would work out. To do otherwise would be to reject God's gift to them.

They were ignorant of the child's heritage, other than that the mother had dressed well and alleged that she was a gentlewoman. As to the veracity of her assertion, they could not tell, as her spoken English had been very rudimentary. Knowing how important heritage and blood were to John's family in particular, it was decided that they would claim the child as their own, relaxation and Mediterranean air being the cause of fertility. Thankfully, propriety and manners would prevent anyone asking more probing questions, and why shouldn't they be believed? There were no witnesses after all, and why should it ever need to be revealed? After much debate and prayer, it was decided that it was in everyone's best interests that the truth of her parentage never be disclosed.

For these same reasons, they had never told the child herself, and she was brought up in the belief that she was her parent's natural child.

A letter had been sent ahead of them to reveal the blessing that had been bestowed upon them. They used the excuse that they had waited to be sure of the child's survival before making any announcement. Every word of the letter was weighed so as to be truthful yet veiled.

Both sets of joyful grandparents had arranged to be at Haversham House when the little family arrived to celebrate the dear child's arrival.

All had gone according to plan, and they were called upon but little for details, as they had supposed, it not being deemed appropriate. The darkness of the infant's locks lent credence to their story and the brown eyes were attributed to kin long passed. The house was in an uproar of felicity, and many prayers of thanks were raised to the heavens.

And so the deception had succeeded and taken root, and family life had passed by like a heavenly dream.

Only now their security had been proven to be an illusion that had been shattered into a million pieces.

Emily rarely came down for breakfast, preferring to take her meal on a tray in her bedchamber. His first decision was that it would be best to address the difficult matter in the privacy of her boudoir.

He knocked lightly on her door, for one moment, hoping that she was still asleep and that he could delay fracturing her peace of mind.

"Come in!" she called lightly, gladness in her tone.

Upon seeing her husband, she patted her bed and bid him sit so that she could embrace him. He allowed the kiss but then went to sit on her armchair, at a little distance. Now she noticed the pained expression his features bore. "My darling, is something wrong?"

"I am afraid it is, my dear. You must brace yourself."

"John, you are so serious, I am alarmed! Pray, tell me the bad news."

He waited a beat, then with pained eyes declared, "We are discovered."

No explanation was needed as she had nursed a buried, nagging fear of discovery her whole life. It was a fear she had learned to live with.

"Who?" she whispered.

Twenty-Two

ENGLAND

Emily Haversham bowed her head and wiped her eyes with the sheet. The decision they had made, which they were so sure was right all those years ago, was at this moment flooding her with a rushing, gnawing guilt. Her breakfast rolled in her stomach. She was suddenly acutely aware of so many sounds in the previously silent bedroom as emotion heightened her senses; her husband's rapid, shallow breaths, the clock ticking, gardeners calling to each other outside, birds singing, unaware that the world had just toppled off its axis. A buzzing fly was trying desperately to get out of the window; she wished she could join it.

She raised her head slowly, her undressed hair forming a veil over her face. She shuddered a breath and whispered, "What do you think we should do, John? She might hate us for not telling her."

"I have thought of little else for the last thirty minutes and I have reached several conclusions. On the one hand, I believe that a lonely, ailing old man who has recently received the joyous news of a hitherto unknown granddaughter deserves to know her, if she desires it. On the other hand, her birth mother never indicated that she desired such a reunion, so I feel sure we would be within our rights to prohibit a meeting. However, as a Christian who is trying to live a life modeled after the Savior, I feel that since this knowledge has been uncovered, we are morally bound to honor the old man's wishes, let the chips fall where they may."

"You mean, by that, I suppose, that our families may reject Francesca as she is not a blood relative and is of unknown heritage. Do you really believe that their love is so shallow?"

"I have every reason to believe that your parent's love will remain unchanged, though they may need time to adjust and come to terms with the deception—for though we had the best motives—it *was* a deception. But when it comes to my parents . . . well, there my hope fails. My mother, particularly, has built herself such an empire around class distinctions that I fear she would rather shun her own granddaughter than lose her standing in society. And I know for a fact that my father is the worst kind of snob, for whom pedigree is more precious even than gold. I suspect their reaction will not be the best."

He pushed her chin up with his finger and looked into her striking blue eyes, eyes now clouded by uneasiness.

She shook her head away and cried, "This was never supposed to happen! Why did this happen? Why? What will I do if she becomes angry? I could not endure it if she left us. She is my world, John. I have poured everything into her, my very heart and soul and if she were to reject me . . ."

"Hush, she will not. You are her mother; you have always been and will always be her mother. She is a good girl, and though she may balk at the news at first, I think she will consider the facts and see that our motives were pure."

"But she will want to go . . ."

"Of course she will! Wouldn't you? Let us go with her. It will be an adventure!"

"What if she prefers it there and decides to stay?"

"She is a grown woman now. I don't believe we can stop her and that would not lead to good relations. We must let her go and hope she comes back. I am certain that she will, eventually."

"Hope she comes back . . ." Emily's face crumpled and John wiped a tear away with his thumb.

"Come now, be brave! We will weather this together! It seems that our decision has been made, and it is the moral one. Onward and upward!"

"Francesca, Mama and I would like to have a private word with you. Come, let us go into the drawing room."

Francesca's pulse quickened, and her stomach clenched. Had someone told her parents of her indiscretion? Had Phillip betrayed her? No! She could not believe it. One thing she could count on for sure was Phillip's dependability and honor. She racked her mind to think who might have betrayed her. Aunt Barrington? Again, no! She was sure that her aunt and uncle did not suspect anything since she had forced herself to be animated and cheerful on the journey back from Brighton.

Had she been told she was to meet her Maker she could not have been more nervous. Her feet felt heavy as cannon balls as she forced herself to cross the hall into the drawing room.

As the door to the room opened the first thing she beheld was her mother, seated on her chaise, with a perfectly terrible expression upon her lovely face. She knew! Francesca was about to mount her defense when her father bid her sit and began to speak. She braced herself, flinching at his voice, and it took her several phrases to realize that he was not speaking about Mr. Ashbourne.

"I am sorry, Papa," she said in surprise. "Can you say that again?"

Emily and John glanced at each other, and it was only with herculean effort that Emily's face did not collapse in despair.

"I said, my dear, that we have had some news that is of great import to you, and we feel honor-bound to reveal it. It will not place us in the best of light, so I hope that you can find it in your heart to forgive us."

Relief bathed her soul like waves breaking on the shore. They did *not* know! They had not called her in for an interview of reprimand and damage control. Indeed, they were asking for *her* forgiveness. She looked again at the stricken face of her mother and ran to her side.

"Of course, I forgive you of all and any offense, without reservation," she declared, holding her mother's delicate hand in her own and kissing it.

"You do not yet know the offense, my darling. You may feel the need to repeal your forgiveness," whispered her mother.

"Now you are scaring me!" Francesca declared, looking from one anxious parent to the other. "Pray tell me and ease my concern."

"For many years after your mother and I married, we were not blessed with children," began John.

"That I know well," she proclaimed. "It has never been a secret."

"'Tis true, 'tis true, but we do have a secret that we have kept for many years."

The scales of concern tipped from fear of exposure to fear of treachery. She let her mother's hand slip from her own and turned to face her father. "A secret?"

"Your mother's health was in decline and so we journeyed to the Riviera—"

"I know, I was born there," she said in relief, hoping that this was the secret.

"Yes, yes you were born there. But the secret lies with how you came to us."

Francesca knit her brows in confusion.

"We had gone to the Riviera for your mother's health, and while we were there, we made the acquaintance of a young woman, an Italian woman. Her name was Mrs. Grimaldi, or so she told us, and she had come to the area for her lying in and was to be joined by her husband. She was a pleasant young woman in the full bloom of imminent motherhood, and she would join us on our daily walks around the village square. After several weeks, she disappeared and we assumed, correctly, that her time had come and she had delivered her baby. After another few weeks, we were surprised to see her again. She had delivered a baby girl, and her husband had gone back to Italy and she was to join him soon. She asked your mother if she would hold the baby while she ran an errand. I was greatly concerned as it was very difficult for your mother to be around infants at that time. However, your mother implored me to allow her the opportunity. If you could have seen your mother's face as she held that baby. It was as though some great injustice had been righted, the last piece of a puzzle fitted in to complete it. Click. We admired and cooed at the baby for some time, and then I looked around expectantly for the young mother's return. She was nowhere to be seen. I began a search in earnest but to no avail. I rushed back to your mother, who looked so much like a Madonna that I was loathe to break the spell.

"Your mother clutched the baby to her at the news, and as she did so a letter fluttered out of the blankets."

He extended something to her. "Here is that letter."

Twenty-Three

ENGLAND

Emily chewed the inside of her mouth as her nerves chewed up her insides. Her eyes focused on her daughter as she read the letter that could forever sever their familial bond. John watched anxiously also, tapping his knee as he waited to see the dawn of comprehension upon his daughter's fine features.

As Francesca read, her face displayed a rapid spectrum of emotions; initially, her brows were pinched tight as she accepted the letter and began to read, then her lips pursed, her eyes widened with shock at the mention of an illegitimate child, then filled with sparkling tears as she clutched the letter to her breast and looked at her mother and father, who were as taut as piano strings, awaiting the verdict that would determine the happiness or misery of their future lives.

"I am the baby." It was not a question, rather a statement.

They need not have feared. Francesca's heart melted and she ran to embrace them. Emily and John began to breathe again.

"Why did you never tell me?" she blurted out into the vest of her father.

"There seemed no good reason. You were our child, and there was no benefit to anyone else knowing. In fact, the opposite could have been true, indeed, it still could be."

Francesca sat up wiping at her eyes, a quizzical look returning to her features.

"You are the granddaughter of Sir John Haversham. You stand to inherit his fortune, but only as the natural heir. Until today, no one knew that you were not, in fact, the natural heir, and this knowledge may have the power to change your future dramatically."

"She says she was a gentlewoman, Papa—"

"Yes, my darling, but she does not say that your father was a gentleman. In fact, we had no reason to believe that she herself was a woman of rank, only her own words. Her clothes were fine, but other than that, we could not tell her breeding, as her English was primitive and she had no maid in attendance or nurse. I hope you see that this did not matter to us. We loved you anyway and made a deliberate decision that we would not share unnecessary information with our family that might prejudice them against you. We could have had no idea that the truth of your birth would ever be exposed."

"Why are you telling me now, Papa?"

His heart took courage at the term of endearment and he cleared his throat. "I received an unexpected visit, early this morning, from the agent of your natural grandfather. It appears that your natural mother has recently died, without children, and upon her deathbed confessed to her father that she had given birth to a child in her youth, so that he might not find himself alone in the world in his old age. It seems that she was truthful, that she was, indeed, a woman of rank, as your grandfather is the owner of a vast acreage of vineyards. He desires to meet you and make you his heir."

Francesca leaned back and let out a long breath.

"The birthmark you bear upon your neck is inherited from her."

Unconsciously, her fingers traveled to the familiar mark.

"It is so much to take in!"

"Of course it is," said Emily. "We will give you time to digest the news and then you must tell us, honestly, what you want to do."

"What I want to do?"

"You must now decide if you intend to claim this gentleman as your kin and whether you want to disclose the connection to anyone, or keep it entirely private. There are ramifications for each course of action, and you must ponder carefully the road you take from here. Forgive us for thrusting this difficult choice upon you. Know that your father and I will support you in whatever decision you make. You are and always will be our daughter."

"But I need your help . . ."

"Of course, we will offer advice, but we feel that you need time to come to terms with everything first. Go for a ride, pray, think, and then come and find us."

                               ❧❧ ❧❧

"I am an Italian." Francesca murmured this repeatedly in her mind in an attempt to make it feel true, but it did not. She was not even sure how she felt about the change in her status, there were too many emotions muddying the field.

She was an illegitimate child, and she knew well how badly that would be received. Indeed, she knew that her parents were correct in saying that she may be rejected by many in society who, at the present, claimed affection for her. Her parents were not mistaken; this was not information to share without serious and careful consideration of the possible consequences, consequences that would change the way people regarded her. Was she emotionally strong enough for the possible aftermath? The more prudent path may be never to mention it and preserve her world intact.

However, she was experiencing a burning curiosity to see the land of her birth mother and the gentleman who was her natural grandfather. She felt an unseen cord, pulling her to travel to Italy and satisfy her inquisitiveness.

Her thoughts whirled around and around, presenting no clear conclusion. After some time of wandering aimlessly, she looked up and noticed that she was almost upon the land of Phillip's family. Phillip! They had not kept company since her return from Brighton by tacit agreement. She appreciated his discretion and was glad of the time to recover from her ordeal. Now that she felt stronger, she knew that he was the perfect person to consult on the matter.

He was so wise and would present a disinterested party who would examine the facts with a degree of distance, helping her make a decision. Dear Phillip. He would not reject her! She urged her horse onward, and as she entered the drive to the Waverley Estate, she saw Phillip preparing to leave on his own horse.

"Hello there! Phillip!"

She waved her whip over her head and the sight in his peripheral vision, rather than her voice, caught his attention. He turned his horse in her direction and cantered over.

"Francesca, to what do I owe this pleasure?"

"I have something of great import to discuss with you, if you are at leisure to do so."

He noticed that her expression was serious and imploring. Not a social visit then. His heart stuttered at the anticipation of what the subject matter might be. "I was going to visit our tenants—but that can wait a while. I have no fixed appointment. Come, let us ride over to the folly and talk in private in the shade of the great oaks."

He trotted over to the area in question, dismounted, tied his horse to a tree and turned to help Francesca dismount. His skin tingled as she placed her delicate hand in his. He wondered if she felt it too and glanced at her face but saw only concern and indecision depicted there. They were in full view of the house for propriety's sake but far enough away to be sure of privacy in their conversation. He sat on a bench and indicated for her to join him.

She perched on the edge of the bench in an attitude of anxiety, fiddling with a handkerchief and unable to look him in the eye. His heart took a dive. *Pray, let it not be that she has decided to marry someone and is seeking my advice on the matter!* he agonized.

Since she appeared unable to begin he said, encouragingly, "There is a matter you would like to discuss?"

"Yes . . ." she hesitated. "You are fond of me, I think?"

His hopes took flight. "Of course—"

"We have been good friends since childhood, have we not? Almost brother and sister, no?"

His hopes crash-landed. He struggled to arrange his features so that his feelings were not apparent. "Indeed . . ." *Where was this conversation headed?*

"Your affections would not be altered if you learned something about me that would change how society viewed me, would they?"

He shook his head in confusion and then intelligence unfolded.

"Has someone spread a rumor about your trouble with Mr. Ashbourne? You can be assured that I will defend you on that score and will contradict the account at every opportunity!"

He saw that his vehemence made Francesca smile and gave her courage to continue. "No, no! That secret is safe, thank heavens! No, it is another matter entirely that I wish your opinion on."

He relaxed.

"Phillip, what would you say if I told you I had been adopted?"

His eyes dilated briefly and then the edges crinkled in amusement. "What would your parents have to say about that? Are you not satisfied with them?"

"Phillip, I am in earnest."

His mind spun momentarily as the facts impressed themselves upon his consciousness.

"You are adopted? But that cannot be, surely?"

"Yes, indeed it is! I have only just learned of it myself, this very morning. An agent of the man who is my natural grandfather, an Italian, came to visit my father this morning. He desires to meet me and make me his heir."

"I think you had better tell me the whole story from the beginning," he said.

⁂

As the tale unfolded, Phillip considered the differences in appearance between Francesca and her parents. He, himself, did not wholly resemble his parents, but in this light, it was clear that Francesca had differences that could readily be explained by this new revelation.

"Now my parents have left me to decide what I will do with this new information. They will support me in any decision that I make but want me to consider deeply before taking any action."

"I suppose there is no doubt that the account is true?"

"None. My parents showed me the letter my birth mother left them, and there is more . . ."

She turned in her seat so that her back was facing him and lifted her hair to reveal the birthmark on her neck.

"My birth mother had the same mark upon her. Very few people know of mine and it is usually covered by the tiny curls on my neck but this man, this agent, knew of it."

She turned back to face him, her dark eyes full to the brim with concern.

"Until this very day, I did not know of my Italian grandfather's existence, now this knowledge has turned my world upside down. There are so many consequences attached to each choice! I am at a fork in the road and know not which is the best one to take."

"Indeed."

His tone made her looked up sharply. "Has this then, changed your opinion of me, Phillip?"

He took her hand gently in his and smiled.

"By no means."

Her shoulders loosened.

"However, the rest of society will not be so forgiving. It is a complicated world we have created, consisting of points for and against our standing in the rankings, and though I hate to say it, your own grandmother is the worst offender." Francesca nodded with a sad smile. "Her reaction will determine how the rest of them receive you, I believe. For my part, it makes not the slightest difference."

He hesitated to add that he loved her either way, though it was on the tip of his tongue, thinking that she had had enough revelations for one day.

"Oh, Phillip!" and she leaned against him, putting her head on his shoulder in an attitude of utter solace. They sat like that for some time; he relished her closeness, she basked in his acceptance.

At length, she lifted her head and engaged his eyes. "Can *you* tell me what to do, Phillip?"

She was biting her lower lip in a most engaging fashion and he had to tear his eyes from her mouth in order to concentrate. "I cannot, but tell me what *you* want to do and I will advise you whether I think it is wise or what some of the drawbacks may be."

"In truth, I feel an extraordinary force tugging me to Italy, an unquenchable desire to visit that place—that it might help me understand myself."

"Are you in a state of confusion, then?"

"The horror of my interaction with Mr. Ashbourne aside, I have lately felt very happy with who I am becoming and am enjoying the new-found freedoms life as an adult has to offer, but this news has undeniably shaken me and I feel that I do not know myself anymore. The person I thought I was is false. I feel an evolving need to satisfy my curiosity about my real parentage and to see the place of my ancestors."

"Then I believe you have made your decision!"

"Yet, will this not upset my parents? Will they not question my love for them? Truly, I know of no one who loves their parents as I do, but will not this desire call that love into question in their minds? I could not bear to upset them and knowing now the heartache they have already endured, being unable to have children of their own, I feel it would smack of ungratefulness. I am torn between my own desires and my unwillingness to hurt their feelings."

"Then describe for them the battle your emotions wage. They have sworn to support any decision you come to, have they not? Tell them that you fear hurting them and ask them to travel with you. Make it a journey that unites you rather than divides you."

"That is an excellent proposition, Phillip! I think I must go. Not knowing would eat at me and render me dissatisfied with my life, I believe."

She gazed toward the house, deep in thought, and he took the occasion to peruse her lovely face, his mind still reeling from the revelation, but his heart steadfast in his affection for her. After a moment he said, "Will you tell your grandparents and the general public?"

"As for the public at large, I will be guided by my parents. I suppose I must tell my grandparents. Mother's parents will be surprised and even hurt by the discovery but I do not fear their rejection. Father's . . ." she let the words hang in the air.

"Let us hope that their love is affixed and true and not subject to the alteration in your situation. You are prepared, though, for a tempering in their affections?"

"The announcement is still so new to my own conscience. I hardly know—but you are right, I will need to steel myself for their wrath and rejection. Poor Mama and Papa. They will feel it too. Oh, perhaps it is too much for them to bear! For myself, it is a path of discovery, but for them, it could be the shattering of their comfortable life. Illegitimacy is such a scandal, is it not? Do you not feel a little revolted by it?"

He turned to her and took both her hands in his. His gaze was penetrating, and he suddenly flashed back to their conversation by the brook at her cousin's picnic. His brow cleared, and his lips parted in a tender smile so that his whole face was alive with tenderness.

"Francesca, I hope that you think me a truer friend than that! The circumstances of your birth are completely outside of your control. You have been raised as a lady by loving parents. Therefore, in my eyes you are a lady. Nothing in this world could change my high regard for you. Nothing."

For reasons she could not fathom, Francesca felt her nose tingle and tears spring to her eyes. She was filled with comfort and peace such that it caused her to smile and cry at the same time. He pulled her close, and she again placed her head upon his shoulder. "Will you come with me, Phillip?"

"No, little one. This is a private time for you and your family. You can make your travels and tell me all about them on your return."

They stood slowly and he helped her onto her horse, smiling benevolently. She noticed that his fair hair hung a little over his left eye and that his smile illuminated his entire face. How could she ever have thought him lacking?

As she trotted back home, she cast a glance behind her and was surprised to see him still standing, still smiling, as she departed.

Twenty-Four

ENGLAND

The air was frigid with an icy silence. The faces of the four grandparents were similar; eyebrows raised, mouths forming an O, eyes wide open, as if life had paused for a moment.

John Haversham stood at the fireplace, having just related the whole story. Emily perched on one of the sofas, awaiting the reaction, thankful they had decided to have this meeting without Francesca present.

After a beat, it was as if someone had pressed a button and all the grandparents spoke at once in a cacophony of sound. John raised his hands for silence and gestured to his father-in-law to speak.

"Why on earth would you do that? Shouldn't you have found an orphanage?"

His wife hit his arm in reproach. "Do you realize how offensive you sound?" she declared.

Emily's face collapsed in disappointment, and a look of deep concern filled her husband's. If this was the reaction of those they hoped would be accepting, how would John's parents respond?

Emily replied, "We had been praying so long for a baby. She was— no, she *is* the greatest blessing ever bestowed upon us."

John's father, Sir John Haversham, spoke out in a loudly pompous tone, "We have grown to love her, of course, but her heritage is completely unknown, you say? That was utterly irresponsible of you! Preposterous! The truth is that you have betrayed us most cruelly and now we find that she is not actually our granddaughter! The deception is inexcusable. She may be the offspring of a peasant for all we know!"

"Father, please moderate your tone! I understand that this has been a shock and that you are angry with Emily and I, but please, temper your opposition."

His father bowed and shook his head muttering under his breath. John looked to his mother, Augusta, whose face was scarlet.

"So rather than a young lady of high rank and breeding, she is a mongrel."

Emily flinched.

"Mother!"

"You have brought this on yourself, John. You have deceived your family. What? Did you think we would embrace the knowledge that our granddaughter is of low birth? For shame! Our family has been noble for two hundred years, unsullied by any vagrant offspring, and now this! It is not to be borne!"

Emily looked to her mother, Lady Davenport, for support. "Now, now everyone," she said, "Francesca has not changed in the space of these five minutes. We know her to be a diligent and respectful child and in all relevant senses a lady. We have known her as our progeny, and she has never given us any cause for complaint as to her conduct or bearing. Indeed, we have never witnessed any evidence from her behavior that she was not, in fact, blood of our blood. She is, in every other respect, an English gentlewoman, in spite of her true parentage."

Emily rushed to taker her mother's hand in gratitude as Lady Davenport continued, "The Bible speaks kindly of adoption. Let us be more Christian in our attitude and take time to adjust to the shock before spouting things while in this emotional state that we might later regret. And, foremost, let it not change our affection for dear Francesca. Hysteria will help no one and will only serve to ostracize us from our granddaughter's affections."

"Thank you, Georgina," said John, relieved to have at least one ally. "You are perhaps all forgetting that Francesca herself was only informed of this a week ago. She has experienced myriad emotions and has frankly forgiven us. *She* has not deceived you. Lay the blame at our feet for that. At the time we could, honestly, see no good reason for admitting the fact that she was adopted and your conduct today has borne that out.

She is a child of God, as are all of us, and is deserving of our unconditional love and support at this difficult time."

His father, Lord Haversham, harrumphed in disapproval, and his mother spat back, "The deception itself is a sin. Were it not for this, this agent coming, you would have continued to deceive us our whole lives. Are we picking and choosing which of the Ten Commandments we will keep now?"

"I suppose that is the true reason for the choice of name, which I thought strange at the time. No one on either side has ever been called 'Francesca.' Indeed, it is rather foreign sounding, and I have always thought so," fumed Lord Haversham.

John looked between his parents. "Please try to understand how hard it was for us to pray for a child but not be blessed with one. None of you has ever experienced that kind of anguish. She was truly a miracle, an answer to our prayers, and it seemed fitting that she be named in remembrance of that blessing. It is a beautiful name in its own right and doubly so as it reminds us of how God smiled on us," he pleaded.

"But it was another lie compounding the first! You said you chose the name because she was born in France close to Italy. Another deception!" cried Lady Haversham.

Emily began to weep.

"What will we tell society?" gasped Lord Haversham, working himself into a frenzy. "We, who pride ourselves on the purity of our blue blood? We, to whom others look for guidance on lineage, proper ranking, and manners? We will be mocked to shame! Ridiculed as hypocrites! Come, Augusta, let us leave this place where we are not given the respect we deserve and carefully ponder how to proceed in this matter."

He stood in dramatic fashion and waited for his wife to rise. They swept from the room. The effect of their departure was like that of popping a balloon and those still present sank as the tension exited the room with them.

"I think we see where their true rancor lies—in how this will affect *them*!" said John.

Lady Davenport patted her daughter's hand. "There, there, my darling girl. We will not desert Francesca, shall we George?" In a brusque manner, he stiffly agreed. "No, no. She is a good girl, and we are fond of her. . . . There is, however, the greater moral question to address . . ."

"What do you mean?" asked John.

"Well, you will have a moral obligation to tell any future suitors of her true heritage. You may pooh, pooh it sir, but breeding is the life-blood of English society and a man deserves to know all the facts before entering into a marriage."

"Of course, Papa," said Emily to her father. "We have concluded the same thing, but as to the greater society in general, do you believe we have a similar obligation? You have been witness to the prejudice from her own family, would that not open her up to unnecessary abuse from those not related to us?"

"I do not believe such a course of action is necessary at this time," he said guardedly. "But we will all need to give it more thought."

"Indeed, I think you need have no fear of John's parents broadcasting it!" exclaimed Lady Georgina.

"The immediate course we have decided on," continued John Haversham. "After much deliberation and discussion, is to travel to France to show Francesca where she was born and then on to Italy to meet her grandfather and visit the land of her mother's birth, without disclosing the reasons for the journey to anyone here. I have instructed the Italian agent to travel back in haste to tell him, Signore Giaccopazzi, that we will arrive in a few weeks.

Upon our return, we will, of course, tell any young man who seeks Francesca's hand in marriage that she is adopted, but feel, as you have validated, no compunction to broadcast it generally."

"You realize that if such a young man decided not to pursue her after your disclosure, he will be at liberty to tell whomsoever he desires," counseled Lord Davenport.

"We shall cross that bridge when we come to it," John sighed. "Poor Francesca is just coming to terms with the change in her fortunes herself."

Lord Davenport, who was pacing by the fireplace, stopped and faced them all, no smile upon his countenance. "Then she should be very careful of the male company she seeks upon her return. Her very future and standing in society will depend on it!"

Part Two

Twenty-Five

FRANCE

The crossing to Calais had been very rough, and more than a few passengers had been green around the gills, including Francesca.

Thus it was that their eventual arrival in Cannes, with its resplendent views of the Mediterranean, had the effect of a good tonic, and Francesca had the sudden and unexpected impulse to share the moment with Phillip.

She was enthralled by the sight of water so blue that it rivaled sapphires, having only ever seen an ocean that was a rather murky green most of the time, and the pleasant sun was a definite bonus. She again experienced the juvenile desire to rip off her stockings and shoes and plunge her toes into the inviting water.

After their arrival, they passed a very pleasant afternoon walking along the coast and then repaired to an hotel in the town of Grasse, a little inland, up in the mountains, so that on the morrow they might show Francesca the villa where they first lived with her and the small mountain town where they had met the woman who gave birth to her. They planned to spend several days there to show Francesca around the entire area where their happy life had begun.

Staying at the same hotel was a middle-aged clergyman on his honeymoon, a Mr. Septimus Sladden and his new wife, Charity. The Reverend Sladden was a portly gentleman of about fifty, and his new bride was not in her first bloom of youth. They seemed well-matched, but Francesca found their company intolerable as the Reverend Sladden spoke in a very nasal tone and was rarely quiet. He seemed to find silence a sinful state, and therefore filled it at all possible costs. His wife was his very opposite and barely spoke a word, though she smiled and nodded a good deal.

"I do believe that Mrs. Sladden married Mr. Sladden due to a misunderstanding," chuckled Francesca to her mother.

"What can you mean?" replied her mother with a smile.

"I believe that she was so used to nodding while he speaks that he just dropped the proposal into the middle of a very ordinary conversation and she nodded, which he took to be an acceptance!"

Emily's smile faded. "Francesca, you should be more charitable! I believe they are very well suited, and Mrs. Sladden told me that this is her first journey outside of England. She feels herself very fortunate."

"Forgive me, Mama. I am still rather new at being a mature adult who keeps their opinions to themselves, but I must say I find him rather annoying."

The sadness of the rejection by her paternal grandparents continued to hang around her like a noose while traveling, but the ambiance of the Riviera eased the pain somewhat. The eternal sunshine, the colorful houses and markets, the narrow cobble hillside streets with upstairs neighbors so close they hung washing lines across the streets from one side to the other, all aided the improvement in her spirits.

On the third day, her father came back to the hotel, gleefully holding aloft a large set of old keys.

"I inquired with the booking agent and the villa Normandie is not occupied until next week! After I told him my story, the curator has been generous enough to let us peruse it, unaccompanied, this very afternoon! I have hired a carriage to take us there immediately after luncheon, and it was no small feat as it is during siesta! I told the driver that he can find a shady tree and nap while we visit."

"Oh, John! That is marvelous!" Emily grabbed Francesca's hands, and they danced a little jig of delight.

❧❧ ❧❧

The approach to the villa was very steep and bumpy, and Francesca held tight to the door handle as they made the slow journey up the hill. At length, they came to an imposing gate that had seen better days but was still grand in its own way. Behind the gate were so many trees that the house could not be seen.

Her father jumped down and took the largest of the keys and placed it into the lock on the gate. After jiggling it several times, they heard a satisfying click and he pushed open the gate as it squeaked on its rusty hinges. Francesca began to hurry up the steep path, but her father explained, "It is still quite a way up, and it is very hot. Let us return to the carriage and save our energy for exploring the grounds after we have seen the house."

The path twisted and turned until, at last, a magnificent pale-lemon villa sprang into view with a filigree iron balcony in every upper window and magnificent French glass doors all across the front of the house below. Ivy decorated the side walls, and to the right, attached to the main house, was a very pretty, covered walkway, bursting with tropical blooms of every imaginable color.

A well-kept garden led up to the front of the house with short green hedges trimmed to perfection in little mazes and a pond situated dead center of the front entryway.

"Oh, Mama! I wonder that you ever left!" cried Francesca.

"Ah, but you have not yet seen the best detail. Let us walk up to the door, and then I will show you my true delight in this house. Uh, uh, do not turn around yet! It will spoil the surprise!"

Though it tortured her, Francesca managed the short journey without peeking, but as soon as she reached the front patio, she turned around and gasped. Whereas the house could not be seen from the gate due to the trees, an unobstructed, panoramic view of the valley was clearly visible from the house. It offered a vista of sharp mountain valleys with succulent green trees and colorful mountain houses, opening onto the Mediterranean ocean in the distance. It was as unreal as a picture, and she again became aware of a fervent, unanticipated wish that Phillip be there to share the experience with her.

"It makes even *me* want to paint! Cousin Katherine would be in heaven!"

"I used to love to awaken in the mornings, open the windows, and take tea on the balcony overlooking this view," said Emily. "It was a perfect way to begin the day. The stresses of home melted away, and I was beginning to come to terms with the fact that I might never have a child. This view was the perfect setting for communing with God, and it became my sanctuary.

"Then, just as I was accepting my lot in life, God blessed me beyond my wildest dreams and allowed me to have a beautiful baby girl. This villa will always hold a special place in my heart."

"Come," said John. "Let us go in!"

They turned, and he applied another key to the lock on the front door. This lock was well oiled, and the key turned easily, the door swinging open readily on its hinges.

The foyer was wide and airy, and a stone spiral staircase dominated the space. Artisans of great skill had carved the stone at the center of the spiral so that the rock resembled drapery entwined with ivy. So delicate was the masonry work that Francesca could not resist reaching out to touch it.

On the main floor was a drawing room whose French doors opened out onto the glorious view. Happily, since tenants were soon to occupy the house, the dust sheets had been removed and revealed French woodwork furniture of the most ornate style. It was a happy room.

At her father's encouragement, they entered the library. It was not as dark as English libraries tended to be.

"I spent many happy hours in this room. I would read for leisure instead of to solve the problems of the estate. It truly was a time of great healing," explained her father.

Francesca touched his arm tenderly. "How could one not be content in such a room as this!" she declared.

They walked on and her mother pointed to the dining room. "We did not use this room at all," Emily explained. "For we did not socialize. We kept to ourselves and enjoyed each other's company, preferring to eat on a little wrought-iron table outside on the veranda. It was like a second honeymoon, was it not, John?"

"Indeed, it was." His face became thoughtful as he reviewed the past, swept back in time by the old house and the memories.

They walked back to the spiral staircase. The stone was cool to the touch and very welcome on this hot afternoon. Some windows had been opened to air the place and a very pleasant cross breeze drifted in.

Her parents were talking quietly to each other, reminiscing, and rather than disturb them, Francesca hung back, reveling in the beauty and tranquility of the old villa.

Upstairs she lingered, looking in each bedroom until she found her parents, giggling like youths. She smiled at the comforting sight. Her father was trying keys in the lock of the window to gain access to the balcony, but the lock was being stubborn. However, after several attempts the key finally turned, and John pushed open the windows. They entered the small balcony that contained a wrought iron bench and a small circular table with two chairs that gave the impression that the occupants had just left. Her parents sat down and bid her sit.

"We spent every morning here together, welcoming the new day and listening to the birds sing. It was better medicine than any doctor could offer," Emily said.

"Were you very sad then, Mama?"

"The doctors had become very concerned about my mental health. The last of my closest friends had just had a baby, and the longing was more than I could bear. The world was all blackness and sorrow for me. I could no longer see the light. This house commenced my cure and you," she said, turning to grasp her daughter's hand, "completed it."

They sat in companionable silence and enjoyed the view for some time. Then her father stirred and encouraged them to continue the tour.

After descending the stairs, they exited the front door and went around the side to a north-facing courtyard that provided shade for the whole day. It had arches and porticoes, statues and sitting places, and was filled to bursting with greenery and colorful flowers.

"This place makes the weather at home seem rather depressing, does it not? Even the light here is different, don't you think, Papa?"

"Your mother used to say the same thing! She believed that the rays of the sun were more bright and clear than in England. Now, let us explore the rest of the gardens, for you have really only seen the formal area. There is a great, vast wilderness of indigenous flora."

After a while, Francesca broke off from her parents and went to do her own exploring and came upon a babbling brook. She listened to its conversation and it brought to remembrance the time at another brook, with Phillip. Had she imagined the tenderness in his dewy eyes? Of course she had! Phillip had had countless opportunities to declare his feelings, if such they were, and he never had. *His tenderness was merely a product of his brotherly concern and his insight into Mr. Ashbourne's character, and besides, he has surely lost his good opinion of me for being so easily led astray by the said Mr. Ashbourne,* she told herself.

She turned from the brook abruptly, deeply shaken by the unexpected disappointment of that realization, and hurried to find her parents.

Twenty-Six

FRANCE

They had roused the driver from his siesta and driven back to the hotel without incident, quietly contented with reviewing their visit.

"You love it too, don't you?" said Emily.

"I can honestly say I would be quite happy to live here for the rest of my days!" exclaimed Francesca.

She looked out of the carriage window and saw a magnificent bird of prey swoop past. She followed his flight path eagerly and then pulled back sharply as he dropped to feast upon some poor dead forest creature. The jarring image burst her mood completely and left her feeling strangely unsettled.

They arrived at the hotel in time for tea and entered the dining room to find a pleasant array of pastries arranged most artfully. Upon looking around the crowded room, Francesca was disappointed to see that the only table with three seats available was with the Sladdens. She looked at her mother and frowned in disappointment. Her mother ignored her and, wearing a bright smile, led the way to the table to join them.

"Have you had a marvelous afternoon?" inquired the Reverend Sladden.

"Indeed, we have! We have been showing Francesca the villa we occupied when she was born."

"Have you, my word! I had not realized that the fair Francesca had been born in these parts. Is that perhaps the reason for her unconventional name?"

Francesca took instant offense at the perceived slight as she had already decided to dislike the Reverend Sladden. Unconventional indeed! It was a perfectly beautiful name!

Her mother, however, was possessed of better manners and chose not to take offense at all. "It is, sir! We had been childless for many years and her coming to us was such a blessing that we chose a name that paid homage to the place where she came to us. I suppose it was rather unconventional, but then her two middle names are in honor of her grandmothers."

"Jolly good, jolly good! I myself have three grown sons, and my dearest Charity has taken to mothering them like a duck to water." He bestowed upon his wife an awkward, twisted smile, more proper in a pimply youth that a man of a certain age. His wife blushed with pride and love.

Her father did not seem to notice the embarrassing show of affection and engaged them in pleasant, if rather dull, conversation. Francesca concentrated on her pastries and the mint tisane that had been brought for her, looking around at the other occupants of the room so as not to have to contribute to the discussion.

Her attention snapped back when she heard the word *Hampshire*, and she shook herself from her reverie to listen.

"—we are very fortunate in the living we were given. Though small, it is perfect for us, and we are next to a much larger parish administered by the Reverend Gray."

At mention of this name, Francesca gave him her full attention. "The Reverend Gray, you say?"

"Why, yes! Do you know the gentleman?"

"Not personally, but a friend of mine has recently made his acquaintance and told me that he is a very kind and genial person."

"He is indeed! What a coincidence that you should know of him. He is the best of men, a credit to our profession. He is ever willing to give me aid if I need it and in fact has loaned his curate to my flock while I am away on my honeymoon."

With her heart in her mouth, Francesca said, "I understand from my friend that they have a grown daughter still at home."

"Your information is accurate, Miss Haversham. I have known her since she was a child, when my own boys were still quite young. She was a lovely child, though a little rambunctious in her early years, but she grew out of it. More than one of my sons lost his head over her!"

He stopped and smiled as if his account were done, avoiding condemning Miss Gray for the indiscretion, of which he must have been well aware. Francesca, though, was strangely curious to have the facts confirmed by a third party, to learn if the Reverend Sladden could throw any more light on the subject, and though worried about how to broach the subject of Miss Gray's downfall without appearing to be a common gossip, searched for the perfect question. She felt humbled that this man, whom she had belittled as a dullard, was loyally guarding Anne Gray's secret, not using the opportunity of distance to indulge in idle talk.

"She never married then? Such a beauty as that, I am surprised." She tried to appear completely indifferent, but the longing to know was building, and she was on a precipice of anticipation. She glanced at her parents, fearful that her attitude would arouse their suspicions, but they were thankfully engaged in a conversation with Mrs. Sladden.

The Reverend's expression fell and he lowered his voice. "I hesitate to share the young lady's story for fear of appearing malicious but as a young lady yourself, let me just say that her story is a cautionary tale to all young ladies of the world and I, for one, do not censure her.

"Sadly, she was led away by a devil and has never recovered. Be very careful always to guard yourself against compromise, Miss Haversham. There are men of evil intent who find sport in taking advantage of the innocent."

He lowered his lids as if in prayer, obviously deeply moved by the memory. Her esteem for the good reverend surged.

With a voice that trembled, in spite of her efforts, she sympathized, "That is the saddest of tales, to be sure." She was reminded that, but for divine intervention, she, herself would have served as a cautionary tale.

The reverend re-opened his eyes. "I was able to repay her father's kindness by taking his daughter away for a season to my married sons' homes to avoid the wagging tongues and try to help her regain some degree of happiness, but it was to no avail, and to this day she is a recluse."

Francesca raised her head, truly touched by the Reverend's kindness. How quickly she had judged him. In fact, she could learn a great deal about true Christianity from Reverend Sladden. She felt truly ashamed. Not once did he chide Anne for bringing her misfortune upon herself. Mrs. Sladden was indeed a fortunate woman.

Her heart heavy from the memories that now beset her, she excused herself as in need of a rest and retired to her room to weep in private.

‿◞◟‿

After several days of travel, they crossed the border into Italy and approached the area known as Florence. After the painful reminder of her brush with ruin, her thoughts had wandered to Phillip more than once. She thanked heaven that he had come to her rescue, and she found herself wishing he was there to share her new adventure.

As they neared her grandfather's property, impatience set her emotions aflutter. It was late afternoon when their carriage pulled into the forecourt of yet another pensionne and her parents made as if to settle in for the night.

"Oh Mama, Papa. Can we not call upon Signore Giaccopazzi this evening? I have waited so long, and I fear that my patience is exhausted!"

"That would not be very good manners, my dear. We ought to send him word that we are in the region and indicate that we can visit him at his earliest convenience. He may still be ailing and require some time before we make his acquaintance. I understand your impatience, I do, but we must maintain decorum. We want him to know that you have been raised properly as an English gentlewoman. He will take great pride in that fact, I do not doubt," said Emily.

Francesca's lips turned down, and Emily glimpsed the child she had been. She patted her daughter's hand. "Come, let us write the letter and move the process along!"

‿◞◟‿

"Signore, they have arrived in Florence," said Mario, handing Giorgio a letter.

Giorgio ripped open the letter with trembling hands. Mario had returned more than two months before, and Giorgio's eagerness to finally meet his granddaughter had been unbearable.

Each morning, hope that today would be the day would crowd his heart then slowly drain away as sunset came. The mental stress did nothing to help the health of his heart. Now, at last, they had come!

"Write back immediately and invite them to dinner this very evening! I cannot bear for her to be in the same place and delay the meeting more! Make haste, make haste!"

Mario allowed himself to be pushed to the desk, a smile upon his lips, and wrote as Giorgio dictated.

As Mario left the room, Giorgio imagined how Francesca might look for the thousandth time. How happy he had been to hear that they had given her an Italian name! He had envisaged her with the thick hair of his countrymen but hoped she would also bear the wild curls of her mother. He had envisioned a round face, then a long face, and finally, a heart-shaped face. None seemed to fit. Would her eyes be dark brown like her mother or light brown with flecks of gold like her grandmother? Would she carry the image of her father? The girl he had conjured was a vague shadow of a woman, and he yearned to see the genuine article and direct his growing love to someone tangible.

He looked down and noticed that he was drumming the arms of his chair in a tattoo. He stopped his fingers but the tattoo continued in his unreliable, old heart. Since his attack, he had been aware that the regular rhythm of his heart had been replaced by a most irregular one. Fear of this was the only reason he was obeying his doctor's orders to rest.

The door opened and Mario returned. Giorgio turned sharply and, beaming with anticipation, said, "Take down what I wish to have for dinner! Everything must be perfect!"

Twenty-Seven

ENGLAND

The normally dignified Lord Haversham was stomping about his study, weeping and wailing and gnashing his teeth as the short, thin banker slowly shook his head. He cleared his throat.

"If you had read our copious correspondence over the last six months, this would have come as no surprise to you, my Lord. We have documented our attempts to educate you on the precarious state of your investments abroad, but you have chosen to ignore it. It has now reached such epic proportions that I felt I had no other option than to come to Haversham Hall in person to inform you that, after you settle our current bill, our firm can no longer represent your family as it will undoubtedly damage our reputation in the city."

Lord Haversham stopped abruptly and turned sharply, roaring, "My family *made* your reputation what it is and *this* is how you repay me? Abandon me in my hour of greatest need? I will see you ruined, Arthur Farthing!" Spittle showered the air around Mr. Farthing's person. He stood his ground stoically, though his complexion blotched and mottled at the abuse.

"If I may be so bold, m'Lord, when this is noised abroad, as it undoubtedly will be in a very short time, your opinions will be worth less than your fortune. I doubt there is a counting house, club, or merchant to whom you owe a considerable amount who will not now join you in your pecuniary distress. It will be like an army of dominoes; as you tumble, so shall they."

Sir John Haversham dropped into his chair, a shrunken replica of his former self, his blustery anger blown out at last. "I have not wherewith to pay you, Farthing. Not two pennies to rub together, if truth be told. What am I to do?"

"Then in my professional opinion you must sell Haversham Hall, as soon as may be."

"It is mortgaged," he replied timidly.

"Not through us!"

"No, I sought funding elsewhere to keep the situation as quiet as possible."

"Then your predicament is far worse than I feared, my Lord. As soon as the bank that holds the mortgage hears of your change in fortunes, they will call in the loan and turn you out. Why did you not take some precautions when you read of the looming troubles abroad?"

His voice cracking and hesitant, Lord Haversham whispered, "I hoped that it would all turn out well."

"With all due respect, my Lord, hope is not a strategy. I will leave you now."

As the door to his study closed, it was as if the very heavens were closed against him and the full weight of his troubles crashed down on his mind, like some dark and sinister force. He could see no hope, no light at the end of the tunnel, no way out. He glanced at the decorative sword displayed on the wall and toyed with the idea of using it to end his misery, rejecting the idea as unworthy of a man in his position; an action that was dishonorable and would only bring further shame to his family.

Where could he turn to find the relief he sought? What was he to do? He craved immediate oblivion, even if it were temporary, and dragged himself up the stairs to his bedroom with a bottle of whiskey.

⁖⁖⁖

ITALY

As their carriage approached the fine Giaccopazzi mansion with its infinite vineyards on either side, excitement was replaced with something more resembling of nerves. It was hard not to be impressed with the rolling hills of green, verdant vines. This was wealth indeed, even by her own family's standards.

Francesca's eyes grew large and anxious. Perhaps her grandfather would not like her. Perhaps he would be disappointed that she was not more accomplished. She looked to her mother, who gave her an encouraging smile, fully aware of the tumult of emotions her daughter was experiencing.

"I think we can be reassured that your birth mother did not exaggerate when she said she was from a wealthy family of good standing in the community!" said John, smiling broadly at the sheer expanse of the enterprise.

As the forecourt appeared, Francesca could see that the mansion was not dissimilar from the style of the villa she had visited in France, though on a much grander scale. The filigree iron balconies were present and the light color stucco on the exterior with many tall windows. However, the lower portion of the house was unique. It was built upon a corridor of arches and boasted a Greek-style portico and stone staircases swept up on either side from the forecourt. It was magnificent.

Before long, the carriage crunched on the gravel. Several servants appeared under the portico, and an elderly gentleman in a wheelchair waved to them from the main balcony.

As they advanced, Francesca was able to study her Italian grandfather. He wore his white beard short and to a gentle point, and it framed his kind, tanned face. His eyes, once dark, wore the lighter look of cataracts but sparkled in anticipation and crinkled at the edges in a friendly smile. His white hair was wavy and thick and reached past the collar of his shirt. She loved him instantly and wondered, abstractedly, if Phillip would like him.

In a moment, the nerves were blown away, and Francesca eagerly descended the carriage. She was only stopped from running up the stairs by a gentle pressure on her arm from her mother and the very slightest of shakes of the head, disapproving of the childish desire. She smoothed down the creases in her dress to use up the nervous energy instead and settled her bonnet on her head. Then her father and mother took her by the arms and ascended the staircase to make the introductions.

They stopped at a comfortable distance from Giorgio, and he reached out his hand to Francesca, who moved forward eagerly to take it. Grasping her hand, he pulled her into a familial embrace, his cheeks glistening with tears. She gladly placed her head upon his breast, returning his embrace. A sense of completeness consumed her, and she felt as though a hole she had not known existed had been filled. She looked up at her parents through tears of joy. She had never felt such an intimate closeness with her English grandparents who were bound by English rules of decorum in showing affection.

John Haversham pulled his wife closer and placed his hand upon her arm.

"Benvenuto in casa mia!" Giorgio said with enthusiasm, and released Francesca so that he could hold her at arm's length and study her features. He was gratified to see that she favored her natural mother very much. He bobbed his head in approval and continued in very halting English, "Please, to come!"

He turned in his wheelchair, reclasping Francesca's hand as though she might disappear like a vision if he released it. Her parents followed.

Francesca looked up as they passed under the Greek portico and was fascinated to see that the ceiling was decorated with the most delicate masonry in a regular pattern consisting of squares, circles, and flowers. It was exquisite work.

They entered a room filled with windows and light that faced a lovely garden. The heady scent of the flowers from outside permeated the room. Giorgio was wheeled next to an armchair, which he patted to indicate that Francesca should sit there.

"Bene," and he indicated for Mario, whom they just now noticed in the room, to come and translate.

Giorgio held out his arms toward Francesca, palms up, in a gesture of presentation, his face infused with pleasure. "Bellissimo!"

"Giorgio say your daughter is very beautiful."

Emily and John bowed their heads to indicate their pleasure. Giorgio continued in a crescendo of Italian, and they waited patiently for the translation.

"Giorgio want thank you for bring your daughter to visit. He say it clear she is much loved. He proud that she grand lady. He say his daughter, Isabella, be proud too."

Another deluge of animated Italian poured forth from the old man.

"He say before this day, his life dark and empty. Your daughter, she come to fill it with sunshine and hope."

Addressing Mario, Francesca asked, "Could you ask Signor Giaccopazzi to tell me about my mother? Ever since I have learned of her I have been eager to know what she was like."

Emily winced and looked down quickly so that her features did not betray her concern. She swallowed hard, and John squeezed her hand in solidarity. As Mario translated, a mixture of delight and sadness settled onto Giorgio's wrinkled face and he nodded. He began his recital and Mario translated after every few phrases.

"She was only child, though, my wife, she have many babies," Giorgio crossed himself in the Catholic tradition. Mario continued, "My wife, she spoil Isabella because she only one to live. Isabella was free spirit. She loved horses. She ride like a man. But she intelligent too. When her mother die, was hard. For me and for her. I work more to deal with sadness. Isabella and me, we drift apart.

"At sixteen I send her to finishing school. The years soon pass and she come back in middle of bad, bad drought. I must save grapes. I neglect her. She spend time with stable boy and horses. Stable boy is very handsome. She very beautiful . . ." His recitation trailed off and he shrugged.

John and Emily looked at each other in concern.

"I had no idea. I blame myself. I failed her," he continued. "I not remember her leaving to go to France. I too busy. I feel guilt now," and he pointed to his heart. "Here." He was silent for a while and then continued, "She come back, I don't know where from but she sad. She not tell me why. I let it go. I forget it. Was easier.

"Time pass. We become friends. I forget her sadness. She marry. A good, good man. But no babies come. Then while she dying she tell me about baby." He put his hands gently around Francesca's face and looked into her eyes, his own moist. "I travel far to find you. God has not forgotten me. He has brought you to me."

He released her face and reached for something from a side table, handing it to Francesca. It was a beautiful portrait of a striking woman with flashing dark eyes, thick wavy hair, and more than a passing resemblance to herself.

Twenty-Eight

ITALY

 iorgio asks if you agree for Francesca to meet her natural father,"
said Mario as he came into the breakfast room the next morning
and bowed to the Havershams.

Giorgio had insisted that they stay at the house instead of the pensionne and had sent servants to retrieve their belongings.

"He promise the man that he would try to make a meeting, but if
not, he understand. Much to think about, no? Giorgio is much tired
this morning. He apologize he not come down. So much excitement."

At the hint of the topic the night before, it had become the matter
of an intense private conversation between the two of them after they
retired. The shocking revelation that Francesca's natural father was a
stable boy had come as astonishing news, as they had assumed that he
was a man of noble birth who was, perhaps, married.

Francesca had been so enthralled with meeting her grandfather and
learning about her mother that she had been oblivious to the disclosure
about her father, but the idea that Francesca would at some point ask to
meet him was broached by her parents in private, and even after hours
of discussion, they had not resolved on a course of action. The alarming
realization that he was of low birth had led them to weigh the options
and had prompted much soul-searching, particularly on John's part.
This fact could damage Francesca's chances for a happy and successful
future, were it to be known. He rejected the notion of making a decision for his daughter based on prejudice, as his own father would, but he

had to acknowledge that her parentage was distinctly objectionable for a man of his rank and reputation, and he hated himself for it. He had wrestled with the question of what to do with this knowledge deep into the night. Now to learn that her natural father was actually expecting to meet Francesca . . .

"I am torn between feeling that he has a moral case for meeting her and—and I am ashamed to admit this—a feeling that we have a moral case for preventing such a meeting," admitted John. Mario bowed in understanding. He well understood the politics of hierarchy.

"You should know that Antonio, that is his name, has climbed from stable boy to head groom. That is something, no?"

"Perhaps we should take the question to Francesca, my love?" suggested Emily.

"I fear that she does not possess the experience and wisdom necessary in making such an important decision. I fear that she will make the decision using only her sensibilities. Once the meeting has taken place, once the introduction has been made, it cannot be undone. He will, perhaps, demand a more permanent place in her life, which would jeopardize any prospects of marriage with a suitable English gentleman. Our first responsibility as her parents is to protect her. We *must* consider her future."

"What about my future?" gasped Francesca, as she looked with fear from her mother to her father, on entering the room.

"I will leave you," Mario said tactfully, then withdrew from the room.

Francesca dropped into a brocade chair, her brows pinched in panic. "We are not leaving already, are we?" she queried.

"No, no, do not fear. We have only just arrived."

Her brow smoothed but her eyes grew curious, "Then what about my future?"

"Your birth father has asked to meet you. It is a matter that will require you to deliberate and weigh different options. Again, I would suggest that you take some time before making a hasty emotional decision."

"If you require it, Papa, but what can you mean?"

"We mean, Francesca that you must decide whether it is wise to start a relationship with him."

"Oh, I see . . ."

"I would advise you to appraise the situation using logic as well as your heart. Your father is not a gentleman as we had assumed; he is a groom."

"Ah. I do not remember that being mentioned. Well, yes, that does change things," she said thoughtfully.

She walked to the open glass doors and leaned against the frame, gazing out at the beautiful gardens. "You mean that this fact might taint me in the eyes of English society."

"We do. Though hard to accept, given the facts as they are, it is one thing to be the illegitimate daughter of an unknown gentleman, but it is quite another to definitely be the daughter of a servant. This connection with the lower classes will have serious repercussions for your future prospects. Think if he were to demand access to you after your return to England. These are all things you must consider carefully."

"But Papa, it seems so wrong to judge people by their wealth and position. Cannot a man be worthy who is not rich or of noble blood?"

"Of course, but you must be realistic. We live in a world where traditions of rank and class are the foundation of our civilization. You cannot snub these social rules without understanding the consequences—to do so will be a risk to your whole way of life and your reputation. Remember the reaction of your own grandfather when he merely suspected that your parentage was not noble. Society at large will be much less forgiving, and your mother and I will not live forever to be your protectors. Your chances of making a good marriage and finding protection through your husband's position, if your birth father is to be a permanent part of your life, are very low, my dear. You may not like it, but it is the world in which we live and you will live or die by its rules, unfair as they may seem."

Francesca sank onto the couch and hung her head in her hands in quiet despair. Emily and John looked at each other in sympathetic desperation. This was uncharted territory indeed.

They all sat still in quiet meditation for some time. John sent a prayer to the heavens and as he sat, the seed of an idea began to grow in his mind.

Francesca slowly raised her head, eyes raw from weeping, "I really do desire to meet him, Papa, but if you think it truly unwise, I will try to forbear."

Her father relaxed his face and suggested, "What if we were to engage the services of a lawyer?"

Francesca's head tilted to the side like a puppy, listening to its master.

"Go on," said Emily.

"I am sure your birth father is an intelligent man. He has risen to be head groom according to Mario, and that is no easy task. He could be made to appreciate the threat his presence is to your way of life if he were to insist on associating with you in England. Perhaps we can draw up a legal document to protect you. Suppose we explain the situation and ask him to sign a contract promising that he will not attempt to visit you in England but that you will come to Italy to visit him on a regular basis if he so desires it."

"Do you not think that will seem rather rude, Papa? Perhaps it will make him angry."

"It will depend on what manner of man he is, dearest. If he is a worthy man, he will be happy that you want to meet him, and the contract will show good faith that you desire to continue the relationship in the future."

"What if I don't like him . . . or you and Mama don't like him?"

"Here is what I suggest. We prepare the document and send it to him before any meeting, allowing him time to overcome any hurt to his pride and giving him time to consider what is best for you. What do you think?"

Emily leaned forward. "It does seem to be a solution, Francesca. It will protect you and give him hope for an association."

"I will think on it, Papa."

Francesca kissed them both and went out into the gardens. She wandered around the tended area and then glided into the rows of vines. The grapes were immature; small and green, but the branches were loaded, which promised a good harvest.

Her mind churned like the bottom of a water mill. Papa was right; her heart wanted to run to her natural father, but she was not a child, and she could well understand the ramifications. A legal document that protected her might be the answer. She was not even entirely sure yet that she was wholly comfortable with the knowledge that her father was of low birth. She had been raised to believe that there were intellectual and social differences between the classes, as well as cultural ones. What if she was revolted by her natural father's manners or way of speech? Did she feel that a relationship with a servant, though he be her father, was beneath her? If he sensed that she was ashamed of him, how would that make him feel? She honestly could not anticipate her reaction, though she hoped that she would behave well. She had felt such an instant kinship with Giorgio. Would she feel such a one with her natural father? The questions chased around and around in her head.

"Francesca!"

She looked up to see her grandfather sitting on a bench and smiling and rushed to his side, seeking comfort.

Though oral language was a barrier, the language of love was universal. He took her hand, placing her head on his shoulder and they sat together in a companionable silence, drinking in one another's presence.

⋙ ⋘

After they had eaten lunch and Francesca had talked about her thoughts and feelings on the matter, John presented the arguments to Mario so that he might translate for Giorgio.

After a short silence, Giorgio spoke and Mario's expression became more serious.

"Giorgio say that he think Francesca's birth father would take offense in beginning, if a contract like this come to him, but after some time he would see that it is wise. But he can see also could make a barrier between them. I Mario agree. It is how I would feel."

Giorgio nodded and continued. "Francesca, it your decision. I met your father. He intelligent man. It is risk, but worth it."

Francesca nodded. "After listening to everyone's opinions and after much consideration on the topic myself, I believe that the legal document is the most prudent way forward, though I do agree with Papa, it is only fair to send him the document in advance."

"Good!" replied John. "Then let us secure the services of a lawyer."

ENGLAND

"My lady, we have rung the gong and his Lordship has not appeared. Shall we begin serving dinner or should we wait . . . ?" The butler pursed his lips in anticipation.

"Well, what could be keeping him?" said Lady Augusta, "Wait a while and I will go in search of him."

A worrying train of thought was standing off the stage in the wings of her consciousness and she shooed it away until it turned tail and ran. She opened the door to her husband's study but it was dark and smelled stale. She closed the door and moved on to the library. It was quiet and heavy.

Ascending the stairs to enter his changing room, she found it was empty as well, but as she swept her skirt behind her to exit the room, she thought she heard a primal, guttural sound. Her first thought was that an animal was trapped in the room. However, as she entered further, she realized that the sound was emanating from the other side of the door. She placed her hand on the cold door knob and turned it slowly, terrified of what might lay beyond. As the door cracked open, no light escaped, and on opening it fully, she could see that the room was entirely black. She felt her way over to the bed and as her eyes adjusted, became aware of a large shape on the bed that was shaking.

"John?" she ventured, in a strangled whisper.

The black shape groaned and she clasped her heart, the ugly fears inching back to the wings of her mind. Going to the window, she opened the curtain a fraction to let in a sliver of light but the figure on the bed moaned and raised an arm to block it.

"Are you ill, John?"

She desperately hoped this was the cause of his malaise as the alternative was too awful to contemplate. The unnerving sound of a grown man weeping shook her to her foundations.

"Oh, that I were only ill!" moaned the figure. "We are ruined, Augusta. Ruined!"

Twenty-Nine

ITALY

The horse bucked, and Antonio apologized for being rough with the brush. As head groom, he was no longer obliged to brush the horses, but today he needed somewhere to exhaust his nervous energy.

Ever since receiving the message that his natural daughter desired to visit him, he had both dreaded and longed for the meeting. The letter had included a legal document, drawn up to protect the interests of the child. It had irritated him. He understood the way the world worked as well as anyone—perhaps better, having had his heart torn to shreds by it and having the knowledge of his child kept from him. *His* child. In spite of the provocation, a tenderness was working its way through his soul.

Tossing and turning in bed during the night, he had reviewed the short time he had had with Isabella, dragging out memories he usually kept deeply buried. Though it had been many years, he still easily conjured up the image of her in full riding habit at the stable doors, silhouetted by the morning sun. She'd had such spirit, so unlike other great ladies who simpered and twittered and did nothing more taxing than needlework.

The horse flicked its head and whinnied and he thought it better to drop the brush and leave the poor animal alone.

He went to his office and shut the door, something he rarely did. Sitting down roughly in his chair, he gazed out the window at nothing in particular, biding his time. A sharp knock on the door shot him from his reverie.

⚬⚬⚬

If it were possible, Francesca was even more nervous to meet her natural father than she had been to meet her natural grandfather. She had skipped breakfast and eaten a very light lunch. The lawyer had written up a legal agreement to everyone's satisfaction, and it had been sent ahead a few days before. Giorgio's doctor had not given permission for the journey, which would take several days, so they were making the trip with Mario as an attendant.

⚬⚬⚬

At last the traveling came to an end in the forecourt of a fashionable villa, set among a large park. Mario went ahead to determine the lay of the land. A stable boy took Mario to an office and he knocked sharply at the door. It quickly opened to reveal a man close to his own age, with curly dark hair that was graying at the temples. He was of an athletic build and appeared more refined than Mario had expected. It was a promising beginning.

Mario introduced himself, and Antonio moved aside to allow him entrance while calling to someone and asking them to go in search of a third party. Antonio then settled himself behind his desk. "I have read the document, though I do not pretend to be conversant with the legal language and have secured the services of a legal clerk from the town who has read it and explained the details to me. I will sign it with him present as a witness. I have just sent a boy to retrieve him from the town. It will take no more than twenty minutes. I must confess, I found its tone quite offensive, but I have accepted the terms."

Mario nodded, impressed by the groom's forethought and intelligence. He, himself, would never sign a legal document he did not understand.

⚬⚬⚬

What could be taking so long? The sun was at its zenith and though the carriage was stationed under a large tree it began to be very hot. The harsh bite of blood filled Francesca's mouth, and she realized that she had chewed the inside of her cheek to pieces. Her mother and father were sleeping gently, due to the heat and the long drive. How they could sleep she did not know! The anticipation was about to undo her.

She looked out of the window yet again for signs of Mario and sank back in utter despair of him ever returning. She harbored real fears that she might find her natural father uncouth and rough and be very disappointed. She despised herself for the thought.

She took out a little mirror from her reticule, pinched her cheeks and bit her lips so that she might look her best, and twirled a curl around her finger. The crunch of gravel signaled the long-awaited return of Mario with the signed document, and she gently shook her parents awake. The time had finally arrived.

⚜ ⚜

Every nerve was standing to attention as Antonio heard the footsteps of several people approach his office. His neck was so tight that it began to give him a headache, and he breathed in deeply to relax. As the party entered the open door, he gasped and put his hand on the desk to steady himself; he was looking at a ghost.

⚜ ⚜

As Francesca rounded the door she inhaled deeply to muster her courage. There were two men in the room, one rather aged with white hair and a beard and the other middle-aged with dark curls and a handsome face. She looked around in some confusion.

"Buongiorno, Senorita Haversham. I am Antonio."

She moved toward him with a hesitant step. He did not reach out to embrace her as Giorgio had. In fact, she could not read the expression on his face at all, so she lifted her hand for him to kiss in the formal manner. After a beat, he took her gloved hand, kissed it, and then bowed. It was all very formal and awkward.

Sensing this, John Haversham stepped boldly forward and shook hands with the man warmly, the effect of which was to crack the eggshell atmosphere. Antonio's tense shoulders dropped in relief, and his face broke into an engaging smile.

"I trust you are not offended by the legalities," said John. "English society is very unforgiving, and I know that you would not wish to harm Francesca's chance at a suitable marriage." He looked to Mario to translate.

Antonio replied through Mario, "I understand. Now I see her, I not want to hurt her future. Please to sit."

Antonio could not take his eyes from his newly discovered daughter. She was her mother's very image, and only the shape of her eyes could he attribute to himself. He was aware that her adoptive mother was valiantly keeping up a polite conversation, but for Antonio it was background, for the room was slowly spinning as the surreal nature of the situation broke over him like a welcome shower of rain in the heat. He felt dazed and a little as though he had had too much wine; pleasantly joyful and feeling that all was well in the world. It was a sensation he was unaccustomed to.

He eventually became aware that the background noise had stopped, and as he dragged his eyes away from Francesca's lovely face, he noticed that all eyes in the room were on him, expectantly.

"I apologize. It is a beautiful dream. I not want to wake." Mario translated.

"Of course," said Emily kindly. "We can appreciate how this changes everything. She certainly changed our world for the better!"

⁂

The next hour was spent in asking and answering questions as though Antonio and Francesca were the only people in the room. He wanted to know every detail of her life in England, her passions, and her heartaches. She in turn wanted to hear of his feelings for her mother and his life since they parted.

Realizing, at length, that this might not be of interest to the whole party, he suggested that they all take a stroll around the grounds of the villa, enabling him to continue his friendly interrogation.

Antonio had never felt such emotions before. His heart, which had hardened over the years of self-imposed solitude, had been softened in just one afternoon in the company of his daughter and the invisible thread of paternal love was thickening to a sturdy rope that would bind him willingly to this young woman for the rest of his life. As she spoke, a part of him mourned missing her childhood, but this was no time for remorse, and he swept the feelings aside. He watched in wonder at her beauty, elegance, and good humor.

As she approached the horses and petted their noses, he noticed that there was a natural affinity between them; something else from him, then.

"You like to ride, yes?"

"I love to ride! It is my favorite pastime. Mama says it is unbecoming to ride so much."

"Like Isabella, then. She would rather ride than do anything else."

"Did she? That explains so much!"

Her parents smiled back as she bestowed a look of triumph on them.

She excused herself from Antonio and went to whisper to her parents, returning to declare that her parents had agreed to stay in the area for the next few days. His heart leaped at the thought that she was not ashamed of him and that her affection for him was growing. A life that had been satisfying but gray was blossoming into many colors.

⋰ᴏᴇ ᴏᴇ⋱

"He is a fine and worthy man, is he not, Papa?"

The carriage lurched and dipped as it traveled back to the pensionne.

"I confess that I am pleasantly surprised at how well he presents himself. It is no small feat to rise from a stable boy with no education to head groom for an establishment of considerable size. He has used his talents and time wisely."

"I am so happy that you approve of him, Papa! For myself, I like him very much. It almost seems an insult to have asked him to sign the document."

"And that is why a young girl needs parents to guide her through this perilous world. You cannot know a man's true character after one afternoon! To his credit, he saw the wisdom of the protection such a document afforded you and was willing to sign it as an act of good faith. Imagine if he had been some ignorant fool who saw in you a chance to make his fortune!"

"I suppose if you put it like that! However, he is not a fool and is very pleasant company. I think it is requisite that I begin to learn Italian, do you not, Mama?"

"I believe it would be a very good idea for all of us, now that we have added an Italian contingent to our family!"

⁂

Over the next few days, Antonio took them to many attractions in the area, and he and Francesca established a solid foundation for a lasting relationship.

As the Havershams readied to depart, Antonio stepped forward to kiss Francesca's hand. Instead, Francesca gave him a sudden hug which he returned without hesitation.

"As per the agreement, we will return next year," said John.

Antonio bowed and quickly turned before his face betrayed the sudden sadness that engulfed him. Francesca was left to watch him depart with a quivering lip and a deep void in her soul.

Thirty

ITALY

*T*he journey back to the vineyard estate seemed much quicker without the anticipation, though on the return she did notice the beauties of the countryside. She was fast falling in love with Italy and was joyful that her new future would include regular visits.

On the second day, the entire party had dropped off to sleep due to the hypnotic bouncing of the carriage when they were awakened by loud, fast hooves approaching and the subsequent braking of their vehicle. John pulled up the blind to ascertain what was happening.

Mario, who rode beside the carriage, was deep in conversation with another man on horseback who was handing him a letter. All three Havershams pressed their faces to the tiny window to learn the reason for the delay. Their question was soon answered as Mario approached and John opened the carriage door.

"It is Signore Giaccopazzi. He is very ill! I must go."

"Of course, of course," replied John.

"Do not delay, Signore. The doctor say he may not last the week."

Emily looked at her daughter, whose eyes had grown as round as an owl's and whose face was tight with anguish. John closed the door as Mario sped off.

"But I have only just met him! It is cruel for him to be taken away just as we were making each other's acquaintance! Oh, I cannot bear it!" cried Francesca.

Emily pulled her daughter's head onto her own shoulder and gently placed a soothing arm around her. Life truly was merciless at times.

⚬⚬⚬

Mario rode hard trying, without success, to keep his concern for Giorgio at bay. Dawn was hardly breaking as he raced into the forecourt of the villa and handed off the horse to a groom. He raced up the stairs without ceremony and made his way hastily to the door of Giorgio's bedchamber. After knocking gently, he was admitted by the doctor whose solemn expression was less than encouraging. The room was dark and stuffy and reeked of death. His throat ached and he swallowed hard. "Is he . . . ?"

"He clings to life, my friend. He is fighting to keep the reaper at bay until Francesca returns, I believe, but I fear he is losing the battle. He suffered another heart attack in the night. His heart is very weak."

Mario went to the bedside and knelt, taking Giorgio's hand in his own. There was a faint flicker of the eyelids but no other recognition.

"We must prepare for the end," ventured the doctor. Mario nodded.

"Did you know that he has written a new will?" asked the doctor. Mario turned his head sharply.

"He called for the attorney after you all left. He was very happy when it was completed and smiled in his sleep. I know only that he has provided for the young woman and yourself, but I have no knowledge of the details."

Mario nodded again and realized that his life was about to change dramatically.

⚬⚬⚬

The Havershams rode all through the night and changed horses twice over the next two days. There was little quality sleep, and everyone's nerves were over exercised. Francesca was unusually terse, but her parents did not condemn it and she was quick to apologize. They ate small amounts and did so hurriedly, merely eating to keep the hunger pangs at bay.

At last they arrived, some three days after Mario had left them. The household staff rushed to welcome them and usher them into the somber house. The day was bright and sunny and filled with the smell of flowers, but the atmosphere inside spoke of sadness.

Mario came down to greet them with a falsely bright expression that duped no one. Francesca grasped her mother's hand.

"He lives," he said. "But the end is near. He asks for you, Francesca."

Emily released her daughter, and with one look back, Francesca ascended the beautiful staircase with Mario. Dread settled in her stomach. She had never witnessed death or dying and certainly never of someone she loved. And she did love him, she realized—fiercely. Although the two had known each other less than a few weeks, Francesca had bonded with her grandfather and her Italian heritage.

As she entered the room, the feelings of aversion were swiftly replaced with compassion, and she ran to his bedside, taking his big hand in her tiny one, wetting it with her tears.

His eyes were closed but on sensing her there, he struggled to open them and attempted to speak, but the power to do so had left him and he resorted to squeezing her hand. Leaning forward and placing her forehead on his pillow, she whispered, "Nonno, ti amo."

His face wrinkled into a smile and his thumb rubbed her own and then, too soon and without warning, his hand went slack.

For some moments, she could not process what had come to pass and hesitated, hoping that he would squeeze her hand again, but after some time, she accepted the truth and the doctor came to lead her down the stairs.

There were no histrionics, just a bone-deep sadness for a relationship that had been cut too short. Her parents perceived immediately the events that had transpired by her expression and enveloped her in their comforting arms.

⁂

The following morning, Mario explained the funeral arrangements. Giorgio had requested a short, private funeral and burial with only his closest friends and new family in attendance.

Francesca was experiencing an emptiness that gnawed at her soul; the bright sunshine seemed to mock the gravity of the situation, but as she stood beside the grave a day later, she thanked God for that same sunshine. It was as though nature itself was celebrating his life, welcoming him to heaven to be reunited with his wife and child.

Upon their return, the attorney who had drafted the document for Antonio arrived and invited them to hear the reading of the new will. Mario translated after each sentence was read.

"I leave the bulk of my estate to my natural granddaughter, Francesca Haversham."

Francesca gave a little gasp, but her father nodded, having expected as much.

"I leave Mario Lombardi, 10,000 lira per year and strongly suggest that my granddaughter retain him as manager of my vineyards for the remainder of his lifetime. I also suggest that Francesca's natural father, Antonio Rossi, be offered the job of head groom for the estate."

Francesca found that she was moved that her grandfather would think of her natural father so kindly and saw it as the perfect solution to maintain a regular relationship with him, should he desire the position.

There were small bequests to people she did not know, and afterward, her father went to speak to the lawyer and Mario. He later explained that the inheritance was a wonderful gift, but the practicalities of living in one country, while being the owner of such an enterprise in another, needed to be sorted out. He spent the next few days carefully planning with the attorney and Mario.

Everyone was surprised to discover the vast extent of Giorgio's fiscal wealth, over and above the enormous value of the vineyards. Francesca had become an exceptionally and independently rich woman.

At the end of the week, it was decided that the Havershams would make their departure and allow Mario time to gain his footing as sole manager of the estate. Word had been sent to Antonio, and he had readily accepted the position of head groom and arrived quickly to fill the position and to bid his daughter a fond farewell.

As they slowly made their way back across Italy and into France, Francesca found her thoughts turning to Phillip again and again and admitted that her affection for him was growing daily. She was eager to share all that had happened but was reticent, given the change in her status. He had been so supportive of her, despite the revelation that she was adopted, that she felt it was appropriate to inform him of certain recent events but instead of a long sentimental letter, she sent him a short note, briefly detailing her change in fortune and describing her grandfather, sharing with him her anguish as his death.

Her parents had discouraged any disclosure of her father's station until her own family had been notified.

More than once as she traveled, the memory of Phillip on horseback, smiling at her as she left his home, came vividly to her mind. The vision induced a yearning to be in his company that was new and unfamiliar. At such times, she would reprimand herself for being foolish; had he not said that he preferred auburn hair and had he not always considered her more as a sister? Furthermore, adoption was one thing, but her father was right, her lowly heritage changed everything. The son of a nobleman might have qualms about marrying the daughter of a servant. She must readjust her expectations of life and consider a future without romance. This admission left her feeling hollow and disconsolate.

John Haversham had thought it more prudent to disclose the nature of Francesca's heritage in person and had sent a letter to Francesca's grandparents, explaining only their sadness at Giorgio's passing and her good fortune in becoming his heir. The remembrance of her grandparents' reaction and fear of an unknown and unpredictable future at the hands of a callous society encouraged a somber mood as the carriage trundled onward, ever closer to impending rejection and loneliness.

Thirty-One

ENGLAND

"There is a letter for you, dear," said Phillip's mother as he entered the breakfast room.

His stomach jumped and he caught a breath when he saw the handwriting, and he hoped his mother could read nothing in his expression that betrayed his feelings. He had not received any correspondence since Francesca left, which was to be expected, but some part of him had hoped she would send word.

He had begun his employment in chambers and was thoroughly enjoying the challenges of the law but had returned home with the sole purpose of ascertaining if he had any mail. He had not told Francesca of his new address and had instructed his mother not to forward any letters as he would be returning home from time to time. His fear that Francesca would never see him as a suitor had prevented him from opening his heart to his family.

He placed the unopened letter by his place setting and ate his breakfast slowly so as to arouse no suspicions. The letter, however, monopolized his attentions, inert and plain as it was.

As soon as he was able to leave without appearing to be rude, he took a walk in the gardens to ensure complete privacy. He ripped open the seal. If a faint flicker of hope burned that she would in some way write that she had missed him or cared for him, it was handily extinguished by the tone of the note. She spoke only of the beauties of Florence and how sweet her grandfather was and how painfully cruel his passing had been. Phillip was astonished to hear of his death and further amazed to read that her grandfather's great vineyard now belonged to her! He wondered how she was coping.

He feared the rest of the letter would say that they were delaying their return because of the death but instead it informed him that they were already en route!

⚬◦❡◦❡◦⚬

The ferry crossing from Calais was even more rough than on the out-ward journey and had necessitated a short stay in Dover for everyone to regain their equilibrium. An unanticipated consequence was that the English coastal environment brought back buried memories of her narrow escape from ruin. She shrank at the memory of how naive she had been and thanked the Lord for her deliverance. She heartily wished that she might never lay eyes on Mr. Ashbourne ever again.

During the journey back to Wiltshire, John and Emily discussed with Francesca the morality of telling any suitor of her true birth. They agreed that it was incumbent upon them to tell their parents, though they shrank from the task, and decided to seek their counsel on the problem. They further discussed the possibility that news of her adoption may have leaked out and already be known abroad. In their experience, people were quick to judge and withdraw support.

Francesca listened as an uninterested bystander. Having just lost someone very dear to her, severing the link to her birth mother, she could not evoke the energy to worry. Though she supposed she ought.

After they arrived home and were settled, John and Emily wrote to their parents to invite them to dine the following week. They would lay before them the facts of the case.

Francesca had found correspondence awaiting her which consisted of invitations to balls and to dine. Evidently, news of her adoption must not yet be generally known. Among them, she was delighted to find an invitation to Annabelle's wedding. She was truly happy for her cousin and, remembering her harsh judgment of the Reverend Sladden, decided to give poor Mr. Doyle another chance.

The night of her grandparents' visit arrived, and she was struck by the stiffness in their greeting, so English and formal. Or was it more than that?

They talked of inconsequential things during dinner and only addressed the weightier matters once they were all together in the drawing room and the servants had left.

John cleared his throat and nervously began, "I am sure you are all anxious to know the outcome of our journey."

Lord Haversham, who had dragged himself out of his depressed state to attend this event, grumbled and muttered in agreement.

"You will be gratified to learn that Francesca's natural grandfather was a man of enormous wealth and land who welcomed us most graciously."

"Notwithstanding he was a foreigner," mumbled Lord Haversham under his breath.

"As you know from our letter, he left almost the entirety of his estate to Francesca as his only living relative."

"How will that work given that she intends to live in England?" demanded Lord Davenport. "I assume she *does* intend to continue on here?"

"Yes, indeed! There is a very capable manager who is more than able to run things and Francesca will make regular visits to oversee that all is well. He has been well compensated in the will, and I believe that he was fond of the old man and will honor his wishes."

"What did you find out about her natural father?" questioned Lady Haversham, lips pursed.

"Ah well, there things are a little more complicated."

"Complicated?" growled Lady Haversham.

John garnered his courage, "The irony is that he was, indeed, a peasant, a stable boy—"

"Good heavens!"

"For shame!"

"—However, he has risen to be head groom of a fine establishment."

"Oh, it is worse, far worse than we had anticipated!" moaned Lady Augusta.

Francesca looked to her maternal grandparents for support, but though less vocal, they too were shaking their heads in sorrow.

"Would that you had pressed for the truth in the beginning, then it might not have come to bear such bitter fruit now," spat our Lord Haversham.

"Father, we have been over this. We believed it to be in Francesca's best interests to keep her parentage a secret."

Lady Haversham stood and turned sharply, throwing out, "What about the family's best interests? If this is exposed we will *all* be ruined!" The muscles of her neck stood out like soldiers at attention.

"Mama?" said Emily, cautiously, to her own mother.

"It is most unfortunate," Lady Davenport said, and, turning to face Lord and Lady Haversham, she continued, "But it cannot be changed, and the charge cannot be laid at Francesca's feet. We are all tainted by the association, and I therefore propose that we suppress the fact. Do you not agree, Augusta?"

Lady Augusta sank down on the chaise with a deep sigh, shaking her head, and holding a handkerchief to her mouth in distress. "What if our secret is discovered by malicious persons? Do you appreciate my standing in society? They will stone me as a hypocrite!" She was working herself into a righteously indignant state of agitation.

"We are perfectly aware of your position, Augusta," Emily's mother responded acerbically. "You have sacrificed many poor souls on the altar of prejudice."

"Perhaps it is time to retire from your career as self-proclaimed judge and jury," proclaimed Lord Davenport. "For it may now bear a bitter fruit of your own sowing! Was it really necessary to hang and quarter people for lack of connections? I believe it is a practice that could well be put to rest!"

"I felt it my responsibility to keep our noble circles pure. I defend the position that our society is stronger because of it! However, I perfectly appreciate the tenuousness of my current situation which, I might point out, is not of my *own* making. I am furious that my children have placed me in this untenable position! You do not understand—"

"Oh, I think I understand very well!" shouted Lord Davenport. "You have undertaken a cruel employment, Augusta, that leaves people's lives in tatters. I confess that I am sometimes ashamed to claim you as kin!"

"For shame! What impertinence! I refuse to stay here to be insulted! John, I insist that you take me home this instant!" Her neck was scarlet from her anger, and her hand rushed to cover it as she leaped to her feet.

Lord Haversham arose and pulled himself to his full height. "This is a bad business, son. A very bad business!"

⊰⊱ ⊰⊱

Lord and Lady Haversham returned home to their own estate in thorny silence, each ruminating over the catastrophe of their personal affairs and the calamity of Francesca's revelation. When they arrived, the butler hurried to convey a letter that had arrived by special delivery. Lord Haversham ripped open the seal and sank onto the nearest chair.

Lady Augusta threw a fleeting, sideways glance at the spectacle, oozing with disdain.

"What is it now?" she fumed, her patience stretched as thin as gauze as she removed her gloves.

"The bank has called in the mortgage on the estate. We are bankrupt. The bailiffs will come soon." He groaned as if in pain.

Augusta Haversham was stunned into silence. She felt stripped, exposed like a peach whose outer skin had been ripped off. He had mortgaged the estate without consulting her! The fool! The fear that had built after he confessed his failures was ebbing away and a furious anger was building in the void.

How dare he hide from her the full extent of their financial difficulties! When he had first mentioned to her that they were running low on funds, she had never dreamed that he was telling her only partial truths. She had been more than happy to conceive a plan to acquire wealth through family connections. It was, after all, a British tradition to gain wealth through advantageous marriages. There was no shame in it. She had gladly encouraged a liaison between her granddaughter and Langley Ashbourne as being favorable to all parties. A little manipulation did no harm. It had worked out extremely well in the case of her son, John, after all. Total bankruptcy, however, was unthinkable. People went to debtor's prison for less.

She felt crushed, adversity being piled on top of adversity. Was it not enough to face the shame of learning that her granddaughter was of scandalous parentage, a fact that threatened her own position in society? Must God punish her further by adding destitution? What had she done to deserve this?

She did not know which loss she felt the most keenly. Her heart was squeezing in her chest, mourning the loss of the life she had built and the virtual crown she had fashioned for herself.

"Do you detest me, Augusta?"

"Yes!" she hissed. "I hate you for doing this to me! What did you expect me to say? The shame is more than I can bear! I deserve better! I am furious that you have brought me down with you! You have lost all my respect! It was your duty to communicate how dire our situation was. I cannot forgive you! I must escape this mess you have made! I will travel to the Continent immediately and do not even think of following me! You must face the consequences of your mismanagement and betrayal alone. I shall be gone by morning."

The desperation Lord Haversham had been fighting to keep at bay plunged back over him with a vengeance. He dragged his tired body up the stairs to his room and curled into a ball of despair, desperately seeking the comfort of drunken sleep.

Thirty-Two

ENGLAND

The most important quality of any lawyer is discretion. Knowing that full well, Mr. Arthur Farthing decided that he must put discretion aside if it could possibly save someone's life. He had experienced a heavy sense of foreboding after leaving Lord Haversham and only managed a fitful sleep in the ensuing days. After failing to receive a reply to his last attempt at communication, he was seized by the concern that he might have blood on his hands if he did not hint at his Lordship's distress to his son.

To that end, he sent an anonymous dispatch to Mr. John Haversham, the son, suggesting that a visit to his father might be in order.

❦

"What can this mean?" John asked at breakfast.

"Of what do you speak, dearest?"

"I have here an anonymous letter that suggests I should visit my father!"

"It must be a cruel joke from someone who has found out our secret and the rift it has caused. My goodness, it did not take long, did it? They must know that your father left here in anger. What else can it mean?"

John crushed the letter in his palm and threw it to the floor, from whence the footman picked it up to dispose of it. Life could be immensely unpredictable and he felt it sorely. But what was done was done and his little family would sustain and support one another through the threatening storm. He only prayed that after the storm had abated, some courageous young man would still venture for his daughter's hand so that *she* might not suffer for *his* sins. It would take a singular character to set at naught the disapproval of society. Would that there was such a man.

As Francesca entered the breakfast room, he made his excuses to leave, lest she perceive the worry upon his countenance. He strode about the grounds but the feeling of uneasiness did not leave him and at length he decided to make the journey to satisfy his own curiosity. If he was not received he would stay at an inn close by his father's residence. Then at least he could be at peace that he had not ignored a warning.

⚬⚬⚬

Haversham Hall was dark when John arrived, and he supposed that his parents were not home. He was greeted on entry by Sanderson, the butler of his youth, instead of a footman, and the butler was wearing a very dower expression.

"Oh, Mr. Haversham, how very prescient is your arrival! We are all in a commotion! Your father has taken ill and refuses all nourishment and ministry, and her Ladyship has left for the Continent. I did not know if it would be proper for me to send word for you and had been wrestling with the idea when here you are!"

"My father is ill? Has he taken a fever?"

"I believe it is a fever of the mind rather than of the body, sir, But more than that, I cannot say."

John felt a punch of guilt as he supposed his own actions responsible for this illness of the mind, but was astonished that it would cause his father *so* much anguish. Did their standing in society mean so very much to them, then? For his own part, society could hang if it no longer valued his daughter.

"Where can I find him, Sanderson?"

"In his bedchamber, sir."

John bounded up the stairs to his father's room before he could change his mind and knocked, bracing himself for the onslaught of criticism he was sure to receive. There was no reply. He knocked again, more sharply this time but still no response. Gingerly, he opened the door a crack and, seeing no shaft of light, entered carefully.

The room was stale and odorous. He picked his way cautiously across the room and pulled back the heavy drapes in order to open the window for some fresh air but dropped them back at the pitiful cry of pain from the bed.

There is no sight quite so disturbing as seeing one's parent regress to a state of childhood. It knocked John's earth off its axis, and his own place in the universe was called into question.

He rushed to the bed, finding his father's hand in the bedclothes. "Father, courage! If society rejects us, we will band together! We will not leave you alone!"

"Oh, my son, my son. Would that it were only a fall from social grace. It is far, far worse. I have been a derelict steward of your inheritance and it is all gone. All gone!"

This was such an unexpected direction of speech that John was temporarily mute. As his brain received and digested this new set of facts, the problems associated with his daughter's birth faded. His father's fortune had been very great, and he had varied interests in America. How could it possibly be gone? Gently, he spoke. "Tell me all, father."

⚬◦❧ ❧◦⚬

John reflected on the Bible's teaching that the love of money is the root of all evil. He had never had to think much about money as there had always been plenty. Now, on the contrary, money was very much on his mind. He had spent the last four hours going over his father's accounts, sinking deeper and deeper into depression with every minute that passed.

He was horrified to see that Haversham Hall was mortgaged in its entirety, and the amount of money owed to creditors made him tremble. The losses sustained in America had resulted in huge debts that could not be repaid in a lifetime. He found letters from Arthur Farthing that had never been opened that warned of the impending doom. How could his father have been so irresponsible? It seemed so totally out of character. Even were John to sell his own home and give his father the proceeds, it would hardly make a dent and would, quite frankly, be throwing good money after bad.

He checked on his father periodically, and, after four hours, Lord Haversham had finally slipped into a sleep from sheer mental exhaustion and no nourishment.

John was irritated that his mother had flown the coop and not been of more assistance, then almost immediately chastised himself, realizing that he was being uncharitable and that she was probably in shock. She was dealing with it the only way she could—escape.

He ran his fingers roughly through his hair and sighed. He was starving and looked at the clock, surprised that it was already eleven in the evening. He rang the bell for some food and when Sanderson appeared with a tray he was more than grateful. Rather than leaving the room, Sanderson hesitated and John quirked an eyebrow.

"It seems most ill-mannered to make such indelicate inquiries at this difficult time, but the staff are up in arms and rumors are rampant. Her ladyship's maid, Mrs. Oliver, left in a hurry with her ladyship and we have been told nothing. I just want to put the rumors to rest."

"What are they saying?" asked John.

"That her ladyship and his lordship have parted ways and that the house will only need half the staff. It's about their jobs, you see. Several of them send their wages home to families that depend upon the extra."

John breathed in deeply and let out a long sigh.

"They are correct then, sir?"

"I am afraid it is a lot worse even than that, Sanderson. I know I can count on your discretion . . . the truth is, Lord Haversham has lost his fortune and owes a great deal in debts. This house has been mortgaged, and with the news of his interests in America failing, I am sure that it is only a matter of time until the bank calls in the loan and the house is repossessed. I am very sorry to have to tell you that *all* the staff, yourself included, will need to look for new positions as soon as possible."

Sanderson's face fell in disbelief, and he staggered to sit in a chair. He whipped out a handkerchief and wiped his forehead.

"I had no idea, sir. No idea at all."

"No more did I, Sanderson. I am more than sorry. We will, of course, give everyone the best references." He knew this was of little comfort and had an idea. "We will give each servant a bonus as a parting gift." It would come out of his own pocket, but he did not want to admit that.

The faithful butler rallied and, standing, said, "I will inform his Lordship that I will stay on until he, himself, departs. I will not leave him comfortless!"

John was so touched by the statement that he did not trust himself to speak and merely nodded as the butler left the room. It struck him that people really did not appreciate just how much their actions affect the lives of others. His father's irresponsibility would bring the whole house to its knees financially, and his own deceit had estranged his family from him and ruined, perhaps forever, the chance for his daughter to have a happy life.

He picked up the next letter from the desk but found that he no longer had the energy to deal with it. He snuffed the candle and mounted the stairs to one of the guest bedrooms, leaving his supper untouched.

꧁ ꧂

FRANCE

A small, colorful bird flew and sat upon the wrought-iron railing of the balcony and gave a deep throated aria for Lady Augusta's entertainment. She watched and listened, intrigued by the celestial sound emanating from the tiny creature. She envied him his uncomplicated life and all at once felt old and tired, the weight of her troubles pressing upon her stately shoulders.

As she looked beyond the bird and out from her balcony, she drank in the warm air and pristine view of the Mediterranean. The ocean had a slight haze upon it and other birds swooped up and down searching for food. Life was so tranquil here and she realized that she would happily stay on, indefinitely, pretending that all was well and that nothing had changed.

Did she miss her husband, she wondered, and was surprised to find that the answer was no. She was outraged and bitter that he had dragged her down to complete and utter destitution. She thanked heaven that her parents were no longer living to witness her disgrace.

She had had some inheritance of her own when she wedded, but it became her husband's property upon marriage, and he had used it to fund his enterprises in America. It was gone now, of course. She did not even have the money to pay for this apartment and had only secured it because the owner was blissfully ignorant of her change in fortune. Just thinking of having to escape without paying left her feeling exhausted.

She had run away from the situation. It had seemed the only logical thing to do—to wait out the scandal from afar. The mismanagement was not her doing and therefore she felt no compunction to support him through the fallout. The plan to marry Francesca to Langley Ashbourne was too little, too late; a finger in the dyke of their financial hemorrhage. Her husband's lack of honesty gnawed at her, and she found that she could not forgive him. Bitter tears stung her eyes and she wiped at them roughly. He was the author of this disaster. Let him suffer alone!

As if this was not trial enough, there was the other matter— Francesca. How could her son have polluted their family tree thus, with the daughter of a servant? The illegitimate daughter of a gentle- man was one thing, but this, this was inexcusable. She had ingrained in her children the need for standards, and John had thrown it all to the wind, bringing her down with him. She could barely think of her granddaughter without repulsion.

Her trials were heavy to bear. Which trial was the greater of the two evils? She might be able to live off her friends to cope with the poverty but the heritage problem, that could not be avoided and it would undoubtedly leave her reputation in tatters. The fine ladies of her acquaintance would snicker and talk about her behind their fans and cut her in public. She could not think of one so-called friend who would stand by her. Indeed, if truth be told, she would not stand by *them* if circumstances were reversed. Her past was littered with rejected souls. She had never before appreciated the power she had wielded in such individual's fates. Where were those she had sentenced, now? She had never given them one moment of thought. Were they languishing in some virtual jail or secluded on a self-imposed island of despair?

She had labored greatly to coronate herself judge and jury and now it had come back to haunt her. Guilt crept into her consciousness, but she banished it before it could begin a soliloquy. She refused to succumb to a weakness of conscience. She should be heralded for protecting the integrity of England rather than being condemned for it!

She thought back to the dark bedchamber, to the admission of her husband's failures. She would have been less shocked had he told her that he was dying. She knew that their reserves were depleted, of course, but *bankruptcy*? She shuddered at the filthy word.

He had continued to lament their situation and beg her forgiveness, but it had all been as background noise. She had assessed the situation coldly in that moment and seen that escape was her only option. She had hurried from her husband's room, castigating him for the whole affair and spitting oaths like daggers. He had failed her.

With a speed that belied her age, she had summoned her maid and commanded that she pack for a voyage to the Continent. Within two hours, they were speeding cross-country toward the ships that sailed the Channel. Her maid had looked on, not daring to ask questions as her mistress wallowed in self-pity and tears.

At length, her weeping had transformed into resolve borne of the need to survive. She had put away her handkerchiefs, washed her face, and stiffened her spine. She would not crumble. She would not falter. By the time they had arrived at the enchanted coastline of the Mediterranean, she had developed a renewed determination.

She had dismissed her maid, sunk onto the bed, and slept for sixteen hours. Upon awakening, the ball of heaviness in her middle had perked awake and stretched, but she noticed with relief that its presence was less powerful, and she had felt capable of surviving another day.

Thirty-Three

ENGLAND

*P*hillip was looking forward to a rare night out at a great lady's London townhome. He had thrown himself into his work and was in sore need of some distraction. The invitation had come through one of the other solicitors in his chambers and he was eager to socialize with people in the great metropolis. He might personally find many ways to criticize the great culture of "society," but he could not deny that life was pretty lonely without social interaction, and as a newcomer to London, his circle of friends was the size of a pin dot.

As a footman opened the door onto the dark and dreary night, the warmth, bustle, and lights spilled out and drew him in. He followed the crush of people, bumping shoulders and apologizing as he went. He craned his neck in search of his legal colleague, making his way to a large room where people were playing cards and engaging in animated conversation. He purloined a drink from a passing footman and with some difficulty, made his way around the room, searching for a face he might recognize, holding his glass high to avoid spilling it on anyone.

"Why, Mr. Waverley!"

He turned back to see a very pretty face framed with golden ringlets, and a delicate rosebud mouth cast in a smile. Beguiling as she undoubtedly was, he was still untouched, except in friendship. He pulled his manners out of his back pocket and smiled. "Miss Fairweather! Well, this is a welcome surprise! Pray, what are *you* doing in London? Are your sisters here?" He looked around hopefully in search of them.

"Why no, sir," she simpered. "I am here with my aunt and uncle, who are acquainted with the family. Do you know Lady Mountbatten, then?"

"No, indeed. I was invited by a third party who is a close acquaintance of hers and was assured of a warm welcome, but I see that the welcome was extended to the whole of London!"

He chuckled good-naturedly and then, hoping to make an escape from the awkward situation, took a step away and turning his head said, "I am trying to find my colleague but there are so many people here that I have failed thus far."

"Then please sit here by me," encouraged Miss Fairweather. "For I am alone at present and in need of company in this great throng, though I do thrill to watch them all."

Phillip waited a beat as he decided how best to handle her invitation without giving offense and sensibly decided that to decline her offer would be ungallant. He picked up his tails and took the seat beside her, looking out at the crowd.

"You left Staffordshire in a great hurry, Mr. Waverley. I did not have the chance to say goodbye. I hope there was no emergency?"

He turned to face her, resigned. "Not a real emergency," he bluffed. "I just needed to return home quickly." It was a lame excuse and he felt like a cad.

"Oh." She looked crestfallen, surely hoping that he had been called away by some great tragedy. Her eyes fell to her hands in her lap.

"It was very bad manners of me to have left without a proper farewell, Miss Fairweather. Can you forgive me?"

She looked up at him with bright, shining eyes and a smile that clearly forgave him all.

"Of course, Mr. Waverley. Perhaps you can sit by me at supper, since neither of us really knows anyone here."

Phillip looked over the crowd in one last desperate attempt to find his friend and save this captivating young woman from any false hopes, but fate contrived against him and so he accepted, just as the announcement for supper was made. He courteously stood and held out his arm just as her aunt and uncle approached. Miss Fairweather made the introductions and they went in to supper.

Initially, the feast passed with lively, yet inoffensive small talk, but as time went on, one lady in their group articulated a comment that struck Phillip's heart like a gong. His blood instantly ran cold and he could not help addressing the lady in question. "I'm sorry, but did you say that Lady Augusta Haversham has finally been put in her place? Can I ask what you mean by such a thing?"

"My dear sir, it is all over London. She has been damaged by the revelation that her granddaughter is actually the child of a stable boy!" The last comment was screeched with a triumphant flourish. "She, who has destroyed the chances of many a worthy person, now humiliated herself! I cannot help but take pleasure in it as she cut my mother some years ago for a rumor that was untrue, as it happens, and my mother never recovered from it. No one who was anyone would accept my mother's invitations after that and she was refused at doors. It took such a toll on her health that she was never the same. I am most fortunate that my dear Henry rescued me and elevated me again in society." She nodded around the table for affirmation, but Phillip could not let it go.

"I demand to know to what source you attribute this vicious rumor?"

"It is no false rumor, sir! Indeed, I believe one of her servants has spread it abroad, and you know how rumors fly from house to house among the servants. I understand that Lady Haversham has fled to the Continent, which would seem to affirm the veracity of the claim, would it not? I hear that she is in hiding until the scandal blows over, but if I am not mistaken there are many of us who have faced the fierceness of her judgments who will willingly fan the flames. I heard it all of my maid yesterday morning."

Phillip blanched and stood abruptly, tipping over his chair.

"My dear Mr. Waverley," exclaimed Miss Fairweather. "What can be the matter? Do you know this person of whom she speaks? Truly, you look very ill! Can I be of assistance?"

Phillip pulled down his waistcoat and said clearly, addressing the other woman, "Madam, I do not doubt that Lady Augusta Haversham may have brought this on herself, but in delighting in her demise you slander a worthy young woman who is completely without fault in the matter. It might be better if you would hold your tongue!"

At his words, the table went silent, which silence spread through the whole room like a bad odor, as adjoining tables felt the tension and pointed hush.

The lady who had uttered the claim flushed to her roots and sprang to her own defense. "Well, I am sure that I meant no offense, but those are the facts, and there are many among us who are not sorry about it!"

The whole room stared at Phillip, who bowed stiffly and abruptly left the room, almost running to flee the claustrophobic atmosphere.

Miss Fairweather filed away her matrimonial hopes for the future with more than a little disappointment while silently championing Phillip for defending the unfortunate.

Phillip did not wait for the footman but pushed open the front door himself and fled down the stairs and out into the crisp, night air, gasping like a man who was being suffocated. He tore at his cravat and pulled it free of his neck as though it were a strangling python. Could it be true that Francesca was actually the daughter of a stable boy?

He ran along the street until he came to a bridge and clung to its railings as his mind tried to make sense of the knowledge he had just acquired. He focused on a leaf bobbing on the waves in an attempt to order his thoughts. Up and down, round and round.

Since Francesca had confessed to him that she was adopted, he had unwittingly fabricated a history for her of his own making. He had taken it for granted that she was the daughter of a gentleman who had compromised a young woman of rank. He had had no facts upon which to base his theory, and he now saw how foolish he was! Like it or not, he was a product of his own rank and era but he hated that his hitherto unwavering support for her was now floundering; he had considered himself quite a forward thinker, not bound by the rules of society, but were not these new feelings of disdain proof that he was a hypocrite of the first order? Her sweet features appeared before his eyes, and he tried to purge the unwelcome feelings of prejudice, but they would not flee! He tugged at his hair and let go a howl of despair. The anguish stripped him of energy and he hobbled along like a drunken man, from post to post, until he could flag a cab.

The jolting of the carriage on cobblestones mimicked the reeling of his mind. He painfully admitted that his love was no longer his equal in rank or birth and that it *did* matter.

His disappointment with his own weakness was acute.

He entered his rooms and flung himself on the bed, emotions still raging. In this delirium, his fevered mind accused him, like a barrister for the prosecution, of hypocrisy and inconstancy. The defense feebly argued the case for the validity of such feelings after a lifetime of societal indoctrination. On and on the two players raged, and Phillip could find no peace.

As the dawn broke, he fell into a disturbed sleep and missed the early morning calls of the news criers, proclaiming the failure of certain ventures in America.

⁂

As the sun steadily penetrated the gloom of his room, Phillip awoke reluctantly with a headache of gigantic proportions. The mercy of hazy consciousness was a temporary forgetting of the misery of the night before, but as he pressed the balls of his hands into his eyes in an attempt to relieve the pressure, the awful memory sprang to life.

He mentally stepped back to examine his emotions only to discover that he was still filled with a kind of abhorrence that further depressed him. He dressed carelessly and scurried away to his chambers, late.

On opening the door to his work place, he found it in an uproar with clerks running hither and thither so that no one noticed his late arrival. He slipped through the crazed maze of people, slumped into his desk, and opened the closest file, but the words merely swam before his bloodshot eyes and he could think of nothing but Francesca.

The excessive noise and commotion barely touched his consciousness, but at length another legal novice, the one he had not found at the soiree of the previous evening, collapsed into the chair of the desk adjoining his, muttering, "Well, this is a bad business!"

Phillip raised his weary head and tried to focus on his colleague but found he had neither the desire nor the energy to understand and dropped it again.

"Phillip, what the devil is wrong with you? Can you not see the mayhem? Fie! Are you not concerned? The crash of ventures in America means we will not be paid by a significant number of clients!"

"The crash?"

"You must have heard the criers and seen the newspapers, surely? It is all anyone is talking of." He examined Phillip more thoroughly.

"Are you ill, man? Indeed, you look very unwell. Perhaps you should go home."

Phillip nodded vaguely and staggered to his feet. Pushing his way through the beavering minions, he knocked on the door of the head of chambers, who was pacing his office, mumbling to himself.

"Sir Edward, I wonder if I might take the day off," he ventured. "I am not feeling well . . ."

"Take the whole wretched week off, sir! It will take us at least that long to work though this mess. And if our chambers are still standing by the end of the week, it will be a miracle!"

He stopped pacing and glanced at Phillip. "Good heavens! Look at you! Are your family's fortunes tied up in this American thing? You look as though Armageddon is approaching!"

"What? Oh no, I don't believe so, sir. I just have a fearsome headache and need to go home."

"Yes, yes, I can see that you are not well. Take the week as you will be of no use to us until we get our affairs in order anyway."

Sir Edward Blythe resumed his pacing and muttering, and Phillip discreetly closed the door.

Upon returning to his dingy rooms, Phillip could think of nothing but ridding his breast of the disturbing feelings flourishing there and sank to his knees, pleading with God to purge the prejudice from his heart, petitioning for the negative feelings to be replaced by the pure love of old. So lengthy were his appeals to the Almighty that he fell asleep and was woken by a pain from such prolonged kneeling. He roused and shifted, continuing to beseech the Lord for the peace that passes all understanding.

Another hour passed while he patiently waited, listening. As he was about to give up all hope, a dawning awareness of a conversion began as a warm peace almost imperceptibly permeated his soul. The sensation grew steadily until it completely filled his heart with a feeling of intense euphoria and he heard the quiet words, "The worth of *all* souls is great in the sight of God."

He repeated the satisfying revelation over and over in his mind and in so doing experienced a serenity that confirmed that the words were true, that man had created class distinctions but that to God, all men were equal. He continued to wait on the Spirit of the Lord.

"True worthiness depends on conduct not rank." The voice was still and small but, like a two-edged sword, it penetrated to his very soul. He thanked God for the clear and unmistakable answer. Tranquility had at last replaced agitation.

He jumped up and, throwing a few possessions in a bag, ran out to the street and hailed a carriage. It was time to go back home, home to Francesca.

Thirty-Four

FRANCE

Mrs. Oliver handed Lady Augusta a letter. She ungraciously snatched the note from her maid and growled, "Who knows where I am? I have told no one! Have you betrayed me?"

The maid held her mistress's gaze with effort and the merest hint of a glance to the left, and resolutely said, "No."

Lady Augusta continued to regard her maid with suspicion as she broke open the seal, not noticing that it was her son's. Dragging her eyes away, Lady Augusta reluctantly read the words and let out an involuntary shriek. "I am saved!"

Mrs. Oliver widened her eyes with interest and Lady Haversham, realizing her error in betraying the contents of the letter, stood up and pushed the maid out the door. Once it was closed she leaned back upon it and read the letter again, this time in its entirety.

Dear Mama,

Firstly, please do not ask how I have found you, if indeed this letter does reach you.

I am writing to tell you that Haversham Hall has been saved from the creditors and there will be a little money upon which to live and keep the servants, if you live wisely.

Ha! What impudence! I have always spent wisely! she thought, but continued reading.

Father has been very low since you left but on learning that the hall will be saved has rallied. Though humbled by his errors of mismanagement, he has gained a renewed desire to live.

"Stupid man! It is all his own fault anyway and if he had died from remorse I should not have cared!" she exclaimed out loud, to no one. She resumed reading.

We should very much like for you to come home and be reconciled to us and perhaps find it in your heart to forgive Father.

"The audacity!" she retorted. She returned to the letter.

We await your response,
Your loving son,
John

She crushed the letter in her fist and looked out the window at the azure sea. She had now been in France for six weeks and had kept mostly to her rooms for lack of money and fear of being discovered. She had to concede that she greatly missed society and the admiration of her peers.

The only obstacle to returning to England now was whether the nature of Francesca's true parentage had become common knowledge. The letter gave no indication. The fear of being humiliated was potent, but the hunger for the respect she was so used to was stronger. The two competing emotions clamored in her mind as she paced back and forth across the room.

After some time, she became aware of a new advantage. She would no longer have to escape the apartment without settling her bill! She would refer them to her husband and he could pay with whatever money he had managed to secure. The arrival of the letter had tipped the scales in favor of return. Not once did she consider to whom she was beholden.

⚜ ⚜

ENGLAND

"Francesca saved us?" cried Augusta Haversham. It was more of a shriek than a question. "I am obligated to that little—"

"Now, now my dear be very careful what you say," said her husband. "We have treated Francesca abominably, and she did not need to save the Hall. In fact, our son warned her against such charity, but she would not be deterred. I fear we are undeserving of such generosity after our conduct."

"Undeserving? Undeserving! We, whose blood runs pure blue, undeserving! This country owes us much for all that we have done. Why, we are the backbone of polite society. Who should deserve the help more than us?" Augusta burst out with flashing eyes.

"I feel compelled to point out that it is not the 'country,' as you put it, that has bailed us out, but our own granddaughter. None of our so-called friends are banging down the doors to help, though the reversal in our fortunes is well known. In fact, Lord Denby sent a letter informing me that those we had thought were our friends are celebrating our demise, and he wrote to warn me against coming into town."

Augusta collapsed onto a chaise. "Our disgrace is public knowledge, then?" she asked, through gritted teeth.

"Oh yes! The plumed and painted birds of London are crowing over our misfortunes. I am afraid that we are reaping what we have so carefully sown. For myself, this kindness on the part of Francesca has rendered me more humble, though I still struggle with the facts of her birth. You would do well to learn that lesson too, Augusta."

"But it is all insufferable! We are to have no money of our own, then? If my parents could see how low you have brought me—"

"I accept all the responsibility for losing our fortunes. I speculated too much and was over confident in my own infallibility. There were signs and recommendations but I was too vain to accept them and now I have lost it all. Rage at me all you want! I have done that, and more, to myself in these last weeks. More from you will not harm me."

"Ah! I am ashamed of you! And now I have not two pence of my own to set up somewhere away from you. I am trapped. Why could you not secure a bigger annual income from Francesca, at least? I should not have returned if I had known there was no income!"

"Augusta, do you have any idea how much money Francesca has put up to save the house and the staff? Dirty money it may be, but remember, she was not obliged to do any of this and could yet change her mind. You had better temper you anger."

"Should she *not* help us? Is it not her duty to her grandparents?"

"One minute you reject her as kin and the next you claim entitlement to her fortune. You must decide where your principals lie, Augusta!"

"You have placed me in an impossible situation, John! Would that I had never been born!"

"You are being overdramatic, Augusta," he sighed. "Our original plan was to orchestrate a marriage with that Langley fellow and dupe the two of them into supporting us anyway, though at that time we were not so destitute. Though the money is tainted, it is offered freely as a gift—the result is the same, is it not? We have been saved from a life of begging from our friends and losing our home. Perhaps that renders the fortune less distasteful. Thanks to Francesca, we can live an agreeable life here, a more quiet life to be sure, but an agreeable one."

"You stupid man! A quiet life is a prison to me. I crave the associations of society and will wither and die here. You must insist that she give us a more generous allowance!"

"I will do nothing of the sort! I fear we must learn to lay on the bed we have made. My horror of destitution outweighs my aversion to the girl's lowly station, and if we give offense, she may withdraw the offer."

"The bed *you* have made! You! Oh, that my life has come to this! I am leaving to stay with Lady Cornwallis in Yorkshire. She will not abandon me!"

Lord Haversham shook his head slowly as she made a dramatic exit. He thought she might.

Thirty-Five

ENGLAND

"Here is yet another one," said Emily, holding up a card declining dinner.

"I am so glad that you did not attend any of the parties and dinners you had invitations to, darling. I fear that people would have been very rude and it would have been especially awkward for you. Are you very grieved?"

"Not at all, Mama. My recent experiences in Italy have opened my eyes to how ridiculous some of our genteel English 'rules' are. These rebuffs are not from people I have particular affection for, and I have the fondest hope that my true friends will continue to support me. After all, I am the same girl that left some months ago, am I not? If society cannot see that, then I think my life will be better without their patronage. And if my hopes are in vain, I can be assured that my parents will never leave me. If that is the worst of it, I think I can endure. Though to be sure, I hope not all my friends cut me." She was thinking of Phillip, who had been suspiciously absent.

"Do you blame us, dearest? Things would have been very different had we told the truth from the start."

"Of course not! I know things are a little complicated now, but intellectually, I understand why you did it. And Isabella was not truthful with you, either." She dropped her voice and almost whispered, "Do you think you might not have kept me if you had known who my father was?"

There was a pause, and she looked up into her mother's eyes searching for acceptance.

"Honestly? I was so desperate for a baby that I would have convinced your father to keep you, even if he had had objections! Had we known, he may have tried to point out the difficulties that it might bring in the future, but I would have swept his arguments aside. I do not regret one day of the eighteen years you have been with us. I hope that you know that you have made my life happy and complete and that this changes nothing for me!"

⚜

They had neither received nor been received when the date for Annabelle's wedding arrived. Annabelle had been faithful and had written to confirm her support. Her parents had needed a little more persuasion.

Annabelle looked resplendent in her wedding finery and wore a very pretty bonnet with her veil. Her happiness was so apparent that it elevated her looks to beautiful. Francesca looked around the church cautiously and saw many people staring straight ahead. It was not a hopeful beginning.

Annabelle was much occupied at the wedding breakfast, and the cousins had very little time together, but Annabelle continued to assure Francesca of her friendship and that of her husband, to which he readily agreed. This warmed Francesca's heart to Mr. Doyle considerably.

Francesca and her parents stayed together, and though everyone was careful of their manners at a wedding celebration, very few people actually engaged them in conversation, and many cast sideways glances at them. The temperature in the room was chill. Fortunately, Annabelle and Mr. Doyle seemed not to notice.

Everyone waved the happy couple goodbye as they left on their honeymoon, and after catching a snippet of whispered conversation about being surprised that such a person would be invited to the event, the Havershams quietly left to return home. The dipping of their toes into the societal pool had not gone well, and they departed for home to lick their wounds and adjust to their new normal.

⚜

Several days later, Francesca was spending time with her horse and confiding in him that she had neither seen nor heard from Phillip when she heard a cough. Turning around she was elated to see that it was Phillip, but immediately following that emotion she hesitated, recent experience telling her that he may not be seeking her company and may simply have come to tell her that they could no longer be friends. She held her breath.

Phillip held out his hand and gave a wry smile. "Do not worry, little thing. I have not come to reject you. Indeed, I have come to attest to my support in person."

She moved to take his proffered hand, and he kissed hers but did not let it drop for several more seconds. She looked up, but he turned his head. "Let us take a walk around the estate," he said, to which she readily agreed and left her horse, putting her arm through his.

"Before you pledge your loyalty, I must ask if you know it all, Phillip? If not, you might feel the need to withdraw your protection after I tell you the whole truth."

"Be assured, I think I know it all, but I would like to hear it from you, just the same."

She recounted in detail the meeting with her Italian grandfather and what she had learned about the woman who gave birth to her. She spoke of her grandfather's hesitance to reveal her father's identity given his low station and of meeting Antonio and feeling an affinity that surpassed class. She explained that he had risen to be head groom for a noble household and how she had offered him the same position at Giorgio's Italian estate, now that it was hers, and how this would afford them the opportunity to build a relationship over time.

"Why did you not tell me this in your letter?" Phillip asked. "Did you fear my rejection?"

"Mama and Father encouraged me to tell no one so that it might not ruin my chances at marriage. They feared that if I wrote about it, someone might intercept the letter and betray my secret. However, in spite of our precautions, it appears my secret has been discovered."

Phillip nodded. "I heard about it, quite by chance, at a reception in London and defended your honor to the spiteful biddy who broadcast it with far too much relish. I am heartily ashamed by their conduct."

"Oh, Phillip, you know not how those words are a balm to my soul. I try to bear the cruelty well, but sometimes it saddens me so. I do not know who could have betrayed us so viciously."

"Ah, well there I may have the answer. Your grandmother Haversham would do well to treat her servants with more kindness. It appears that one of the maids was eavesdropping at a door and announced the story below stairs. Before the butler could put a stop to it, the tale had spread through the whole village. The maid has since been dismissed. It is wise to treat *all* people with dignity and compassion, as your grandmother has learned to her sorrow!"

"She will find the shame of it very hard to bear. She and grandfather Haversham were particularly upset about the adoption and said some rather harsh things, which lead to an argument with my Davenport grandparents. It was all very distressing."

"How do you feel, now that all of society knows your secrets?"

"I hardly know. I have already experienced the cold shoulder of society at Annabelle's wedding. I confess, it was hard to bear and makes me want to become a little recluse. On the other hand, several friends and family have written to assure me of their continued support, which is heartening and I am most grateful for it.

"The hardest thing to bear is the fact that I can never marry. That is a hard truth to accept." She turned her bowed head slightly and looked up at him through lashes that were wet with quiet tears.

He lifted her chin with his finger and she dropped her gaze to the floor, the lashes sweeping her cheeks tearing at his heart strings and bolstering his courage. "Never marry?"

With a broken voice that mirrored her emotions, she explained, "Our plan had been to tell the whole truth to any young man who asked for my hand so that he might make a decision based upon all the facts. We would never have deceived anyone who wanted to marry me, but we felt it important to preserve the reputation of the rest of the family by not making my father's station in life public. I am sure that no young man would have followed through with the proposal once he knew the truth but there was a wisp of hope that someone that really loved me might be able to overlook my past, that there was such a man.

"Now that the whole world knows my history, I suppose I am a pariah and no young man will even allow himself to be in the same company with me, let alone court me. Thus, I will become a wealthy old maid and spend far too much time with my horses." She managed a tearful smile.

He raised her chin again gently.

"I am such a man," he whispered.

She blinked to clear her vision and stared back, trying to read his sincerity. He held her gaze and she noticed the soft, gold flecks hidden in the green irises of his intelligent eyes. She glanced at his lips and then back at his eyes and swallowing, whispered back, "Phillip, do not say such things out of pity for me. The world is yours for the taking, and I would not have you limit your chances because you feel sorry for an old friend. I cannot allow you to throw your life away like that."

"Is that what you believe?" He pulled away from her and, holding both her hands, forged on. "Francesca, I have been such a fool! I have loved you these past twelve months and been unable to confess it for fear that you did not reciprocate my feelings. And then you seemed so taken with Mr. Ashbourne—"

She flinched at his name.

"I have loved you for so long and never disclosed it. Not even to my closest friends or family. I was in agony those months you seemed to favor him, and when I heard of his proclivity to ruin the reputations of the rich and young, I rushed to find you and protect you. I was not there by happenstance, Francesca. I had come to warn you." He paused. "I love you! I want nothing so much as to make you my wife. The only remaining question is to ask if you think you could come to love *me*."

She pressed his hands with hers and declared, "But I love you already, Phillip! I had much time to reflect on my travels and found that I was missing no one but you. I berated myself for foolishness thinking that you regarded me only as a sister figure, but my heart would not obey. I was blinded by . . ." She hesitated. "By Mr. Ashbourne, for a little, but it became all too clear that his feelings were not genuine. I was flattered by his attentions, but I fault only my youth and inexperience on that score. And I came to realize that it was *you* who I loved and you who I thought of every night as I fell asleep. When I learned of my father's station, it was rejection by *you* that I feared the most!"

He pulled her to him in a short, powerful embrace and then released her gently, hovering near her lips with his own and drinking in her sweet, heady breath. On opening his eyes, her expression was encouraging, and he finally brushed her lips in a tender kiss. The electrical charge was so intense and so immediate that he was taken aback, and, desiring more of that which he had imagined for so long, he softly pressed his mouth against hers. She melted into his arms and kissed him back with fervor, then pulled away to rest her cheek against his jacket. Encircling her about with his arms, he rested his own cheek on her head, feeling a completeness of joy such as he had never before experienced.

The tiger-like primal protection that had been awakened when he had found her with Ashbourne, now roused with a roar and prowled around. Phillip wanted nothing more from life than to take care of and cherish this dear soul for the rest of his life.

After several minutes in this heavenly pose, Phillip dropped to his knee. "Francesca Haversham, will you marry me?"

"You would be willing to have me even knowing that I am no longer considered a member of high ranking society?"

"I am willing. I love you as I have never loved anyone and cannot imagine a life without you."

"Then yes, Phillip! Yes!" He stood and held her close, his lips touching her hair.

"What will your parents say when they know all?" she whispered. "Do you think they will give us their blessing?"

"Honestly, I have no idea. They have known and loved you all their lives and I would hope that this will change nothing for them, but I have lately discovered that you cannot always predict how others will react, even how you, yourself will react."

She lifted her head but he pulled her closer so that he could make his confession without witnessing her reproach. "When you told me you were adopted, it was of little consequence to me."

"I remember," she murmured, "it gave me hope while I was gone."

"I have not always been so constant. I am ashamed to say that when the full facts were thrust upon me, I wavered. We are so indoctrinated where the classes are concerned, that I confess my love did falter."

She let out a little gasp, but he held her closer.

"I hated myself for it and fell to my knees, asking the Lord to change my heart, for I did not desire this prejudice to take hold. He answered me, and through the grace of His Son gave me a new heart! His Spirit told me of your great worth in His eyes, and I was undone. You are a remarkable woman, and nothing can change that. I love you and will always love you. I am now forever yours."

She raised her head and with no trace of hurt or disappointment cupped his face with her dainty hand. "Thank you for sharing this with me. It gives me such comfort. Your parents' attitude is quite another matter. They may not desire to overcome their first reaction. Can you endure it if they reject me?" she asked timidly.

He moved away a fraction, the easy smile replaced with the confidence of conviction.

"From this day forth, I will remain loyal to you through good times and bad. I have pledged myself to you in marriage—there is no turning back. If my parents have difficulty accepting the circumstances of your birth, then we will be patient and allow them time. But I will not be deterred, Francesca. You are the same dear girl that ever you were, and nothing will prevent me from making you my wife!"

⊷⊱⊰⊶

When Phillip went to John Haversham to ask for his daughter's hand in marriage, John was cautiously optimistic. "I feel obligated to tell you—"

"If you are going to tell me about Francesca's birth father, I can put your mind at ease as I know it all, sir."

John burst into a radiant smile of relief and shook Phillip's hand vigorously. "You are a true gentleman!" he proclaimed and patted his shoulder. "I cannot tell you how happy Mrs. Haversham will be! This is the thing that we had feared the most, that the revelation would prevent Francesca from having a full life."

John's expression changed to doubt, suddenly, "You are not doing this out of some sense of misguided duty, are you Phillip? You *do* love her?"

"Let me assure you, sir, of my devotion and of the deep love and admiration I have for your daughter. She is the choice of my heart and my head and has been for some long time."

⊷⊱⊰⊶

Lady Waverley's face blanched as Phillip told her all they now knew about Francesca's heritage. His parents did not go about much in society, and so even her adoption was news to them. She dropped into an armchair and heaved a great sigh, looking at Francesca with pity.

"Well, my dear, this must be a great shock to you!"

"I confess that it was at first but I have had time to come to terms with it and I have had the opportunity to meet my other family and come to love them."

Lady Waverley looked as though she had tasted something sour but said, "For a young lady raised as you have been it must have been an . . ." she searched for an appropriate word, "adjustment."

"My grandfather was a very wealthy and respected land owner and even my natural father has made something of himself. It would be very cruel to reject him because he has not had the opportunities afforded to me, do you not think?"

Lady Waverley most certainly did not look like she agreed, but was gracious enough to keep her own counsel and merely smiled weakly.

"There is more, Mother, Father," began Phillip, and he took Francesca's hand in his.

"More!" gasped his mother, eyeing their entwined hands. "More?"

"I have asked Francesca to be my wife."

An uncontrolled little yelp escaped his mother, and she coughed to cover it, sending her husband an alarmed look.

"You know we love Francesca as her own person," said his father. "And bear no grudge due to the change in her circumstances, but have you thought through all the ramifications of such a union? Although this has come as a surprise to us, we will make allowances because you are our son and given time we hope to able to accept all this, but you must appreciate that others will not be so charitable. They may persecute you, and they will certainly cut you. You may find yourselves extremely lonely and without many friends. Furthermore, the ripples of your decision will not only affect you, they will affect all your family by association."

"You are right, Father, and we have not come to this decision lightly. You and mother are not much in society and neither is my brother. As your heir, he will not have to deal with prejudice as he would if he had to find his way to earn a good income." He turned to Francesca and continued, "If I find my chances to succeed in the law revoked because of my alliance, that is a sacrifice I am willing to make! Francesca now has a great fortune, independent of the Havershams, and we will want for nothing material. I daresay I can find fulfillment running an estate just as Father has. Though I favor the law, it is not my burning passion, and I can see a life of happiness without it. I cannot see such a life without Francesca by my side."

His father nodded but still wore a grim expression. "I see that you will not be deterred. And you can be assured that we will certainly not separate ourselves from you entirely, though it *will* take time to come to terms with everything, I must be honest!"

"Father, I appreciate your honesty and understand the need for time. However, we have determined that we would like to marry in two months, and because of the circumstances, we would prefer a small wedding with little fanfare. Do you think you might be able to attend? We understand if you would rather not."

Lady Waverley looked to her husband who said, "Give us some time, Son. Let us digest all this and make a decision when our emotions have calmed down."

Phillip and Francesca acquiesced and took their leave. Once outside the house, Francesca breathed a sigh of relief, "Well, that went better than I had expected!"

Thirty-Six

ENGLAND

*E*mily placed the letter beside her luncheon plate and lifted her gaze to the ceiling, trying to imagine what it had cost her sister to write the note. She loved her sister, but she feared for anyone who crossed her. And to think that they had *all* been taken in by the gentleman in question!

The door creaked open and Francesca came in and placed a kiss on her mother's cheek. Noticing the sorrowful expression on her mother's face, she asked, "Have you received bad news, Mama? It is not grandfather, is it?"

"No, no. Sit down, darling. This concerns your cousin Katherine."

Francesca's eyes flew to her mother's, and she gasped.

"Do you know already, then?" Emily asked.

"No! But I confess that I have suspected something was wrong for some time, but Katherine would not confide in me."

"It is terribly shocking and will bear bad fruit for some time I fear. It appears that Mr. Langley Ashbourne, who we all thought so virtuous and dashing, has compromised Katherine with a promise of marriage, which he has now withdrawn!"

Francesca blanched but her mother was so upset by the letter that she did not notice and continued, "Since your ball, it appears that Katherine has sunk into a depression that has necessitated her removal to a sanitarium. In recent days, at the encouragement of her doctors, she has admitted to the secret engagement and its withdrawal. My sister, your aunt, flew into a rage and commissioned someone to find the young man so that your uncle might confront him and force him to honor his promise.

His whereabouts were discovered, and your uncle accosted him, but Mr. Ashbourne resisted his demands, declaring that he was engaged to be married in a few weeks and was therefore not a free man. Your uncle subsequently made a threat of exposure to which Mr. Ashbourne retorted that he would, in turn, expose their daughter for the coquette that she is."

Francesca's stomach dropped in fear.

"Your uncle was apoplectic and demanded that Ashbourne retract his accusations and admit that they were false. Rather than back down, Mr. Ashbourne challenged your uncle to check with his daughter before setting events in motion that he might later regret.

"Your uncle backed down in a daze, vowing to return when the accusations were proven fictitious and Mr. Ashbourne had the bad manners to laugh in his face. We were sorely mistaken in that young man's character!"

"Indeed," murmured Francesca, looking down at her hands folded in her lap.

"But there is more!" exclaimed her mother, slapping the letter with her palm. "His accusations were true! I can hardly believe it, but your cousin, upon being told of his allegations, broke down and confessed all. My poor sister!"

Tears sprung to Francesca's eyes and she took her mother's hand. "Mama, I am so sorry for Katherine."

"You do not blame her, then?"

"No. Who am I to cast blame on anyone? We know not how Mr. Ashbourne tempted her. I, for one, will not stand as her accuser."

"But you are trembling," said Emily.

"My emotions are all in chaos at the thought of how wretched Katherine must be, her reputation in tatters. I, who am in need of friends, will not cast her off but will offer her my compassion and love . . ." She bit her lip and gathering up her courage pushed on. "Mama, I must disclose that . . . that Mr. Ashbourne attempted to ruin *my* character while I was in Brighton, but thanks to Phillip, he was thwarted. He truly is an evil and wicked man."

Emily looked up locking eyes with her daughter and placing a hand on her shoulder cried, "What? When was this? Why did you not confide in us? When was it?"

"I was too ashamed. Mr. Ashbourne followed us to Brighton," she whispered. "I believe he planned to entrap me into a marriage for my money. If I had to guess, I would say that when he discovered that Katherine will not inherit any money, he dropped her like a hot iron. Phillip has found out that he and his father are about to be turned out by the creditors, like my grandparents. Mr. Ashbourne and his father are so desperate that they care not who they hurt in their plans to fill their coffers and maintain their estate."

She coughed on a sob, and Emily wrapped her in an embrace, waiting for the tears to abate. "Tell me everything, my darling," she encouraged, and Francesca gladly laid the burden of guilt at her mother's feet, afterward rejoicing in the freedom of a clear conscience.

"So, you see, I can never condemn Katherine for there, but for the grace of God, go I. There is another too, Mama. Phillip met a shadow of a girl in Hampshire who fell victim to Mr. Ashbourne some years ago. Perhaps the lady to whom he is currently engaged is also marrying against her will."

"We must tell your father! Perhaps it is time to unveil Mr. Ashbourne to protect others!"

Francesca sniffed and nodded, "Yes, Mama. I think it is time. If he chooses to spread rumors about my virtue in retaliation, it can hardly hurt my reputation any more than it already has been, and given that I have found happiness with Phillip, it is a sacrifice I am willing to make, as Phillip knows the truth and will defend me to any who dare to slander."

⁂

Some days later, Emily saw an announcement in the Times which read,

> *Langley Ashbourne and Caroline DeMontford, widow,*
> *were married April 3, in Hampshire.*

At that moment, John entered the room having just returned from town to commence the unveiling of Mr. Ashbourne.

"Do you know of her, John?" she asked, showing him the announcement.

"Yes," said John with a malevolent gleam in his eye. "I have just this minute arrived home to tell you of her. It is all the talk in town. As you know, I went there with the express purpose of exposing Ashbourne and found that I was too late. He was already married. I did, however, feel compelled to learn what I could of the matter. Mrs. DeMontford is ten years his senior and not a woman to suffer fools. From what I hear, she saw straight through his devious plans to marry her for her money and was happy to be party to it. She was well aware that Langley was in need of funds, and she was in want of a handsome husband—and a title.

"By all accounts she is a social climber of the basest kind and enticed her first husband into marriage rather scandalously. He was a much older, ailing, wealthy man, and she set her sights on *his* money. He was no match for her wit and charms, and they married after a very short acquaintance, much to his family's distress. He died not twelve months after their marriage, leaving everything to her.

"Now a widow of dubious character, I suspect she calculated that her star might rise on the arm of so dashing a man as Langley, who is to inherit his father's title, and so she set her own trap for him. I imagine that after his altercation with your brother-in-law, he knew that the true nature of his character was about to be revealed and that he should play his hand quickly to secure his bride and her money before she could change her mind. However, if the accounts are true, and I have no reason to believe they are not, she has turned the tables on him and engaged a solicitor before her marriage to protect her money from the Ashbournes! He will be allowed only a modest stipend; the rest will be held in a tight purse!

"The irony! It is no more than he deserves! The scoundrel! I confess, I am rather gratified to hear that he will get his punishment. I think his new wife will lead him a merry dance, and may he curse the day he met her!"

※ ※

The peal of the organ rang out, and Francesca shifted the bouquet in her hands, taking her father's arm. She felt completely calm as they proceeded down the aisle, nodding at Annabelle and a few other close friends. They walked slowly down the aisle of the sparsely filled church that was brimming with a riot of colorful blooms.

Her Davenport grandparents were in attendance, but Grandmother Haversham was conspicuously absent. Francesca smiled at Grandfather Haversham. He had become much more affectionate of late. She nodded to Phillip's parents, who had decided to attend at the last minute.

Phillip turned around and bestowed upon her that smile she loved so much, the one that creased his features from the corners of his eyes to his masculine chin, his face bursting with devotion and satisfaction.

When they reached the front of the church, her father lifted her veil, placed a dainty kiss upon her cheek, and placed her hand in Phillip's. As they repeated their vows, Francesca took time to thank God that her trials had helped her see that the man who stood beside her was her perfect match. Without the clarity that they had forced upon her, she might never have come to realize his true value and instead been billowed about by the vagaries of the world, shunned and lonely.

They might face opposition and cruelty from those who judged her harshly, but she was confident that with Phillip by her side, they could endure any storm that might threaten them. It was an adventure she was anxious to begin.

Epilogue

The baby was gurgling happily as Phillip bounced him on his knee and his great-grandfather offered him a finger to chew. Francesca smiled and glanced at the deeds to the villa Normandie, which lay open on the table. After honeymooning there, she and Phillip had decided to purchase it so that their family might enjoy winter vacations there.

They had completed their grand marriage tour by staying in Florence at Francesca's estate. Mario had faithfully fulfilled Giorgio's request, and the vineyard was thriving. Though awkward at first, Phillip and Antonio had forged a solid friendship.

English society had been slow to forgive or forget the crime of Francesca's birth, and though they valued its approval but little, Italy afforded a relaxing place of escape.

Lady Augusta had sentenced herself to solitary confinement, never allowing herself to associate with her great-grandson, and was miserable as a consequence. Her fears had all been realized and the great society that had once lauded her now ridiculed and abused her and she was despised and eschewed at every great home. Rather than take solace in her family, she renounced them, furious that she had been given such a paltry allowance upon which to live and disgusted by the pollution of her family tree. Her husband sought refuge quite often in the home of his son or granddaughter.

The Havershams and Waverleys had recently been apprised of the fact that Langley Ashbourne, upon finding out the legal obstructions to spending his new wife's wealth, had had an outburst of hysterics and threatened to find his amusements in other quarters. His wife, who was more than his equal in the art of manipulation, shot back that if he chose to pursue such a course, she would cut him off entirely and spread the history of his wicked dalliances with noble young ladies, thus curtailing his ability to move around in society freely. They had forged an icy truce.

Within six months, Langley's father had died of heart failure, and they had inherited the title of Lord and Lady Ashbourne, which assuaged their hostility toward each other to some extent.

Katherine had continued to be downcast for the better part of a year but had, at length, met a courageous captain who had rallied her spirits and who had proposed at the end of three months. She had felt compelled to confess that she had been indiscreet in her past, to which he replied that he, himself, was not as white as the driven snow and what was past was past. She readily accepted his proposal.

Miss Fairweather had accepted defeat gracefully and had set her cap at Annabelle's cousin, William. She was in the process of reeling him in.

And what of Miss Gray? Phillip, who had maintained his acquaintance with that admirable family, learned that she had been encouraged to visit and succor the poor of her father's parish and had found, therein, a large family whose mother was sickly who greatly benefited from her benevolence. Finding a purpose, she had greatly improved but never socialized outside of her own little corner of England.

As Francesca perused the happy scene before her, she considered how much she had learned and gained in the crucible of her trials. Though painful to endure, the experience and love she had acquired was more than enough compensation. She was happy and loved. What more could one ask?

Discussion Questions

1. One of the main themes of this novel is prejudice. The prejudice in the book is not one we really face today, but we have many others. What are other prejudices that have come and gone? Are there any today that affect relationships?

2. English high society was built on a strong set of rules. Are there areas of our modern lives that have lots of "rules" created by arbitrary, unknown people? Can you identify any of these "rules"?

3. Phillip came to know that the "worth of all souls is great." Do you think our modern culture adheres to this philosophy, or is the worth of some souls deemed greater than others?

4. How is social media like regency high society?

5. What problems do you foresee in Francesca and Phillip's future?

6. We know from Jane Austen's writings that arranged marriages and marriages of convenience were common during this era. Our culture allows people to choose their own spouses, and it does not always work out well. Can you see any benefits of arranged marriages? Can you see someone from this era lecturing us on why their way is preferable? What might some of their reasons be?

7. Do you believe Francesca's parents made the right decision in keeping her adoption a secret at the beginning of the novel? How do you think the novel would have unfolded if they had been honest about her low birth from the beginning? Would Francesca have had the happy childhood that is the foundation of her life?

8. Francesca is naïve and inexperienced at the start of the story. What characteristics of Langley attract her in the beginning? Over time, what characteristics of Phillip's does she learn to value?

9. Phillip believes himself to be a forward thinker, an open-minded, modern man, until faced with the crisis of admitting that Francesca's low birth is an issue that he struggles to overcome. Do you think that is a problem in our modern society? What are some modern issues that so-called liberal-minded people might take issue with?

10. Lady Augusta is someone we can love to hate, but toxic personalities are common in many families. Do you feel that she deserved her fate? Should she have been punished by the full consequences of her actions, as her son suggests? Would you have liked to see her punished more?

11. Langley is a narcissist and a serial predator. Was his punishment enough? What do you think his future holds?

12. Giorgio is distracted from parenthood by his vineyard and his own sorrows. What things distract us from being effective parents today? How are our modern distractions affecting society as a whole?

Acknowledgments

I would like to thank God for giving me a nudge, my husband for believing in me and encouraging me, Lisa McKendrick for dragging me to Storymakers, my book club for their support, and Jen G and Stina V for reading my manuscript and telling me not to give up.

About the Author

Julie A. Matern was born and raised in England and has bounced around America as an adult with her husband and family. After dabbling at writing for years, she finally got serious and wrote a children's book inspired by her grandmother's experiences during World War II. It was so rewarding that she tried her hand at Regency romance and found her passion. She now lives in Utah, where she misses her grandchildren who live far, far away. You can learn more about Julie at www.juliematern.com.

Scan to visit

www.juliematern.com